DEATH
STRANDING

DEATH STRANDING
Volume One

DEATH STRANDING
Volume Two

DEATH STRANDING

BY HITORI NOJIMA
BASED ON THE GAME BY HIDEO KOJIMA
TRANSLATED BY CARLEY RADFORD

TITAN BOOKS

Death Stranding: Volume One
Print edition ISBN: 9781789095760
E-book edition ISBN: 9781789096583

Published by Titan Books
A division of Titan Publishing Group Ltd
144 Southwark Street, London SE1 0UP.
www.titanbooks.com

First edition: February 2021
10 9 8 7 6 5 4 3 2 1

Death Stranding by Hideo Kojima/Hitori Nojima
Copyright © 2019 Sony Interactive Entertainment Inc.
Created and developed by KOJIMA PRODUCTIONS.
All rights reserved.
Cover illustration by Pablo Uchida
Original Japanese edition published in 2019 by
SHINCHOSHA Publishing Co., Ltd.
English translation rights arranged with SHINCHOSHA Publishing Co., Ltd.
through The English Agency Japan Ltd.
English translation copyrights © 2021 by Titan Publishing Group Ltd.

Carley Radford asserts the moral right to be identified
as the translator of this work.

A CIP catalogue record for this title is available from the British Library.

Printed and bound in the United States.

CONTENTS

CHARACTERS

Deadman - A member of Bridges and an ex-coroner. He is in charge of BB maintenance among other things.

Die-Hardman - The director of Bridges, an organization created specifically to rebuild America. A close associate of Bridget.

Bridget Strand - The last President of the United States of America. She has devoted herself to rebuilding the UCA to reconnect a broken world.

Amelie - The leader of Bridges I, who went out west to rebuild America. She is currently being held in Edge Knot City.

Sam Porter Bridges - A "porter" who has rejoined Bridges for the first time in ten years. He is heading west as Bridges II.

Higgs - A member of Homo Demens who is trying to prevent the rebuilding of America and accelerate human extinction.

Fragile - The young, female leader of the private delivery organization Fragile Express.

Heartman - A member of Bridges who hopes to unravel the mysteries surrounding the Death Stranding and the Beach.

Mama - A mechanic from Bridges involved in the development of the Q-pid and Chiral Network.

VOCABULARY

Bridges - An organization created by the last President of the United States of America, Bridget Strand, for the sole purpose of reconnecting all of the disjointed cities and people across the ex-USA and rebuilding America.

Death Stranding - A mysterious phenomenon that affected the entire world. When antimatter stranded from the world of the dead comes into contact with the living, it causes a voidout.

BB - Bridge Babies. Artificially created "equipment" that allows its users to sense the presence of the dead.

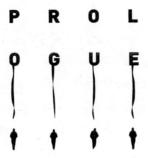

PROLOGUE

This child's special.

Countless faces were staring at him. They edged closer until they filled his entire view, before disappearing. Faces he had seen before, faces he might see in the future, faces he would never encounter and faces that died long ago; they all appeared before him and vanished. Pinned down like an insect under a microscope, he was unable to move. All he could do was let them examine him.

Which are you? A face he didn't know swam into view. *Am I connecting to you? Or are you connecting to me? Where are you? Are you in the past? Are you still alive? Are you in the land of the living? Or the land of the dead?*

Somewhere in the distance, a whale was singing. The

sound of a mating call. *But is it? Couldn't it be crying out in sadness?*

One of the many staring faces, a woman, split from ear to ear, becoming one giant mouth. Small canine teeth crowded the mouth right to the back of its throat. It made a disturbing tearing sound as it gnawed through the invisible wall that protected him. The stench of rotting organs surrounded him. He watched a star explode, followed by a vision of a world full of the microscopic life that was first born to these lands. He slid down its throat, mingled with its gastric juices, before being pushed through its contracting and relaxing intestines. Finally, he was expelled from its anus.

A wave washed over the naked body, the *ha*, that was soiled with blood and excrement. A simple lump of flesh, it had neither hands nor feet. An enormous wave broke overhead, before bursting into a million water droplets and showering down upon him. His *ha* began to develop exponentially, its ageing and growth accelerated almost as if being struck by the timefall. Eyes, a mouth, ears and a nose burst forth as it took human form and sprouted both arms and legs.

This child's special.

The feeling of being held and protected by someone else reassured him, yet... When he looked back up, he was once again surrounded by countless faces.

"Where are you?" he was asked as he began to feel his own body fade away. A bottomless fear crashed over him like a surge of water.

And so, his dream ended.

Now it was time to wake up.

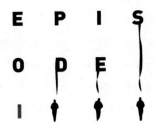

SAM PORTER BRIDGES

"Sam Porter Bridges."

His eyes opened at the sound of his name, and a woman's face appeared before him.

"You're finally awake, Sam Porter Bridges."

Sam flinched as his mind pieced back together his last waking moments.

He had sought shelter in a nearby cave to avoid the timefall. After unloading his gear he'd lain down for a much-needed rest and must have fallen asleep. He couldn't have been out for long, though.

"I'm sorry," the young woman apologized. "I didn't mean to scare you like that."

She wore a black rubber suit, protecting her body from her neck down.

"What're you doing here?"

The woman smiled faintly at Sam's question.

"Trying to stay dry, same as you. Timefall's let up."

Sam shifted his gaze to the entrance of the cave, where the storm of time-accelerating rain had passed and faint rays of sunlight were beginning to peek out from the thin layer of cloud cover that remained. Thankfully, it had moved on before the dead awoke.

"My name is Fragile." The woman held out her hand, encased in a black glove. Sam frowned. He didn't have time for this. He pretended not to notice her offer and made his way over to his pack.

Sam knew the mark depicted on the back of her suit. The unmistakable logo of two bony hands gently cradling a package. "Yeah, I've heard of ya."

"That right?" Fragile asked musically. "I've heard of you too, Sam Porter Bridges. The Man Who Delivers."

Sam continued sorting his gear, ignoring her. It wasn't like this woman would have really known the real him, anyway.

"You want it?" Fragile suddenly held something out toward Sam's face. A bug-like creature wriggled and squirmed between her finger and thumb. "A cryptobiote a day keeps the timefall away." She popped the live larva straight into her mouth. Her noisy chewing sounded almost animalistic as Sam glanced back at her.

"Wanna come work for me?" Fragile's smile softened her

features, erasing the feral expression. "Must be tough out here on your own…"

"Yeah? I thought Fragile Express had plenty of people."

Fragile Express was a delivery company that operated in the central regions. Ever since civilization had collapsed, they had chosen to deliver supplies to those affected by the disaster and had dedicated themselves to supporting recovery efforts. Unlike Sam, they weren't freelancers, but an organized force made up of many people and resources whose mission was to help this world. Without a functioning country, a delivery company like them was indispensable, forming essential lifelines to isolated communities.

"Plenty of traitors. Not much left of us now, save for a few honest folks. And on top of that…"

Fragile removed the glove from her right hand. Her hand looked like it belonged to someone else entirely. Covered in wrinkles and blemishes, the veins that protruded from beneath the skin only served to accentuate the boniness of her fingers. They were the hands of a decrepit old woman. "Not much left of me either. Got soaked from neck to toe."

Fragile squinted into the distance, caught in a memory. Her eyes misted like she was holding back tears, but there wasn't a trace of a wrinkle on her young face. She put her glove back on, concealing the timefall-marred skin beneath the black suit that protected the rest of her body.

"I can't help you with that." Sam didn't know what she

expected from him. No one could get back the time that had already passed or been lost. "I make deliveries. That's all."

Fragile opened her mouth as if about to respond, but she was cut off by a static-buzzed voice calling out from Sam's codec device.

<This is Bridges Central Dispatch. Freelance contractor Sam Porter Bridges—receiver is standing by for drop.>

Perfect timing. Sam picked up his baggage, hoping that she would get the message.

"Headed into town?" Fragile picked up a small piece of baggage with a single hand. Her other hand was holding an umbrella. It was a slick, angular thing made of hi-tech black and clear panels, looking more like a star or crystal formation than any umbrella Sam had ever seen. "Watch yourself. Those things never stay gone for long," she muttered, as if to herself, as she twirled the umbrella between her fingers. Sam nodded silently and left the cave. At that moment, a scrap of paper slipped out of his breast pocket to the floor. As Sam rushed to pick up the scrap, Fragile's voice came from behind him.

"The timefall fast-forwards whatever it touches. But it can't wash everything away. The past just won't let go."

Sam hid the scrap of paper from Fragile's view. It was an old, faded photograph showing a much younger looking Sam, along with two women. He looked awkward, but one of the women was smiling. The other woman's face was blurred, almost impossible to make out on the blotch of faded paper where the drop of timefall had landed. Sam didn't need a photograph to recall her face, though. It was a face that he could never let go, but would never get back.

"I'll see you around... Sam Porter Bridges."

Sam folded the photo and slipped it back into his pocket before turning around to find that Fragile had already vanished.

CENTRAL KNOT CITY

The man's image vanished as if by magic, leaving Igor Frank with a memory of the man's scarred forehead and the luster of his red jacket. He knew it couldn't be true, but he swore that he had felt the warmth radiating from the man's body and smelled his sweat in the air. The man's optical 3D form had felt so real. The hologram had stood there, breathing in and out, staring straight into his eyes to pass along the order as if the projection was truly alive. Ironic, then, that the man's workname was Deadman.

Igor left his private room and ran through the lifeless hallways of the underground Knot City. Only minutes had passed since the hologram of Deadman had delivered the news.

\<A corpse has been discovered in a residential area.\>

Despite his calm voice, the eyes behind his spectacles had lost some of their composure.

\<Sorry, Igor. We only just found it. It looks like it has been around forty hours, so we're in a hurry. You're the only guy we've got.\>

The hologram of Deadman lowered its head. The surgical scars across his forehead were soaked in sweat.

\<Headquarters knows that you're a part of Bridges II and in the middle of preparing for that. This will be your last mission as part of the Corpse Disposal Team. But, look–\>

Igor flashed Deadman a look. He knew there was no time to waste. He only had a few hours. And there were very few Corpse Disposal Team members. If Igor was even slightly delayed, it was very likely that he could kiss goodbye to everyone in the city.

Igor gestured toward some equipment on the wall and asked if he would need it. Deadman nodded silently. This wasn't going to be a straightforward disposal. As Igor put on his uniform and picked up his equipment, Deadman spoke again.

\<I'm sorry I had to put you up to this. But there are arrangements for someone to come and help. If he's on time, he should be arriving at the

distro center soon. I can guarantee his track
record and abilities. I'm sure that he will be able
to help you save the citizens of Central Knot.>

So, there was still someone worth a damn on this continent? Someone who could actually do something good for this dead-end world?

<I've sent his profile over to your device. Check it over later. Sam Bridges is his name.>

With that, Deadman's hologram disappeared.

The noise and vibrations of the truck's motor resonated through Igor's body. On his left, the driver kept one hand on the wheel while wiping at the sweat on the back of his neck with the other. Igor instructed him to stop the truck before the front gate. He had worked with this driver many times before. Igor's job was transporting corpses from isolation wards to the incinerators. Every day was like walking a tightrope. If he put a single foot wrong, he wouldn't just be risking his own life, but the lives of everyone in the city. Normally, he at least had the gift of time, but not for this job. There wasn't a second to spare. If he was just the slightest bit late, the corpse would go necro and cause a voidout, wiping out the whole city.

The truck slowed down as they approached a figure. Igor could barely make out the man's features through the glare of the distribution center lights behind him. He seemed to be a match for the man in the profile, though.

The truck rolled to a halt and the hydraulics hissed as metal groaned against metal, lowering the cabin closer to the ground. Igor exchanged looks with the man outside. Faint frown lines were etched between the man's eyebrows. Igor thought that it was because he had seen the Bridges mark on the outside of the truck. *So, this is the savior who is going to get us out of this mess.*

Igor opened the door and climbed down from the cabin. He strode forward and held out his hand.

"Igor. Bridges Corpse Disposal."

Their supposed savior averted his eyes from Igor's hand. Igor realized that the man wouldn't take his hand, but he kept it held out regardless. "Sam Porter Bridges, I presume."

The man's face twisted in a wry grimace, which Igor took as a yes.

Igor remembered the notes on Sam's profile: a freelance porter who suffered from DOOMS, he had been a member of Bridges up until around ten years ago. Ever since his time in Bridges he had displayed symptoms of aphenphosmphobia and couldn't stand physical contact with others.

"What happened?" Sam may have refused to shake Igor's hand, but at least he met his gaze directly.

"Look, gotta get a move on. I'll explain as we go. Come on," Igor said, turning back toward the truck's trailer. Sam's footsteps followed behind him. "Come and take a look."

Igor climbed up onto the trailer and gestured toward a piece of cargo fixed to the center. It was around the same length as an average human male, a big, lead-colored chrysalis.

"He's got a date with the incinerator," Igor explained.

Sam climbed up onto the trailer, and inspected the dead man in the body bag. "How long since he flatlined?" Sam asked, fixated on the body. It was clear Sam understood the peculiarity and urgency of the situation.

"We don't know the exact TOD, but I'd say it's been upwards of forty hours."

Their eyes met. "He wasn't quarantined?"

Sam's voice was a mixture of anger and confusion.

"He wasn't sick. This was a suicide." The word alone brought back the details from Deadman's briefing and Igor was brought face-to-face with the weight of their mission.

"Oh… Jesus," Sam muttered, staring at the body.

"We're just lucky we found him at all. We got him on ice ASAP, but who knows when he'll go necro."

As he explained the situation to Sam, Igor couldn't help but feel like he was covering for the dead man. Dying undetected and undiscovered and eventually going necro meant turning into the ultimate weapon of destruction. Unless you were a baby who was blissfully unaware of the concept of death, there wasn't a soul on the planet who didn't know that. Suicide no longer meant killing only yourself, it involved other people now, too. To put it bluntly, suicide was an act of terrorism.

"Where are you taking him?" Sam's voice sounded somewhat reproachful.

Brushing it off, Igor booted up the device on his wrist. The device projected a map in front of them. "Closest incinerator is to the north."

Icons representing Sam and Igor's current location along with the location of the corpse incinerator were displayed on the map. Sam screwed up his face.

"This route's crawling with BTs. Sure you can't use another?"

"I wish I could, but there's no time." They had no choice; the corpse had been discovered far too late.

"Then just burn the poor bastard right here," said Sam.

"And put all that chiralium into the air so close to town? Can't do it."

Igor looked back toward the town. Sam was right, though. Burning the body right here instead of attempting to make their way through a route infested with "them," the BT monsters left behind from former corpses, was the safest option.

But the chiralium released when a corpse was burned lingered for a long time, and exposure caused all kinds of issues: depression, apocalyptic nightmares, even suicidal thoughts. And this was the entrance to the city. It would have to be abandoned, severing the links with the few cities left and those outside.

"Hey. We can do this. We just need someone like you, with DOOMS."

Sam didn't answer. He simply removed his glove and felt the body bag with his bare hand.

The skin from Sam's palm to his wrist turned red like an allergic reaction. DOOMS sufferers were afflicted with the ability to sense death. The rest of the skin hidden under Sam's uniform was probably covered in goosebumps and also turning a dark red. Sam removed his hand and inched his head closer to the body bag. He was sniffing at the "death" emanating from the body. A deep line crinkled between his brows.

"Well, he's already in the first stages of necrosis. If we don't hurry, this place is a crater."

There was no other choice but to aim for the incinerator.

"So how 'bout it? Can we count on you?" Igor asked.

Sam leaned back away from the body and nodded. Igor offered his hand once more. "Then Bridges hereby enters into a contract with Sam Porter."

Sam glanced once at Igor's hand before turning back to the corpse. So, he could touch a corpse, but he couldn't bear to shake the hand of a living person? Igor shook his head, resigned.

"It's Sam. Just Sam." Sam began retightening the straps

holding the body in place in the trailer. Igor kneeled down beside him and followed suit. "And I can't spot BTs. Just sense 'em," Sam muttered as he adjusted the belt around the body's ankles. Igor understood. The notes had warned as much, but it was still a big help. Normal people like Igor couldn't even sense BTs. If he didn't have specialized equipment that could sense the world of the dead, he wouldn't have a clue where "they" were. Igor tapped on the equipment attached to his chest. "That's why we came prepared."

"A Bridge Baby, huh?" Sam observed.

"With its help and you, we'll be able to stay one step ahead of 'em."

Igor's words were more to convince himself than anyone else that it would be alright, but he tried to hide his misgivings by taking the end of the cord attached to his abdomen and connecting it to the jack on the pod.

In an instant, the world turned upside-down. A mass of heat ran all the way up from Igor's tailbone through the top of his skull. The world began to twist and distort, a consequence of the tears that were forcing their way out of his eyes. Sam's face now appeared deformed like an abstract painting.

No one could accurately explain the origin or theory behind this equipment. It was a system that appeared at around the same time the world got this way. It took the form of a Bridge Baby, a newborn suspended in a transparent chamber filled with amber fluid, who could connect the world of the living and the dead, but it had been artificially developed.

The Bridge Baby twitched a little in the pod connected to Igor's chest. Bubbles formed and popped within the artificial amniotic fluid.

"Makes me feel like shit every time." Igor wiped away the tear running down his cheek, sniffed, and looked at Sam.

"Well, you are plugging into the other side."

To Igor, Sam's words sounded muffled, like he was speaking through a thin veil. He still hadn't managed to master the tuning of all his senses. His field of vision was unstable. He closed his eyes and massaged his eyelids. Somewhere in the depths of his ears, he thought he could hear the laughter of the Bridge Baby. His eyes snapped open in response, only to find the stiff look on Sam's face, his gaze locked on the pod. Igor could still hear the laughter of the Bridge Baby.

"Roll out!" Igor shouted to the driver. There was no time to spare. Whatever the case, this corpse had to be disposed of thoroughly and correctly. They had to deliver the body to the world of the dead and make sure that it could never come back.

The motor revved and the truck began to move out. As they drove through the gate, the sun disappeared in the sky. Thick black cloud was the only thing that awaited Sam, Igor, the truck, and the corpse.

†

Igor booted up the device on his wrist to check where they were. If they continued like this then they should make it in time. It was a big "if."

"The world was different when I was a kid," Igor piped up, holding onto the handrail in the trailer. If he didn't say something to take his mind off their mission, it would overwhelm him.

"America was a country. Anybody could go anywhere they damn well pleased. No need for couriers like yourself."

Sam was staring off into the distance. Igor couldn't tell if he was listening or not, but that didn't matter. Igor needed to speak, to say anything to hold back the overwhelming fear of what they were attempting to do.

"We had highways, airplanes, hell, you could even visit other countries! Hard to imagine it now. As you can see, the Death Stranding poked us fulla holes. Fucked us beyond all recognition. And if you were lucky enough to survive, the timefall came and washed you away..."

Highways, planes, other countries, America. They only existed as words now. Concepts for things lost in the Death Stranding. It was surely only a matter of time before the words did too. Things were the first to go, followed by language. The name of colors, animals, food, vehicles... The names of feelings shared between human beings. They would all disappear eventually. And even if the words did survive, they would no longer have any connection to reality.

They would be sacred and devoid of meaning. America was breaking down into an abstraction, a set of ideas without basis in reality. It was becoming more or less like God.

Eventually, the generation who were born after America disappeared, like Sam, would become the majority. Then America really would be like God: only the word would remain. Along with the issue of devotion. Like a religious cult driven by their burning belief and fervor, the country would most likely become responsible for tragedy after tragedy.

That's why people like Igor, who actually knew America, had to take it back. Before it became like God. Before the timefall washed it all away. Before monsters destroyed this world.

"Then those freaks from the Beach showed up. Not that I have to tell you."

A slip of the tongue. Igor glanced at Sam, but Sam's expression gave nothing away. The lack of reaction spurred Igor on.

"The worlds of the living and the dead all mixed together... And that's when folks started holing up in the cities. And couriers like yourself got put up on a pedestal."

Igor had been about to say how that included himself and the other corpse disposal teams, but his words died in his mouth. Before them stretched a rainbow. Not a normal rainbow, curving up from the ground toward the sky.

Instead, its arch was upside-down, bursting from the clouds down toward the ground and back up again. An evil bridge that carried monsters over from the other side.

Igor pointed at the inverted rainbow. Sam surveyed the sky, most likely already aware of it, and then turned his gaze back down to the body bag in the trailer.

A black, tarlike substance was leaking out of the dull, lead-colored body bag. Especially out of the abdomen area. The cries of the BB rang inside Igor's ears. His view of the world around him distorted once more. Countless specks were flowing out of the black mass and floating up into the air. When he looked a little closer, he could see them each spiral upwards, twisting into a single, thick rope. It was the first time that Igor had ever witnessed it.

The *ha* was beginning to go necro and the *ka* that was seeping out of it was trying to drag the Beach here.

The Beach was a place between the world of the living and the world of the dead. It supposedly wasn't a part of the physical world, but a special "place" that existed in a different dimension. Normal people like Igor couldn't sense it, unlike those with DOOMS. When they tried to explain what they were able to see, they often described the world of the dead as an ocean and the boundary that connected that world with this one as a beach. The sea, mother of all life, became synonymous with the place the dead returned to. And when the dead crawled out of that ocean and across the

Beach to become stranded in this world, it became known as the Death Stranding.

Sam held his hand out over the body and felt the abdomen where the twisting black thread rose from the navel. His palm turned an angry red instantly.

"How much farther to the incinerator!?" Sam shouted. Tears were streaming from his eyes. The body bag was almost entirely covered in the black mass now. The sky was darkening in response.

"This guy's about to pop!"

"Shit. We're gonna have to cut through the BTs!" Igor tapped on the rear window and signaled to the driver. The truck accelerated and changed course to the left. Igor tightened his grip on the rail and crouched down low to avoid getting thrown from the trailer. This close, he got a good look at the body. The necrosis was spreading, farther gone than he'd ever seen. Igor didn't know how many bodies he had moved before. Most of them were safe; they had been able to estimate the time of death. All Igor and his team had to do was collect terminal patients from the isolation ward once they had reached the end stages of whatever was afflicting them. Even when they received corpses that had died suddenly in accidents, there was still plenty of time to spare before necrosis set in. This was the first time that Igor had needed to transport a corpse that was ready to blow.

Igor wondered what it was like inside the bag. The body

had probably already decomposed into an unimaginable number of minute particles. The body bag was probably the only thing left to give the remains any semblance of shape. It was a casket of soft woven synthetic fibers. Once unbound, the mass would cease to look like a body at all.

The truck leapt up into the air. Igor and Sam gripped onto the handrails with all their strength. A wind powerful enough to stir up the ground beneath them blew from behind, throwing the two men around like ragdolls in the trailer. As Igor squeezed his eyes shut to brace for the storm of dust about to bear down on him, tepid drops of water began to fall on his cheek.

His skin tightened. An itch quickly became a pain, spreading across his entire face. He'd felt this before—the sting of rapid aging. Where the water touched his skin, it left a trail of wrinkles and gray hair in its wake. Sensing the timefall, the hood on Igor's uniform automatically deployed, covering his head, Sam's doing the same opposite him.

The timefall didn't care, driving down harder and harder.

When they looked up, the entire sky was filled with black clouds, dark as the tarlike substance pouring out of the body bag. The light of the sun was completely blocked out and a pall of darkness covered the landscape. The same way the timefall snatched away time from whatever it touched, the chiral clouds it fell from stole all sense of night or day. No matter how many times Igor had experienced it, it was something he had never gotten used to. The world felt suddenly wrong, and there was no way to orient himself.

The headlights of the truck pierced this blanket of darkness and illuminated the torrential sheets of timefall. As Igor focused on gripping the rail, his nostrils were hit by the smell of the sea, though they were nowhere near any ocean. The salty air flooded his senses and sent tears streaming down his face as he breathed in the unmistakable stench of the world of the dead.

The motor whined and the headlights blinked off. In this world of only rain and darkness, the truck had lost all power and stalled. The driver was shouting and was struggling to get the motor going again. "Don't worry. This is just a temporary blackout," Igor shouted through the rear window, trying to keep his voice steady but it came out full of panic. Timefall interfered with electromagnetic waves and frequently brought down electrical systems. But they usually restarted after a while.

"Calm down." Igor was no longer just repeating that for the driver's sake, but his own sake too.

As if his prayers had been answered, the driver's seat lit up as the headlights blinked back on. Igor looked at Sam with a faint sense of relief when he noticed that Sam's focus was toward his left shoulder. The tip of the Odradek sensor mounted on his shoulder had opened up like a splayed hand. Waves of chills, nausea and dizziness washed over Igor, combining with the smell of the ocean.

The dead were inching nearer but Igor had no idea which direction they would come from. The nervous Odradek was flickering open and closed as if trying to grip onto the very sky itself. It was the only equipment they had that would coordinate with the Bridge Baby to show the position of the dead. If the BB sensed the dead, the Odradek would show where. But how could it not find them in an aura of death this thick?

"Sam, can you see anything?"

"No, nothing!" Sam shouted back, temper flaring. There was no doubt that Sam could also sense the presence of the dead all around them, his DOOMS ability just as highly tuned as the Odradek's mechanical sensor. He peered out of the trailer through the dense cloud surrounding them. Igor rapped on the pod. *C'mon, help me out. Where are the monsters?*

Something like a whine came from the baby and the Odradek began to swing around wildly, like a broken windmill.

"This BB must be busted or something," Igor said.

All of a sudden, the motor roared back to life. The tires screeched across the ground beneath them and the truck began to shoot forward once again. The driver thrust his foot down hard to escape the aura of death that was engulfing them. Igor gripped the handrail even tighter so that he didn't get thrown off. The numbing stench that had been offending his nostrils felt like it passed through his nose and out the top of his head. The rotating Odradek came to an abrupt stop.

The robotic claw folded into a cross and pointed directly in front of them. That only meant one thing.

That's where they were. The truck was headed straight for them.

Igor tried to yell at the driver to change direction, but it was too late. The truck was shuddering hard as it raced across the rugged terrain and the air was filled with the screams of the driver and the screech of the brakes. Igor could see a large black handprint stuck firmly to the windshield over the driver's shoulder, but its owner was nowhere to be seen.

Igor's body lost all sense of weight. He thrust his hands out, groping for anything to hold onto. There was nothing to grab. He was screaming something, but couldn't seem to form any words. Igor was thrown from the trailer and smashed into the ground.

Igor awoke to the sound of groans. He picked himself up off the muddy ground and looked around. The groans were very close. The truck had tipped over on its side. Beneath it, Igor found the source of the pain. The driver was pinned, his whole lower body hidden under a pile of metal. He was frantically twisting his body and waving his arms as if trying to fight off a wild animal. Drenched in timefall, his face had already transformed into that of an old man. It was contoured with deep lines and his hair was a snowy white, but the groans that pleaded for someone to save him still betrayed the man's youth.

Knowing that he had to save him, Igor started toward the truck when he noticed a movement from the corner of his eye. It was Sam. He was walking in the direction of the body bag which had been tossed out of the trailer with them. He was half-dragging his right leg behind him. The blackened body bag began to glow gold where it used to cover someone's face. It looked like a casket with a warped golden mask stuck to the front. Countless minute particles were welling forth from the stomach area, stretching out into a single thread that rose up and beyond into the sky.

This was the final stage of necrosis. The step before humans transformed into monsters instead of passing on peacefully.

It was a scenario that he had only ever heard people tell stories about. A process that he had been lectured on when he was first assigned to the Corpse Disposal Team. And now, it was playing out in front of him.

When humans die, their *ka* escapes their *ha*. This was a concept that had been investigated by the ancient Egyptians and explored the two elements that made up life. When the body, or *ha*, necrotizes and lingers in this world, the soul, or *ka*, becomes lost in search of it. It remains in the area where it died, looking for it for the rest of eternity. Bodies had to be burned immediately to let the soul know that there was no longer a body to go back to. If the body wasn't burned, the soul would become a Beached Thing and continue to search for the living.

The last thing they needed was another body going necro. Igor slid his arms under both of the driver's armpits and braced his feet against the ground to try and pull him out. But the driver wouldn't budge. All Igor could do was try and ease the screaming driver's fear and pain.

"Shut up! Don't even breathe!" Igor turned back toward the sound of Sam's voice and clasped both hands around his mouth, realizing his mistake. The driver followed suit.

The cross-shaped Odradek pointed above them and began spinning rapidly, illuminated with the orange warning light that meant BTs were right there.

Just as Igor and Sam couldn't see the BTs, the BTs couldn't see Sam or Igor. They sought out the living by homing in on breathing and other sounds. For those without a high level of DOOMS, the only sign they were near were the oil-slick handprints left behind as they hunted.

A handprint appeared on the door of the overturned truck right at Igor's side, before another then another, making their way farther and farther down the vehicle. A BT was groping for them in the dark.

Igor held his breath, praying he wouldn't make a single sound. That was the only way they were going to get out of this mess.

His prayers were answered. The sickening black

handprints traveled away from the pair. Igor turned to thank Sam for raising the alarm, but he was about to speak too soon. The body bag began convulsing. It shook violently, twisting and contorting the bag, but soon it started to lessen. The shuddering grew gentler until it stopped altogether.

The straps binding the body bag snapped apart loudly one after the other. A sticky, tarlike substance pooled on the ground underneath the body as small particles of glittering dust floated up from the golden death mask that had formed on the outside of the bag.

Sam looked up. "Shit. It's necrotized."

The handprints returned as if they had heard Sam's murmur. Or, maybe they were here for the newly necrotized body—their new friend. All Igor could do was watch the trail of handprints as he kept his hand firmly clasped over his mouth.

Sam fell backward into the mud, scrambling to get away from the handprints, his hand also clasped tightly over his own mouth. They seemed to be confused. *Were they after Sam? Or the body? Please be heading in the direction of the body.* Igor was praying again, but no luck. The handprints began to move toward Sam. Those whose deaths had been interrupted—the necrotized dead whose *ka* never made it to the other side—relentlessly pursued the living.

Sam held his breath, dragging his leg as crawled backward. He could now see how much blood he was losing from it, even in the darkness. Despite this, Sam threw Igor a look that urged him to escape. The handprints stopped. It was almost like they were carefully considering something. Igor couldn't let this opportunity that Sam had given him go to waste. He strained his arms to try and prize the driver free once more.

But the driver was already past his breaking point. He began to wail in agony, couldn't stand the pain any longer. That roused the monster. The handprints changed direction toward Igor and the driver, no longer lost but focused. They were coming at full speed. That wasn't all. Igor could feel the presence of the dead from the truck behind him. They were surrounded.

Igor let go of the screaming driver and stood up. Silently, he begged the driver to be quiet. The driver's screams were leading the dead right to them.

If you were unlucky enough to get caught by the handprints of the dead, they would try to embrace you. The living and the dead together. Matter and antimatter. When two things that were never supposed to meet were brought together, it created an immense explosion.

"Help me! HELP ME!"

The driver kept screaming. Those screams were proof that he was alive. Those screams were giving the dead something to aim for as they swarmed closer. Igor took out his handgun and pointed it at the driver. The dead didn't want the dead. If the dead embraced each other, nothing would happen.

Igor readied his trigger finger. It felt so heavy that it didn't feel like his own appendage anymore. Before Igor could gather his resolve to pull the trigger, the dead grabbed the driver. Unable to move out of the way, the driver's body was yanked out from under the truck by an invisible hand and dragged into the air.

"Sorry."

Igor's bullet pierced the driver's head and he died instantly. The dead lost interest in the driver immediately. Igor knew what he had to do next.

He shot a look at Sam that said he would be putting his faith in him to finish the job. But behind Sam, a figure appeared on top of the overturned truck. Following Igor's line of sight, Sam turned around. It was too dark to make out the figure's face, they were wearing a hood and cloak. Against their chest, a BB tank glowed red. The figure raised a hand into the air and pointed at something.

Igor could smell blood mingling with the stench of stagnant water. The insufferable odor of rotting fish. The smells crashed over him in a single repulsive wave. His head was splitting and feverish chills ran up his body. He was going to puke.

Right at that moment, a howl pierced the thick cloud cover.

It was neither a cry, nor a scream, nor a growl, but rather

a dreadful noise that could shatter the resolve of any man.

The Odradek transformed into a cross shape and pointed toward a space in the sky.

The baby on Igor's chest jolted around, pressing against the glass, then pushing away to hide.

It was here.

Igor's feet slipped. The ground beneath him was no longer solid and had begun to stream away. The new, liquid ground coiled itself around Igor's legs. Numerous pitch-black arms erupted from the water and tried to drag him down by the legs. They groaned with an insufferable hunger. He searched frantically, the ground around him had transformed into a sea of tar. There was no sign of the original terrain anywhere. Like a sea in slow motion, the tar around him swelled unnaturally and collapsed in on itself. The truck was gradually sinking between the waves and the silhouette that had stood atop it had disappeared once more.

The arms pulling at Igor's legs fought harder to tug him into the churning tar. He chose not to look down at his feet, but rather up above his head. This was the end. The silhouette of a giant human figure towered over him. The head was obscured by cloud and the hands were gripping multiple ropes that were connected to the ground. The shadow yanked on the ropes, ripping up the ground to expose the innards of the Earth.

If he was eaten by that monster, it would cause a voidout.

That's what his manual had told him. Worst-case scenario.

The dead who had necrotized retained a lingering attachment to this world—not just to their own *ha*, but to all living things—and became stranded here, unable to move on to the world of the dead. And, if the dead, who were made up of a chiral substance like antimatter, came into contact with the living, it caused a voidout. Who the hell could have experienced that and lived to tell the tale in a manual? Igor thought it strange that such thoughts would cross his mind at a time like this.

"Run!" he screamed.

He gathered the last of his resolve. He was so sorry that he had gotten Sam involved in this. Igor ripped the pod off his chest and threw it in Sam's direction. Then he pointed the gun up at his chin. Just before he could pull the trigger, he was swept off his feet. The enormous shade lifted him into the air, his world turned upside-down for him and the bullet misfired in the wrong direction. He couldn't keep hold of the gun.

"Run!"

It was no longer a command, but a plea. He needed Sam to escape. If only he could buy him enough time to get away. Igor stretched for the gun, but it was no use. He took the knife from his waist and plunged it into the left side of his chest. But he hit the connection unit for his pod. Once more. He tore open his uniform with the tip of the knife, gouged into the flesh until he scraped up against a rib. And again. His pectoral muscles resisted as they tried to protect his heart from the blade. Again.

The invisible hand swung Igor around as it tried to prevent his suicide.

Igor could see Sam still standing there. He was holding the BB to his chest.

Run. Just take it and run.

Igor heaved a last burst of strength and thrust the knife into his heart. He didn't feel any pain. In fact, he didn't feel anything at all. It was beginning to fade.

His body and consciousness separated. Death wasn't like simply flipping a switch, it was a process that passed through phases. There was no such thing as a quick death. Igor's *ka* knew that. Which meant that right now, at this very second, Igor's body was not yet dead.

And with that, the giant consumed Igor's body.

The dead and the living met.

Then came the voidout.

Igor and the giant both disappeared. The figures transformed into energy with immense speed, before swallowing, annihilating, and disintegrating everything around them. Central Knot City disappeared and Sam Bridges and the BB were consumed by the force of the voidout.

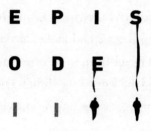

EPISODE II

BRIDGET

—BB, can you hear me?

There was a voice. Someone was staring. There was a light behind them, so it was impossible to make out who it was. Sam couldn't ask them who they were. He couldn't speak. He couldn't move. His arms and legs were bound. He couldn't get free. Tears were running down his cheek, but he couldn't even wipe them away.

—BB, I'll protect you.

Sam heard a voice and opened his eyes.

He sat up with a start, trying to drive away the nightmare he had just been having, but slumped back down helplessly as he felt a pull. There was a dull pain in his right wrist. He was in handcuffs. The other cuff was attached to a bedframe. He tried to yank his arm free, but all that did was worsen the pain in his wrist. The cuffs weren't going anywhere. He wiped away the tears running down his cheek with his free hand.

He took a deep breath and looked around. He was in a room that he had never been in before. He had no idea why he was there and he certainly didn't know why he was chained up. No matter how much he twisted, he couldn't even sit up.

His exposed arms, back and chest were covered in the handprints of the dead, but these were merely a sign of his repatriation from the Seam. What worried him was the injection marks on the insides of his elbows.

He knew it was useless, but he gave his right arm a shake. The metallic clanging of the handcuffs against the bedframe echoed around the room.

"Oh, you're awake. So how does it feel? To be back in the world of the living?" a voice suddenly asked him. The man was wearing a long red jacket and was built like a barrel. Sam spotted a cuff on his right wrist.

He hadn't even sensed the man entering the room. The man approached with footsteps that were far too light to belong to such a massive body. Sam looked up to see a forehead lined with large horizontal scars. They didn't make his face unpleasant, though. Perhaps it was because of the gentle light that filled the eyes behind the man's glasses.

"Don't worry, I'm a doctor. Well, a coroner. Originally."

It clicked into place. His shiny red jacket must have been

his medical uniform. When Sam looked a little more closely, he could see something that resembled a stethoscope hanging around the man's neck.

The man held up his cuffed hand and twisted it in one smooth motion. The action was so quick and natural that it made him look like some kind of magician. The cuff attached to the bedframe opened in response. Sam could now at least get up from the bed, but the other cuff still hung from his wrist.

As he sat up on the bed, Sam examined the cuff and then the man more closely.

"Call me Deadman. I'm well acquainted with the dead. Not like you, of course. Contrary to the name, I've never actually died."

Not flinching under Sam's stare, the man called Deadman held out one of his hands. Sam ignored it. He couldn't touch someone's hand like that. Moreover, he couldn't think of a single reason to shake this man's hand. Especially when he was responsible for cuffing a sleeping man to a bed. Instead of a handshake, Sam decided to try removing the other cuff.

"I would advise against that. I'm no expert, but I can assure you it's for your own protection. See." Deadman rolled up the sleeve of his jacket and showed Sam his own cuff, as if he was trying to indicate that he and Sam were in the same situation.

"So, I'm a prisoner?"

"These aren't handcuffs, they're cutting-edge devices that keep us all connected."

"Us?" Sam repeated back. Deadman gestured at the wall behind him.

Sam turned around and came face to face with a symbol of a spider's web stretching across the North American continent.

"Oh. 'Us.'"

"Yup. Bridges." Sam thought he caught a hint of pride in Deadman's voice.

"Humanity's best hope for the future—or avoiding extinction, if you prefer," Deadman muttered, showing Sam the badge on his lapel. It was the same as the motif on the wall.

"Right. Where am I? What time is it?" Sam asked.

Ignoring the question, Deadman raised his hand again in the same swift movement as before. He removed one of the cuffs and showed it to Sam.

"Watch me. Try pressing it against your skin like this." Deadman clamped the cuff back around his wrist and encouraged Sam to imitate him.

Sam placed the cuff back around his own right wrist. He felt a pain pierce his skin for a split second and let out a yelp.

"That just means your body's got a good connection to the cuff link. Look, look! The cuffs will watch over you twenty-four hours a day. That is to say, we will. We're here to help."

A monitor floating in the air displayed Sam's vitals, including his temperature, pulse, blood pressure and brainwaves, along with the date and time.

"What the hell... Two days?"

Sam had never slept this long after returning from a voidout before. Someone must have done something to put him out for longer.

"During that time, we took the liberty of collecting fluid samples from you," Deadman explained, unabashedly. Sam touched the needle marks on his right arm.

"You're a repatriate. That makes you very special."

There wasn't a sliver of guilt. Deadman didn't even try to hide the curiosity in his voice when it came to Sam's unique ability to survive voidouts. His manner was more like an academic than a doctor. Did he also know that if Sam's body was damaged for any other reason, his *ka* would not be able to come back to this world, nor would it be able to pass on to the world of the dead? His *ka* would be forced to eternally wander between the two. Nobody could understand how frightening that thought was, certainly not this man. This man who had drawn Sam's blood and other fluid while he was passed out in a coma just to satisfy his own curiosity about Sam's anatomy— nothing more than an academic endeavor.

"What happened to the CD guys?"

"Central Knot was obliterated in the annihilation. Place is a crater."

A light flashed in Sam's mind and he bit his lip. The voices of Igor and the driver filled his memory and Sam hung his head in shame.

"The only ones to get a continue were you, for obvious reasons, and your broken Bridge Baby." Deadman made the whole thing sound utterly mundane. He must have known all about Sam's DOOMS. That would have been par for the course if he was part of Bridges, though.

"Is it alright?" Sam asked.

"It's been marked for disposal. Didn't work anymore. Why keep it?" Deadman replied.

They disposed of it even though it had returned from the other side? Sam couldn't fathom what the hell they were thinking.

Deadman stared at the ceiling, lost in his thoughts.

"We lost everyone. Igor and the driver from Corpse Disposal. Most of the Implementation Team and Second Expedition Team. Every soul in Central Knot City, including HQ. All of the area around where you and the others caused that BT to voidout is just one huge crater. The light and shock from the voidout reached all the way over here. Capital Knot City may be close to Central Knot City, but we never expected something that intense." Deadman removed his glasses and rubbed the corners of his eyes. "We're at our base in Capital Knot City now, or should I say our new headquarters. Sudbury seemed the logical choice. But our Implementation Team has been decimated, and there's only so much they can do in two days. Things here are a mess. Fortunately, the director and his support team were out of town at the time, so the chain of command remains intact."

He sounded like he was trying to convince himself that things were still okay. Central and Capital were the largest cities on the East Coast and happened to lie adjacent to one another. It was a miracle that Central was the only city to get annihilated.

"I hate to do this so soon, but I have a job for you." Deadman's expression softened, and the haggard look on his face disappeared as though it had been an illusion. Meanwhile, Sam was still lost for words. The BB, Igor, Knot City, and the Bridges Implementation Team were all gone, and once again he was the only person left behind.

"This pattern is from when you repatriated?"

Deadman had circled behind Sam and was making no effort to hide his curiosity. But putting aside everything that had happened while he was asleep, Sam couldn't hate this man, despite himself. Normally, Sam would have kept the other man at a distance and given him nothing but silence, but for now he let Deadman inspect his handprint-covered body. Maybe it was some kind of atonement he could offer for those who had died. The numerous handprints all over Sam's body were a record of his crimes and punishment— an endless cycle of death and rebirth.

There was most likely a new mark somewhere on his

back where Deadman was looking. A brand to remember the voidout and his subsequent repatriation.

Deadman reached forward with the probing manner of a doctor, but Sam withdrew his arm as soon as he sensed the life emanating from Deadman's fingertips. It was an animal reflex, the instinctive behavior of a creature trying to evade capture.

"I see…" Deadman nodded, neither angry nor surprised. "Aphenphosmphobia? No wonder you were out there alone. Where no one could touch you."

Sam gave up on finding a reply. He was alone. Not only was he rejected by death, but he couldn't even stand the touch of the living.

"I'll try to be more careful, Sam." Pulling his hand away, Deadman pointed to the trolley in the corner of the room. "So, the job is an urgent delivery."

Laying on top was a small attaché-case-like briefcase.

"I need you to bring the president some morphine."

"What president? America is gone. You talking about the mayor of Central Knot?"

"No, no, no, no. Not the mayor. America lives on, Sam. The president is in the final stages of cancer—in critical condition—but there's still time."

"Why me?"

"Look Sam… Do as I ask, and I promise it will all make sense."

"Why don't you do it?" Sam asked.

Deadman shrugged, shook his head, and smiled at Sam.

"Because I'm not really here."

Deadman approached Sam. The large lines across his forehead stretched out across Sam's vision. The traces of the bulging stitches on his clothes, the hair roots and peach fuzz along his hairline, and the faint layer of sweat on his skin were all visible. Still, Deadman walked straight toward Sam. Sam tried to move his body to avoid a collision with the man, but there were no traces of all the things that made a person human, their breath, their odor, their body heat. None of the things that a man with aphenphosmphobia like Sam tried so hard to avoid. So, he really was a dead man. He only really understood afterward.

Deadman's body passed right through Sam.

There was a hint of pride in his voice, like a magician who had managed to trick an entire audience, when Deadman began to speak again from behind Sam.

"Apologies. This is just a hologram. I'm actually over in the Isolation Ward. In the big triangle building." Deadman signaled toward the other side of the room and approached the trolley.

"Here is the morphine."

Deadman reached out as if to pick up the case, but was unable to grab anything.

"Bridges hereby enters into a contract with Sam Porter."

It was all an act. Sam shook his head and glared at Deadman.

"Come on, you've got morphine there. What's this about? Tell me the truth."

Where did this act begin? Sam was asking himself. *Who wrote it? How far has it come to fruition?*

"The truth, Sam, is that America's last president wants to see you in person."

Sam wasn't surprised.

"Are you really about to say no?" Deadman asked.

Someone extremely close to the president was pulling the strings. Sam was sure that if he went along with it, not only could he meet the president, but the mastermind behind all this.

Sam decided to follow Deadman's instructions. That way, he would be able to see if Deadman really was some kind of magician. Sam picked up the container.

"Very good. I'll see you in the Isolation Ward."

Deadman nodded. His large body seemed to defy gravity as it floated upward. The outline of his long red jacket lost its form and expanded. Then the body burst into a thousand pieces and scattered through the air. Only his smile remained in the void as he disappeared. Sam Porter Bridges left the room to deliver the case. To accomplish his duty as a courier.

CAPITAL KNOT CITY // ISOLATION WARD

Deadman stared silently at the room on the monitor. Now that Sam had left, there was no one else there.

He sensed someone stood beside him. There was no need to check who it was. The man who was waiting for Sam was stood beside Deadman, watching the monitor.

Sam would be here soon, following the rail laid down by Bridges to deliver his cargo.

Unfortunately, Deadman had no idea what Sam would be thinking as he walked to the Isolation Ward. But it didn't matter. He'd have plenty of time to find that out later. He could get to know Sam then.

It was three years ago when Deadman was first brought into Bridges, and he first heard the name Sam Porter Bridges spoken about in hushed tones between the upper management of the company. He was the one and only Man Who Delivers.

He was a repatriate who could survive voidouts, the worst calamity to plague mankind. Deadman had also heard that if Sam lost the *ha* that would be repatriated back into this world, then he would be doomed to wander the Seam between worlds forever. In other words, his soul would never pass onward to the world of the dead. That made him immortal in a cruel sense.

Deadman had heard the rumors about Sam. But he had only ever heard of him in terms of a mythical vaccine in the face of the extremely mysterious Death Stranding phenomenon. Deadman understood that. He was just a figment of the imagination of a person who was desperate for someone like Sam to be real. But the Bridges members insisted that he existed. If he was indeed real, Deadman wanted to meet him. He wanted to study him, to understand him. If he could understand him, then he could shine a light on the connection between the living and the dead. It could help the man given the working name of Deadman make peace with himself.

He was very much looking forward to their first real meeting. His brief appearance as a hologram didn't count.

"Sam is here," Deadman told the man next to him, as he left the monitor and exited the room. He needed to make the preparations to greet the porter.

Doctors and nurses clad in red uniforms crisscrossed the elevator hall. Deadman could hear them talking about the condition of the president as he walked past. As he headed toward the hall, Deadman found himself straightening his jacket. Sam would be here soon. Eventually, the display told him that the elevator had arrived.

"Sam, it's me. Deadman." He held out his hand as Sam exited the elevator, but quickly caught himself. "Sorry! My mistake."

Sam ignored Deadman's apology and presented the suitcase.

"I'm afraid the president's condition has deteriorated."
Deadman took the case and inspected the contents. The
ampoules of morphine were arranged neatly. "Thank you.
This will help to ease the pain... and allow her to speak
with you in these final moments."

Sam's expression clouded over.

"Her?" Sam exclaimed.

"The first and last female President of the United States.
Surely you remember her? She raised you."

Sam remained silent. Deadman thought this might happen,
but an uneasiness that he couldn't explain hung in the air.

This man *was* Sam Bridges, right?

Sam should have known that the current President of the
United States was a woman, and he definitely should have
known that she was his mother. So, what was with that
dumbfounded response? Maybe he wasn't Sam, but someone
else? Or did he want to deny that he was Sam?

Deadman led the way to the president's office.

His handcuff reacted to something in front of the door
and permitted them to enter. Deadman ushered Sam into
the room.

Welcome.

Someone had gone to great lengths to recreate the Oval
Office in the basement below the Isolation Ward.

It was an elliptical holy ground that had witnessed

generations of people dedicate their lives to the office of the President of the United States. It was a place where successive leaders, led by their ideals and the world around them, had worked themselves into the ground. It was an altar for the highest-ranking sacrifice that this godless country had to accept. In the middle of the room was a bed covered with a dome.

Deadman moved to the side so that Sam could see. Sam gasped behind him. Deadman nodded toward the bed.

The room was dazzlingly bright, with large windows stretching almost to the ceiling behind the bed, flooding the room with light. Another man stood beside the bed, his back to Sam.

"That's the president's right-hand man, the director of Bridges," Deadman whispered into Sam's ear.

As if he had sensed their presence, the man turned around. Even though he had long withdrawn from active duty, he still had the body of a soldier. His face was covered with an iron mask, dark and skeletal.

"Die-Hardman?"

Sam and Die-Hardman had known each other far longer than Deadman had been on the scene. Deadman approached the bed and checked all the medical equipment organized around it, from the ventilator to the EKG and AED, before turning his gaze toward the patient. Dozens of tubes extended out from the frail body on the bed—a breathing mask, a drip, cords monitoring vitals like pulse and blood pressure. She looked like a butterfly caught in a spider's web. Or perhaps she was more like a golden orb-weaving spider, right at the center of its own magnificent web. She may have been fragile, but she was a leader reconnecting the rest of a country on the verge of extinction with strong and delicate threads.

"Sam… I never thought we would be meeting again like this. Ironic, isn't it?"

Behind him, Deadman could hear Die-Hardman speaking to Sam.

"What's it been, Sam, ten years? Look at us—a bunch of deathless freaks, meeting like this…"

Die-Hardman waited for an answer, but it never came. Only the rhythmic electronic noises emitted by the ventilator and EKG pierced the silence.

"Yeah, well, good to see you, too. President's waiting." He moved closer to Sam, his voice a low growl. "It's your mother. Bridget. She's a bit out of it, but I know she'll recognize you."

Deadman adjusted the bed, raising it so that the president was sitting up. Her eyelids fluttered open slightly.

As the president grimaced, Deadman whispered into her ear.

"Madam President, we've brought Sam."

The president smiled weakly. Deadman beckoned Sam

over, who finally approached the bed. The president let out a pained sound. She lifted her frail arms and attempted to remove her breathing mask. Deadman tried to convince her not to, but a nod from Die-Hardman stopped him in his tracks.

Deadman gently removed her mask.

Her voice was little more than a croak, as if she was using all her willpower to squeeze it out from the depths of her throat. Her face had grown even paler in these few moments since waking.

"We'll leave you two alone," Deadman whispered into the president's ear. He left her bedside to make room for Sam.

"Sam. I knew you'd come back," Deadman heard from behind him as he and Die-Hardman exited the Oval Office.

No one was left in the room but a son who had just returned from the world of the dead and an aged mother who was about to depart for it.

CAPITAL KNOT CITY // PRESIDENTIAL OFFICE

"Are you doing alright?" the president asked. There was less life in her eyes these days. She had a gentle smile on her face, but her gaze was unstable and roaming. She tried lifting her arm, searching for Sam. Sam backed away from the bed slightly, unnerved by the thin and fragile-looking limb.

The president closed her eyes. All Sam could hear was the beeping of machines and the president's ragged breaths.

A sudden movement in the corner of his eye caught his attention. An antique quill sat in the pen holder atop the president's work desk. Sam felt like he had seen it somewhere before. The feather of the quill was swaying rhythmically and its movements seemed to match the timing of the president's breathing exactly. She breathed in and then out. The feather moved up and down to that exact rhythm. Sam was transfixed by it.

"Yeah, I know you hate me," admitted Bridget.

The quill suddenly became still.

"Amelie—"

"Amelie?" Sam asked.

"You remember Amelie went west. Took her three years to cross. She's trying to rebuild the country."

Sam couldn't bring himself to look at Bridget. He focused on the quill instead.

"Still going on about that, huh?" Sam muttered.

"You're the one I wanted to send, Sam. Time's running out."

The president was having trouble inhaling her next breath.

"Sam, help Amelie."

Sam was urging the quill to start moving again.

"She needs you," Bridget pleaded.

Sam shook his head. But the president couldn't see.

"You can make America whole."

Finally, it clicked. Bridget had told him about the quill before. It was the quill used by the Founding Fathers when they signed the Declaration of Independence. The gravely ill president had inherited it from her forebears.

"Sam, if we don't all come together again, humanity will not survive."

"We don't need a country. Not anymore," Sam countered.

"We do. Alone, we have no future."

A broken, whistle-like sound came out of the president's throat. Her eyes were tightly closed as she tried to endure the pain. Sam averted his eyes. He didn't want to see her like that. He wanted to grab the quill and snap the antique in half.

"No, America's finished. Bridget, you're the president of jack shit," Sam snapped.

The president's eyes gently opened and she looked right at him.

"Sam! Listen to me. Lis... Ah..."

Sam felt a burning pain in his left wrist and jerked backward in surprise. But Bridget was clinging to him. Despite her condition, he couldn't get her off. The pain of her touch seared his wrist.

"Sam!"

Her voice reverberated around the office and she wouldn't let go. Sam's aphenphosmphobia was turning his left arm a dangerous shade of crimson. He twisted his body, crashing this way and that to try and wrestle his hand free.

Bridget was falling out of the bed and the cords and tubes attached to the medical devices all disconnected with a pop.

The stand that held the drip crashed forward onto the desk, hitting the quill. The ominous pen that still seemed bound to Bridget was surely broken…

But it wasn't harmed at all. The pen that had immortalized the pledges of the founding of this nation had survived, would continue to survive—to commit the future dreams of the nation to paper, too.

Bridget had fallen on top of Sam. She was crushing him. Not just with her touch, but the weight of the nation behind her.

Sam couldn't support her any longer and fell backward. Bridget was clinging to him with the strength of someone in the prime of their life. Bridget's face was illuminated by the light streaming into the room. She crawled toward him, black ink pooling beneath her from the tubes ripped from her flesh. She reached for his wrist, her fingers brushing his skin.

"So you are willing to help me."

"No, I—"

Sam tried to rip the cuff away from his wrist to shake Bridget off, but she smiled at him. It was a look of understanding. The cuff was a symbol of Bridges and proof that he had sworn to rebuild America. But he didn't want it. He shook his head. Bridget's smile was fixed as her gaze sunk to the floor.

A photograph had fallen onto it. It was the same

photograph that Sam had almost lost in the cave. There, between an awkwardly smiling Sam and a woman whose face had been worn away by the timefall, stood a younger Bridget. The dying woman recognized it, and put her hand on Sam's chest. She tried to speak but her eyes fluttered closed one last time and she collapsed to the floor. Sam could have sworn that he'd heard Bridget thank him.

He was still unable to let go of the past. At least, that was how Bridget seemed to have interpreted the photo. Her mind had been made up. This was the president's Oval Office. The sacrifice who determined the path of the country was the master in here.

—I'll be waiting for you on the Beach.

Sam heard a voice. He searched for its source, but the panicked screech of the monitors echoing around the room drowned out every other noise. He didn't hear the voice again, only the machines and the incoming commotion from the door.

The device on Deadman's right wrist suddenly began to vibrate violently. A biometric warning flashed up on the monitors. When he looked up, the door was already open, and the director was already running through. Deadman rushed in behind him. The large window was covered in black and the dome that had once straddled the bed to protect it was lying on the floor like an empty shell. The work desk was thrown into disarray. On top of the desk, the pen still stood upright, perfectly poised. There was no noise except the harsh warning beeps of the machines.

"Madam President!" Die-Hardman shouted out to Bridget, who was still draped over Sam. Sam raised his arms into the air in a daze. He looked like a soldier making a plea of surrender.

Die-Hardman lifted up Bridget's body and rushed it back onto the bed. Deadman, along with the nurses who had rushed into the room behind them, began to attempt to resuscitate her. He placed the breathing mask back over her face and started up the AED. He kept calling Bridget's name into her ear, but there was no response. Bridget's body began to transform into a state that Deadman knew all too well. She was going cold. Her *ka* began to separate from her *ha*.

All around him was the sound of sobbing.

Looking up, Deadman saw his fellow Bridges members gathering around Bridget's bed and grieving for her. They had assembled from locations far and wide to stand at the deathbed of the last President of the United States of America.

America had fallen. It had fallen before the very eyes of her freshly repatriated adopted son.

The son was sat with his back against the wall, looking stunned in Deadman's direction. Bridget's still-fresh handprints covered his exposed arm. They were simply marks from the physical rejection that Sam's body had shown her still living flesh, but they were the only traces left of her life now.

"Listen. No one can know that the president is dead. If word gets out, Bridges is finished. Now, what happened here does not leave this room. Do you understand?" Die-Hardman whispered to Deadman urgently.

Deadman nodded and looked back toward Bridget. Her death would be celebrated by those who had no interest in rebuilding America. Bridget had been the great backbone to those who still believed in this country. If she disappeared, everything would collapse. The lights flickered. The dome of the bed contorted and disappeared. Then the desk, the sofa, the carpet... Then the portraits on the wall went, the elegantly curved border of the window and the gently blowing curtains. Even the finely crafted door. One by one they all disappeared.

In their place was a cold floor and walls that dully reflected the light. Even the bed had been stripped of decoration and transformed into a functional and basic medical bed.

The only remnant of the president left in the room was an American flag that drooped from the rafters.

That was fast, Deadman thought to himself. The moment the president died, the hologram that had been projecting the veneer of the Oval Office shut off. The holograms of those who were located far away disappeared too, and the place where the men were now stood had turned back into a standard hospital room. Although now it felt more like a morgue. They had to be quick and dispose of the body properly. Even if the dead body in the room used to be the president, she would receive no special treatment. Death came to all human beings equally.

Deadman was in charge of disposing of the body. He couldn't even begin to mourn the president's death until he had finished the prescribed disposal procedure. He gave some instructions to his staff and then attempted to contact the Corpse Disposal Team, but Die-Hardman took charge.

The director bent down in front of Sam and looked him in the face.

"Sam. Before she died, the president made a contract with you." He was quiet, but the tone of his voice told Sam that he had no choice in the matter. Sam glared at the director.

"What are you talking about?"

"As a member of Bridges you're going to work with the rest of us to rebuild America." The director pointed at the cuff around Sam's right wrist. Deadman may have been the one who had fitted it onto Sam while he was asleep, but the director was the man who ordered him to do it—Deadman was very aware of his role in the events that led them all here.

"You think you can recruit me? Like she tried to?" Sam tried to break free from the cuffs. The director nodded.

"Well, she succeeded," Die-Hardman replied.

Just as Deadman had suspected. The director already knew this would happen. If that was the case, Deadman knew that he also had a duty to fulfil as a member of Bridges.

"Director, the cancer spread throughout her entire body," Deadman said. "Harvesting organs is out of the question, and there is no need for an autopsy. Her body needs to be cremated before she necrotizes."

"Cause if we don't, this place'll turn into another crater," the director replied, his eyes still fixed on Sam. Deadman nodded and crouched beside the director.

"Listen, Sam. We don't have any porters right now."

Sam frowned at Deadman.

"Igor is gone, too. All the other CD teams were annihilated in that last voidout."

Sam looked away. Deadman kept pressing on.

"But the president's body has to be burned. This is no ordinary transportation. This job has requirements. DOOMS. Repatriate. There is no one else that we can ask. No one else who can even do it. The road from Capital Knot City to the incinerator was compromised in the voidout. Now, the only way there is on foot, through the mountains. But the chiral density there is off the charts. It's got to be BTs."

"So me. Why?"

"Sam, you're already on the clock," Deadman replied, pointing to the cuff on Sam's wrist. Sam raised his right arm and tried to smash the cuff against the floor, but all that followed was a dull echo. Sam raised his arm to try again, only for the director to grab it.

Sam's arm immediately began to turn red. The director continued to speak, acting as though he hadn't even noticed.

"Now get it done, Sam Porter Bridges."

"The president was a symbol of American reconstructionism," Die-Hardman said as they placed the president's body inside a body bag.

"She worked tirelessly to bring the nation together again. And without her, there would be no Bridges. She deserves a funeral with full honors. But we can't give her that. If she dies, America dies."

"Without her, Bridges will cease to be," said Deadman.

"Her cremation must be carried out with the utmost secrecy." Die-Hardman's voice was taut.

"Even if we pull it off, what then? Who's gonna take her place?" Sam voiced his opposition. "Face it. America's history."

Nothing had changed since the last time he was here ten years ago. They still embraced the same slogans with the same religious zeal. Their persistence riled him up inside.

"Sam, America isn't dead yet," Deadman argued.

Sam raised his eyebrows. Hadn't Die-Hardman just said it himself?

"He just said that it dies if Bridget dies."

"She may be lost to us... but we still have an America worthy of the presidency."

"Sorry, what?" Sam pressed Deadman, but the director admonished Sam in return.

"Let's not get into it now. What matters is that we're going to finish your mother's work and rebuild America as she intended. That's the reason Bridges exists. So take the first step, Sam, and deliver the president's body to the incinerator."

"That's right, Sam. She may be the president, but if we just leave her then her body will necrotize like any other." Deadman continued to make his case.

"We cannot let Capital go the same way as Central. You're the only porter here now," Deadman said.

Bridget's dying words replayed in Sam's memory. *If we don't all come together again, humanity will not survive... I'll be waiting for you on the Beach.*

Deadman lifted up the body bag. Together with the director, he loaded the body onto Sam's back.

It had been almost two hours since Sam departed Capital Knot City. He had just crossed a river and his work pants were sticking to his legs uncomfortably. His pants were supposed to be waterproof, but constant use had taken its toll and worn them down.

If Sam could keep this pace then he would be at the incinerator within a few hours. Normally, he would have transported a corpse by truck, but the crater caused by the recent voidout had completely destroyed the road. There was no choice but to transport it on foot. He had also been forced to go alone so as not to attract any attention to the death of the president.

The cuff link on Sam's right wrist began to vibrate. It was a codec call from Deadman. Sam couldn't help but groan.

Deadman and the director called this cuff a device. They claimed the gadget wasn't meant to restrain Sam and they had only fitted it so they could remain in constant communication. Yet he couldn't remove it. No matter how the pair tried to explain it, this cuff was nothing but a chain to keep someone in check.

<Sam, can you hear me?>

They obviously didn't give a damn about Sam's circumstances. They may have carried the moniker of "Bridges," but it was clear they only cared about where they were coming from, not who waited on the other side. Sam decided not to respond.

<You're making good time, but be careful. You'll soon be approaching BT territory.>

"I know."

This may have been the first time he had to take the route between Capital Knot City and the incinerator on foot, but

it was by no means his first foray into the area itself. There
had been an increase in the number of jobs to the Capital
and Central areas in recent months. The East Coast of North
America had once been the political and economic center of
the United States. It's the reason why Bridges had established
their base there, around the home of the presidency. To Sam,
it was a place that held many painful memories, but also gave
him nostalgia for happier times in his childhood. Back then
he could never have predicted what cargo he would have to
transport through here someday.

<Hey, Sam. I'm sorry to have to ask, but do you
see any signs of necrosis yet? The president had
terminal cancer. Her entire body was afflicted with
cancer cells and we have no idea how that might
affect the time limit for necrosis.>

Sam kicked out at a nearby stone. If they were going to
force him into transporting this body, they should have
mentioned any possible problems earlier. He hated their
hypocrisy. They were pretending to protect him when really
all they had done was enslave him.

"I know where the BT territory is. I also know a way to
get around it. I don't know when Bridget is gonna necrotize,
and frankly, that isn't my responsibility. All I know is if we're
not lucky, then that's it."

<I get it, Sam. I'm sorry. Normally, necrosis
takes forty-eight hours, but sometimes it's

different. Sometimes it comes faster, so I'm a
little concerned.>

Sam didn't sense any kind of lie or scheming in
Deadman's faltering voice. He really did seem to be worried
about Sam and the rate of necrosis.

"I won't tell you to trust me, but I'll make sure to clean
up this mess of yours. Once this is all over, I'm gonna have
you remove these cuffs. This is the last job that I do for you."

Sam couldn't keep the anger out of his voice. Deadman
let out a fuzzy laugh and cut off the communication.

The grass of the plains fluttered in the wind. The
incinerator was just past the hills in the distance. It had been
built in a basin to try to prevent some of the spread of the
chiralium that was emitted as a corpse was burned. The BT
territory that Deadman had identified over the codec call,
where BTs roamed and life and death uniquely existed
together, was right next to the incinerator. To be honest,
Sam didn't know exactly where the area was, but with his
experience and his ability to sense BTs, he had a good idea.

It didn't appear that there had been any change in the
state of Bridget's corpse yet. It had still only been a few hours
since she had died, and it didn't look like any of the accelerated
necrosis that Deadman was worrying about had occurred.

There was no need to rush. It wasn't as much of an
emergency as the job that Sam had taken, along with Igor,
from the Corpse Disposal Team. It may take a little more

time, but it would be better for Sam to circumvent the BT territory. Sam closed his eyes and focused his consciousness. Using his whole body as an antenna, he increased his sensitivity to his surroundings.

Then he took a deep breath and began to walk.

All so that he could deliver Bridget Strand—not only the President of the United States of America, but the mother who had raised him—to the world of the dead uninterrupted.

CAPITAL KNOT CITY OUTSKIRTS // INCINERATOR

As soon as he emerged from the narrow path flanked by cliffs, the landscape before Sam opened up into a vast basin carved out of the mountains. At the center was a large squat building with angled sides, funneling up into an enormous chute. The incinerator.

Sam jolted his shoulders to readjust the position of the cargo on his back. He had managed to go around the BT territory just as he had hoped, and there were still no signs of necrosis from the corpse. Now he just needed to deliver the load. It was almost over. Bridget's body would be burned and her *ka* would be sent to the world of the dead. And she would never be back. It would all be over. America and the nightmare of its revival, too.

The gate to the incinerator scanned Sam and let him in.

Inside the structure, large pillars stood at evenly spaced intervals. The almost nonexistent lighting cast deep shadows throughout the empty space.

Sensing Sam's approach, a round pillar rose up from the ground. It was a delivery terminal that handled the receipt and consignment of cargo.

Humans were treated as cargo after they crossed over to the other side. A *ha* devoid of a *ka* was nothing more than an object. The only people who visited this place were the corpse disposal teams. There were no permanent staff, so the facility had not been maintained. Broken windows had been left as they were and there had been no attempt to repair the cracks that ran through the concrete floor. It didn't look like a place where someone would want to have their final send-off.

Following the guidance of the terminal, Sam removed the cargo from his back and carried it over to the specified area. The floor slid open and the device prompted Sam to place his cargo on the block. It was done.

Just then, something white softly fell from Sam's shoulder. It was a feather. It was the feather from the quill on Bridget's desk… But that couldn't be. That feather was nothing more than one fragment of an illusion that had been employed to make a simple hospital room look like the Oval Office. It was a simple hologram. Sam shook his head. The feather fluttered down until it landed on top of the body bag. The fireproof glass doors closed and flames emerged from the burners.

The feather was engulfed in seconds as the body bag went up in flames. The *ha* inside had also begun to burn. *Goodbye, Bridget. Soon your* ha *will be gone and your* ka *can pass over to the world of the dead peacefully. Hopefully along with the dream of America you had.*

Sam realized that his eyes were closed.

It was a funeral for a dying America. Sam watched the final burial rites for the dreams of previous generations in silence. It was over. America was over. There was no need to concern himself with America any longer.

Sam opened his eyes and turned to leave the place where the dream of rebuilding America had met its demise.

`<Good work, Sam. But I have one more job for you.>`

The sound of thunder roared through the building as if trying to drown out the voice. It was a sign that timefall was on its way. Sam frowned. Burning Bridget's body had released enough chiralium to send its concentration throughout the entire area through the roof. There was no doubt the timefall was on its way, which meant he had no time to listen to Deadman's new request.

`<Sam, burn the other cargo while you're there.>`

This time it was Die-Hardman on the other end. The other cargo?

The cuff link vibrated. The screen projected in front of Sam displayed the details of his job. The first part was to incinerate Bridget's body. The next was to burn BB-28.

<It's BB-28. It's the unit Igor was assigned.>
Sam could hear Deadman's voice again, but Sam didn't
understand what he was talking about. <It was hooked up
to you when we found you in the crater.>

Sam checked his backpack. Inside was a small case, and
sure enough, inside was the BB pod that Igor had entrusted
to him.

<It's flagged for disposal.>

Sam removed the pod and peeked inside. The fetus was
lightly floating in the artificial amniotic fluid. It was even
moving its hands and feet like it was swimming.

<Central Knot's gone, and our headquarters along
with it. Because that thing didn't do its job. At
least, that's how Bridges sees it.>

"But it's still alive."

<It's just a piece of equipment. The concepts of
life and death don't apply to it. It can't be
repaired. And it can't survive outside the pod.
Pity it if you want, but the decision has been
made. It has to go.>

So it's not to be killed, it's to be disposed of? Sam looked at the
BB in the pod. So, the kid's to be incinerated? No matter
which way you looked at it, it was a baby, not just some lousy
piece of equipment.

<The director approved the order.>

Another clap of thunder echoed through the room. It was so loud that it rumbled through Sam. The cuff links had fallen silent and the connection with Deadman had been cut off. The lights of the incinerator building flickered out and the structure was cloaked in darkness. It was a blackout. The timefall began to rain down.

The temperature dropped sharply. Sam felt goosebumps prickle all the way from his back to the nape of his neck. They were coming. The baby in the pod that Sam was clutching to his chest trembled as he moved to the window, careful not to make a sound. He needed to see what was going on outside. The rain battered the cracked glass of the window before it melted into liquid and began to ooze down from the frame.

Outside, a black mass leapt out of the darkness and hit the window hard. It was a huge handprint. Sam pulled back, his breath caught in his throat. They were here. Sam held his breath and focused on the outside of the window. Before he knew it, tears were rolling down both cheeks.

The handprints searched for life inside the room. First, they traced the edge of the windows, before discovering a crack in the glass, whereupon they entered and descended the wall toward the floor.

Sam backed away from the prints until he was pressed against the wall, then made a beeline for the exit. His flesh flashed cold with every step and waves of chills and nausea assaulted him. The rain thrashed down harder and harder. Even if Sam had wanted to look outside, he wouldn't have been able to. He closed his eyes and tried to sense the BTs' positions.

Sam felt immense pressure, which meant there must be dozens of BTs surrounding the incinerator. All of the corpses that hadn't been incinerated in time were swarming the area.

All of a sudden, the codec exploded back to life and pierced Sam's eardrum. The voice belonged to the director. <Sam, what's your status? Chiralium density is still increasing!>

Any increase was proportional to the proximity of the world of the dead. That meant that the world of the dead was closing in.

If Sam couldn't get out of there, the dead would never give up their search for him. If he stayed, there would be another voidout. He couldn't make another crater. This was Bridget's final resting place. And for many people before her, too.

Sam had to protect it.

The baby moved inside the pod under Sam's arm. He had to protect him, too. The only ones alive here were Sam and the BB. He had an idea.

Sam grabbed the umbilical cord that was stowed with the pod. He wasn't sure that his plan was going to work, but he and BB had repatriated from the Beach together. That meant that they were most likely compatible. Sam plugged the end of the cord into the socket in his abdomen.

Nothing happened. Sam checked the connection and shook the pod. The baby kept its eyes closed as the artificial amniotic fluid sloshed around. It didn't react in the slightest. So it really was defective. Or maybe it was already completely broken.

—*Hey.*

Sam urged silently, not daring to make a noise. In his head, he told the baby that it would be coming home with him. He heard the baby laugh.

An electric shock ran up through Sam's abdomen and hips before shooting up his spinal cord. His brain began to scream and his consciousness exploded. His skull was demolished, his scalp was torn off and the outline of his *ha* faded. He could see a vision of the baby laughing inside the pod. Sam returned a smile. His consciousness had incorporated and converged with the BB. He was keenly aware of the new connection they now shared.

The Odradek activated on his left shoulder and began to search out the dead.

And then, he saw them. The shapes of the dead getting beaten by the rain.

What was going on? Sam's breath caught in his throat. It was something he could never have imagined. Human figures were suspended in the air, but connected with an umbilical-cord-like tether that snaked up out of the ground. When Sam concentrated, he could see that the silhouettes were formed of minute particles. The particles writhed irregularly, forming the shape of a human. It looked like they couldn't see Sam. All they could do was hear the noises and sense the breathing of the living. Sam would have to try and conceal all evidence of his presence to escape past them.

It was lucky that he had the BB.

Normally, all Sam could do was sense the presence of the BTs, but the BB augmented his abilities. Now he could see them, too.

He covered his mouth with his right hand and held his breath. Then he took his first steps out of the incinerator building.

The timefall was falling in sheets. At this rate he would be soaked in an instant, and he wasn't sure how much shelter from the rain his hood would be able to offer him. If he dawdled, the rain would eat through his deteriorating porter suit and age the skin beneath.

Sam dropped to his knees and followed the outer wall of the incinerator building.

The tip of the Odradek was giving off a white-blue light and restlessly opening and shutting as it probed the space through which the dead were drifting. They still hadn't found him. If he continued following the wall, he should be able to get out of the area.

Sam stroked the pod on his chest. *Come on, BB.* As if to answer him, the Odradek pointed out in front of Sam. It had transformed into a cross shape and was fixed in position. The amber warning light glowed brightly. They were approaching. Sam stooped down closer to the floor and held his breath again. The hair on the back of his neck burned hot. A rotting fish smell pierced his nostrils.

There was a huge crash right above his head. Sam didn't need to look to know what it was—a big, black handprint.

He couldn't move. He had to remain still.

After holding his breath for so long, Sam started to feel dizzy. His vision began to blur and the sound of the rain seemed to come from a great distance.

The ground had slushed up into a sticky, tarlike substance. The handprints followed the wall downward, leaving imprints right beside him. A red streak flowed into the depression in the ground: Sam's blood was leaking out through a tear in his boot.

The invisible hands were lost. Every time they groped outward, they were pulled back in again. Suddenly, the handprints changed direction, as if they were afraid of something they should not touch and went away. After a while, the Odradek's petals shifted from the shape of the cross to its normal configuration. The BTs must have retreated for now. Sam began limping through the timefall again, dragging one of his legs weakly behind him.

Once the rain weakened and the skies ahead became whiter, the Odradek fell completely still and Sam could finally relax. They had escaped BT territory.

Inside the pod, the BB had its thumb limply in its mouth. It appeared to be sleeping. Sam wondered just how much stress the BB had endured, being surrounded by so many of the dead. He stroked the pod and let out a deep sigh of appreciation.

`<Sam, come in.>`

It was Deadman.

`<Did you connect to that BB?>` Deadman asked excitedly, not even waiting for an answer. `<That one's defective. I've never even heard of someone like you, with DOOMS, using one before. It's too dangerous. When someone with DOOMS hooks up to a BB, your feelings and memories cause feedback, like with a speaker. It can cause autotoxemia. Not even you can come back from something like that.>`

Sam ignored Deadman and looked up at the sky. There were no longer any clouds lingering there to bring the timefall. The outline of the sun was a little fuzzy, but the road ahead looked free of danger. Now, Sam just had to get back.

Then he could remove this damn cuff and go back to being Sam Porter.

The only worry that Sam had left was this BB. He wondered if it was really as defective as Deadman claimed.

Maybe it was broken because they had overused it? Sam peered into the pod mounted on his chest. The baby continued to float in the amniotic fluid with its eyes closed.

It wasn't the first time Sam had used a BB. There were porters who used illegitimate BBs, and Sam occasionally borrowed BBs from them. So, he recognized the disturbing truth in Deadman's words. Although the reality was probably even worse than Deadman imagined. After equipping a BB, a feeling of hopelessness would overwhelm him. The nausea and chills he could endure, but it was the depression and suicidal urges that really got to him. It was all because he had DOOMS.

But this BB was different. Sam didn't feel any of the after-effects that he usually felt when he used other BBs. It could have been because they had come back from the Beach together, but whatever the reason, he felt a special affinity with this one.

That's why he had wanted to save it. Maybe he could do something with the Bridges tech.

The gate leading into Capital Knot City came into view.

<It's a miracle either of you made it back.> Deadman's codec call put a dampener on Sam's spirits as the Odradek at the gate scanned Sam and ushered him in. <We've been monitoring you both the whole time. You're good, but that thing… I'm sorry, but that BB has been pushed beyond its limits. Disposal is the only option.>

Deadman's words stopped Sam in his tracks. If he took this kid back to the ward, it would be disposed of. Sam tried rapping on the pod with his knuckles, but the BB didn't respond. It didn't matter if he called out to the pod, stroked the pod, or shook the pod—there was no change. Sam unplugged the cord and removed the pod from his chest unit. If he reconnected it, maybe he could get the pod to restart. Without the cord plugged in, the window of the pod turned black, so Sam could no longer see the BB at all. When he picked the pod up and cradled it, the only thing he saw staring back at him from the dark glass was the reflection of his own face. He hated seeing his own sad expression and looked away.

He heard laughter.

It wasn't just his imagination. The BB in the pod was definitely laughing.

With a spark of renewed hope, Sam reconnected himself back to the pod.

The BB's laughter echoed inside his head. It was reassuring, high-spirited laughter. Good.

Sam closed his eyes and tried to feel the connection with the BB.

Don't worry—

—BB, I'm your papa.

All of a sudden, Sam heard a voice he had never heard before. A face that he didn't know was staring down at him.

It was a strange vision, almost like he was seeing it through a haze. He was somehow struck by both fear and nostalgia. Sam shook his head to rid himself of the hallucination. As the distribution center gate opened, Sam unplugged the cord, removed the pod from his chest, and made his way down the slope.

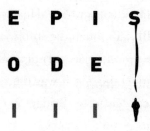

EPISODE IIII

AMELIE

Deadman trotted up behind Sam, who held the pod under his arm. "Thank you. Good job. We couldn't have done it without you. Are you still angry about the BB?" Deadman caught up to Sam, who remained silent.

Finally, Sam stopped walking.

"I'm not your errand boy." Sam turned around and thrust the pod into Deadman's belly.

"Well, in any event, it seems it owes you its life," Deadman replied, looking at the pod.

"No. We owe the kid our lives. You, too."

Deadman took the pod into his arms and nodded. Sam's expression remained angry and in his heart, Deadman understood why. He knew that the cargo he had burdened Sam with was unreasonable. He had forced Sam to meet the president—his mother—on the verge of her death, and then forced him to go and burn her body. He had even asked him to incinerate the BB. Although the stuff with the BB hadn't been planned, the rest of it was part of a ploy to get Sam to carry something much bigger. It was the revival of a once-abandoned plan conceived by Bridget over ten years ago. Sam would have to go on a journey.

"As you say. I shall look after it," Deadman conceded.

That's why Deadman decided that he would take responsibility for fixing the BB. He looked Sam straight in the eye as he promised to take care of it. Knowing what was coming next, Deadman suggested that Sam make time for a shower to wash away the dirt and fatigue of the day.

Sometime later, Deadman was waiting for Sam. The director stood beside him. They were in the same hospital room as before, which had been restored to its former glory using holograms to once again project the decor of the Oval Office. The domed bed was now gone and had been replaced with thick curtains that hung all the way down the full-length windows. The American flag and the Great Seal of the United States hung at half-mast. The room was dim, as if it itself was in mourning for the president.

Sam hadn't chosen to come here. And now that he had completed his mission, Deadman knew he would demand to be released from the cuff link and be left to resume his normal life as a porter.

The door automatically unlocked. It had recognized Sam's link. It creaked open and Sam entered.

The director gestured for him to approach.

"You did well, Sam. Thank you. Bridget may no longer be with us, but her legacy has a chance to live on." The director opened his arms wide as if to hug him.

Sam scowled and turned on his heel.

"Sam… listen to me," the director shouted after him.

Sam stopped.

"America, Reconstructionism—her dream isn't dead."

"I don't wanna hear it." Sam's voice was filled with fury. The director simply held his finger up and wiggled it as if he hadn't heard. Then he motioned for Sam to look behind him.

"This is the face of our new hope. Our new America."

It was a somewhat theatrical motion. At least Deadman thought so, as he followed the director's lead and shifted his gaze.

Light bloomed so brightly Deadman felt like the air itself was alive.

Eventually, he could see the form of a person inside it. It was a woman clad in vivid red clothing.

Her dark blond hair swayed as she stepped forward solemnly. Those light green eyes of hers were fixed upon Sam. It was she who was the sole light source within the room.

"Amelie?" Sam asked.

So, Sam hadn't forgotten about her after all. Not that he should have.

The director nodded and gave way to the woman.

"My mother may be gone, but I'm here," Amelie said, stepping in front of Sam, smiling and holding out her right hand. "And you, Sam. You're here, too."

Sam didn't so much as glance at Amelie's hand, his scowl still etched on his face. Amelie's expression betrayed a flicker of disappointment.

She let out a shallow sigh and lowered her arm.

"Been ten years since you saw each other, right? And in all that time, she hasn't aged a day." The director attempted to move the conversation along.

Amelie smiled again and spoke up once more. "He knows why. My body's still on the Beach. I don't get to grow older."

Deadman had heard of her story. All about the president's daughter's unique birth and constitution.

Amelie was not constrained by the time of this world. She was living in the time of the Beach. That was supposedly why she never aged. Deadman joined Bridges three years ago, but the Amelie standing before him now was exactly the same as the Amelie that he had first met back then.

"But you do, Sam. You look good." Amelie stared radiantly at Sam. A special connection that Deadman couldn't even begin to describe permeated all of the looks and words exchanged between the two.

"So you're serious, then. About 'reconnecting' everyone and everything?" Sam's barbed question was directed toward Amelie, who didn't seem to be perturbed in the slightest and steadfastly returned his stare. In the end, it was Sam who broke eye contact first. He looked around as if to ask for help.

"Someone has to succeed Bridget, Sam. More importantly, someone has to carry on her legacy and see our country rebuilt," the director explained, stepping in for Amelie. He walked over to Amelie's side and raised his voice as if to make a proclamation. "Samantha America Strand. Our new president."

As if signaled by the proclamation, a hologram of the North American continent appeared before them. It was an extensive map that stretched from one side of the room to the other. Amelie and the director stood in the center. They looked down upon it like a goddess and her obedient servant upon their creation.

"We'll reconnect all of the cities. Under Amelie's leadership, we'll reestablish the UCA. The United Cities of America. This is how we'll rebuild our country."

They wanted to revive the legend that was America. Bridget and the director had concocted this plot years ago, and had formed Bridges to put their plan into motion.

"But we'll need your help to do it, Sam." The director looked at him.

"No. I'm through with this. I said my goodbyes to all of you when I said 'em to Bridget."

Sam turned his back on them and made his way toward the door. It almost looked as if he was trying to escape from the giant hologram of the UCA.

"We never forgot about you, Sam," Amelie called out. She rushed after him, moving from the center of the continent toward the part of the map that showed the East Coast. The map undulated with each step she took. "You ran away."

Sam stopped.

"You cut us off," she continued.

"Amelie put together an expedition—the best of Bridges I—and went west."

Sam turned around. His expression had stiffened. Deadman couldn't tell if he was angry or confused.

Amelie spoke up, to confirm that what Die-Hardman had said was true.

"It took us three years, but we managed to make it all the way to Edge Knot City."

"All the way to the Pacific? Jesus…" Sam sounded surprised. He had realized that the Amelie in front of him was a hologram.

It was understandable that he was surprised. He must have wondered how on earth such a lifelike hologram could reach here with such weak telecommunication infrastructure. It was actually thanks to all the data on Amelie that HQ

had acquired over the years. Amelie may have been far
away, but her hologram had been fleshed out with locally
stored information on her voice, her expressions, and her
mannerisms.

Bridges I had been split into an advance team and a
backup team when they headed out west. The main objective
had been to make contact with the cities and the people
scattered across the continent, and approach, or even
persuade, them to join a rebuilt America; or rather, the new
United Cities of America.

At this rate, human beings—a species that requires close-
knit society and cooperation to survive—were going to go
extinct. That's why they had to band together under the flag
of the United States of America. It was this message from
Bridget that Amelie had taken west.

That trip couldn't have been peaceful. They would have
had to travel through BT territory and avoid the timefall. And
that's not all. Radical groups of separatists and isolationists
would also have hampered their journey. The only weapon
they would have had in the face of all that would have been
Amelie's ability to sense BTs, along with her pedigree and
charisma as the legitimate daughter of the president.

As they attempted to convince people of a future with a
rebuilt USA, Amelie and the others had established

infrastructure and facilities along the route. That infrastructure would become the foundation of the Chiral Network, which in turn was to become the backbone of the UCA. The name "Knot City" was a title that Bridges bestowed to any city that was considering joining the UCA in any capacity.

Amelie had continued her journey for three whole years. Now it was time for Bridges II to deploy. But Bridget had died before they could. And what's more...

"The team was wiped out, and Amelie was taken." The director updated Sam on the current situation.

"Amelie and the others reached Edge Knot City. But that place is effectively run by militant separatists."

Separatist and isolationist groups believed that nations suppressed the freedoms of their people and squeezed their rights. They were completely opposed to the resurrection of such a system, especially when it had already collapsed. One extremist group who believed in such an ideology and liked to express it through violence was a dangerous group called Homo Demens. They had no qualms about killing their fellow men, and would often leave their victims to become BTs, along with the craters in their wake. When had the finish line that Amelie and the others were aiming for become infested with those rats?

"I'm not being kept in a cell or anything like that. I'm allowed to use their facilities and to speak with you whenever I want. I just can't leave."

"It's all to safeguard the continued independence of Edge Knot City. That's what her keepers are saying, at least. Amelie's their insurance policy."

Sam's expression stiffened.

"Guess that means that not everyone is on board with this 'rebuilding America' thing."

Bridges had dispatched expeditionary forces to attempt to turn their dream of American reconstructionism into a reality, but instead they found isolationists and separatists taking more and more radical action in retaliation. The corpse that eradicated Central Knot City had originally looked like a simple suicide, but Bridges was now of the opinion that it could have been planted by a separatist group that had snuck into the city. Amelie may well have been trapped in a city way out west, but even Bridges' home turf in the east was exposed to the threat of terrorism. If people like that were going to reject any form of connection, then Deadman wished they would just live out their lives and keep to themselves. But since violence and terrorist acts were also a kind of communication, didn't it mean that they also craved connection?

To Deadman, that was a fundamental question that needed answering.

"More than a few would rather stay isolated. Keep to themselves, go it alone. Like you, Sam. They think that America can only be rebuilt by force—by men who tell them what to do, who take away their freedom and put them in shackles," Amelie explained.

"And what did you put on me, huh?" Sam immediately snapped back. He raised his arm to show them the cuff link.

"You're no better than the Demens. Just another kind of cult."

"They're not shackles, Sam," Amelie protested. "They're a symbol of our bonds."

Deadman couldn't help but put a hand on his right wrist. He could sympathize with what the director was saying, Sam's feelings of opposition and Amelie's logic. Humans were human, and as such, no perfect freedom or ideal collective could exist. People wouldn't be able to go on living if they didn't shut their eyes to things sometimes, or sacrifice things sometimes. That's why Deadman thought that it made sense for the handcuff-like device to be a symbol of Bridges. Whoever had thought it up was a genius. It was a tool to shackle, but it also symbolized open communication. Bridges had never tried to hide that contradiction.

"That's what we need right now: not to stand apart, but to come together. To form chiral knots and reconnect."

"Sam, we want you to go west and finish what Amelie started." The director also raised his cuff link and approached Sam. "The people she left behind have been hard at work setting up Chiral Network terminals. But these terminals are still isolated. We need you to bring them online."

The director held out a small metallic case in front of Sam, and opened the lid with a flourish. It contained six pieces of metal on a chain. It appeared to be floating, like it was defying the laws of gravity.

"And for that, you'll need a Q-pid."

This was the vital piece of equipment that would let them rebuild and reconnect America. Without it, all those places would just be points on the map. Disconnected and isolated.

Deadman didn't know how the idea of the Chiral Network had come about. When he had joined the organization, they were already moving from the planning stage to the testing stage. The plot was conceived by someone in the Strand family around the time of the Death Stranding—Bridget's ancestors had always been heavily involved in making great contributions to infrastructure, ever since America's founding—and Bridget was the one who was going to put it all into motion. Those were the rumors that Deadman had heard, but he had no idea if they were actually true.

All he knew for certain was that Bridget was the woman in command when it came to actual implementation. Connecting cities via physical means like flight routes, railways, or highways was effectively impossible. All they could really do was develop a good enough communications system that could provide an adequate substitute for physical connection.

The Chiral Network was lauded as the means to achieve

that goal. Amelie and the others had established the physical foundations: the cities that Bridges had named Knot Cities, along with any facilities that would connect and support them.

"We need you to use that Q-pid and get the Chiral Network online. And Sam, you're a porter. We want you to take all the goods that each city needs with you. And when you get to Edge Knot City, find Amelie and bring her home," instructed Die-Hardman.

"Please, Sam. We need you," Amelie's hologram pleaded, stepping toward Sam.

Sam shrank back and shook his head as if recoiling from Amelie's continent-spanning determination.

"I'm Sam Porter 'Bridges' now. I'm not a Strand. Hell, I'm not even part of this outfit. You all saw to that. I'm not getting involved with you or anyone else ever again," Sam stated bluntly, turning to leave.

"Wait!" Amelie rushed to block Sam's path.

A sad smile flashed across Sam's face and he stopped. Amelie was holding both arms out as if to embrace him, but Sam simply passed straight through her.

"See? It's like I'm not even here. Same as it ever was," said Sam as he exited into the corridor.

"Sam! Hold on." The director followed after Sam. Deadman's cuff link began to vibrate at the same time.

It was a call from the staff. Deadman wondered if the

director would be able to persuade Sam.

He glanced back at the hologram of Amelie, now all alone in the room, and left.

"Yeah, covering the world in cable didn't bring an end to war and suffering. Don't act surprised when it all comes apart if you try to do it again." Deadman could hear Sam flaring up at the director behind him, but he had to rush off in the opposite direction.

"Alright, alright, Sam. Just take it easy." The director's attempts to quell Sam's anger reverberated down the hall. "You don't have to commit to anything now. Why not get some rest?"

That's right. You rest up, Sam. You already know what has to be done. You're the only one who can do it.

Deadman was muttering to himself, his breathing getting more and more ragged as he ran, clutching his chest. He was greeted by a member of staff wearing a red medical suit. He held a pod in his arms.

The BB was spinning around inside the artificial amniotic fluid, bathed in an amber light, a similar color to diluted blood. Not only had it saved all their lives, it was also the only thing that still tied Sam to them. He had risked his life to protect it. The baby appeared to be recovering and Deadman had to get it back to him.

He turned on his heel and returned to where Sam and the director were still arguing.

"The necessary maintenance has been completed,"

Deadman announced over the director's shoulder. Caught by surprise, Sam fell silent.

Deadman held the pod up so that Sam could see for himself.

"Various adjustments and fine-tunings have been made for your benefit. You can use it again."

That's right, Sam, you can use it.

"For once, it would seem that DOOMS and BBs are a good combination!"

This little guy is your support. A BB comes in handy for traversing all those hellscapes dominated by monsters. But you get it, don't you, Sam? You understand that this piece of equipment has no other reason than that for existing, don't you? The BB twisted around in the pod. *Are you okay with putting an end to that reason?*

Sam made a puzzled expression as he tried to figure out what Deadman was getting at.

"Or perhaps the two of you have something of an affinity for one another?"

Submerged in the fluid, the BB laughed silently like it was in agreement with Deadman.

Sam bit his lip and took the pod. He had decided to help rebuild the country. Deadman just knew it.

Sam was walking in the direction of the first waystation that he was supposed to bring online: northwest of Capital Knot, past the incinerator where he had disposed of Bridget's body.

As Sam took a step, he felt a sharp pain in his right foot.

It stopped him in his tracks and reminded him of how long he had been walking.

Sam looked behind him. He was already far enough away that he was unable to see the silhouette of Capital Knot. Rolling hills stretched before him. Groups of boulders were scattered here and there like lonely tumors on a giant's back, and short vegetation covered the surface of the land like a woven green carpet.

He could hear the sound of the rapids he had just crossed in the distance.

It's like an entirely different planet.

He still remembered Bridget telling him that as a young boy. (*No, that might have been me, Amelie.*)

But why did she say that? I was born here. The world has always been this way.

A completely different world existed in the movies that Bridget used to show him.

Groups of buildings that pierced the skies. (*They're called "skyscrapers."*) Big metal vehicles that flew through the air. (*Planes were used to fly through the sky.*) Long thin boxes that used to whizz through the ground. (*That's the subway.*) Sam had seen things like trucks and bikes before, but the first time he ever saw a highway that they would race along was in a movie.

The old cities overflowed with many man-made things

that were interwoven with flowing rivers, thick groves of trees, and other green accents. Those cities had long since disappeared and now humanity was reduced to cobbling together modest cities in nooks of wasteland.

Sam wondered where those skyscrapers had gone. Where had the planes and subways and highways disappeared to? It was rare to come upon any trace of their past existence.

All evidence that humanity had ever prospered had completely vanished.

This was a whole new world.

It was a primitive world that had existed since before humans, since before they began to pollute it. That's why it was so harsh on humans, who were relentlessly assaulted by invisible monsters while rain stole their time away. It was no longer a place for them.

That's why humanity built those ugly cities and holed themselves up in them.

If this really was a different planet, then we must have been banished from the old one.

This is a world of the exiled. We are the children of the exiled. People like us have no right to rebuild metropolises filled with skyscrapers. No, it's me—Sam Bridges—who has no right. That right was taken from me ten years ago. So why am I being made to carry this cargo?

That's what he wanted to ask Bridget, but he was never going to get an answer now.

Sam checked the weight of the container on his back and began to walk again.

The scent of the air changed faintly. It was a sign that timefall was on its way. After searching for a little while, he stumbled upon a small cave, which he had to crouch to enter.

Sam sat down and took a deep breath. The Bridges-issued boots that he had changed into just before he left Capital Knot City were already dirty and covered in countless scratches. As he undid the laces, he felt some of his weariness melt away. The pain in his foot also grew fainter.

Thunder rumbled in the distance. Sam tried giving his pod a stroke, but there was no response. The Odradek on his shoulder remained still. The timefall may come, but it didn't look like those things would appear along with it. Once he had sheltered here for a while, he would complete the rest of the journey. In the meantime, he decided to catch up on some shut-eye and quickly fell asleep.

In his dream, he could smell something familiar.

He could faintly hear someone singing. It was a song that he had heard many times throughout his childhood.

London Bridge is falling down, falling down.

How long had he been asleep? He tried clapping his face with both hands to wake up.

He could hear the waves.

He could hear footsteps approaching on the sand.

London Bridge is falling down, falling down.

His eye was drawn to vivid red. Her blond hair swayed in the breeze.

My fair lady.

"Sam? Listen." Amelie was standing on the sandy beach in her red dress. "It's a funny word, 'strand.' It has three meanings."

Sam nodded.

He realized that he was on the Beach. It must be a lucid dream. This Amelie was one he had met before.

"A 'strand' is part of a rope or bond."

A huge wave surged up behind her.

"While 'stranding' means being washed up on the shore."

The wave crested over her head.

"And being 'stranded' is when you can't go home."

The crested wave broke into a million raindrops and rained down on her.

Amelie kneeled down before Sam and looked him in the eye. Sam could no longer hear the sound of the waves. It had disappeared along with the sandy beach.

Now he was back in the cave. *But it feels like I'm still dreaming. Sam, listen.*

"I'm stranded now, Sam. Here on the shore of the Pacific. Thousands of miles away... but our bond still holds." Amelie opened her arms and removed a dreamcatcher from around Sam's neck. *When did that get there?*

He never hung this charm against evil spirits around his neck unless he was sleeping.

Then I must still be dreaming.

Amelie smiled as if she was able to read his thoughts.

This was the conversation that he had with Amelie before he departed Capital Knot City.

I'm probably just turning it over in my dream.

After agreeing to go west, Bridges had provided Sam with time to prepare and a room in which to get ready. It was in this room that Amelie's hologram had once again appeared, this time with tears in her eyes as she called out Sam's name.

"Sam? Listen. You are Sam Strand."

"No, I'm not. Not anymore. My name is Sam Porter Bridges."

A tear ran down the hologram's cheek before physically falling onto the back of Sam's hand.

No, this is just another illusion caused by the dream, too.

Sam had already had enough of bonds and strandings and not being able to go home for a lifetime. That's why he stopped being a Strand and began his life as a Porter. Now it seemed that he hadn't managed to rewrite his destiny as well as he had thought.

Unless Bridget abandoned her ridiculous plan to rebuild America, Sam would never be able to escape it. That was the only conclusion Sam could come to as he watched from the sidelines.

Die-Hardman, the director, and Bridget when she was

still alive, had wanted Sam to take on the mission to reconnect America. He was sure there had been some kind of plan in motion to guarantee things ended up this way.

"You're free, but we're still connected. Don't tell me we're not."

Those words echoed around Sam's head as if they had come from multiple apparitions of Amelie. She took Sam's hand and placed the dreamcatcher back into it.

She went to get up and promptly kneeled down beside Sam. She embraced him and whispered into his ear, "Come back, Sam."

Sam was unable to move.

"I'll be waiting for you," Amelie said as she turned her back and departed. An enormous wave suddenly surged toward her like the palm of a giant and engulfed her. Sam raised his voice to make her stop.

He was woken by his own shout.

Sam had fallen asleep in the cramped cave, clutching his knees. In his hand was the dreamcatcher.

He knew he had been dreaming, but the difference between dreams and reality was getting harder to distinguish.

He retied his shoelaces and stood up.

CAPITAL KNOT CITY // WEST // WAYSTATION

The waystation was a Bridges facility used for the relay of goods and data.

As Bridges I had moved west, they had constructed or serviced multiple types of facilities across the continent.

This was the facility closest to Capital Knot City.

It was where George Baton, a man who always got up at the exact same time every day like clockwork, found a small smear of blood on his way to the shower booth from his basement living quarters.

It was a small thing that could easily have been missed had he not been paying attention.

He had a bad feeling about this. Worried that someone had been injured, he decided to skip the shower and rushed toward the communal area. Around this time, the staff would usually be assembling in the meeting room/kitchen area after completing their morning duties. But George couldn't see another soul. All he could hear was the humming of the air-conditioning unit.

It was understandable. His teammates were probably feeling discouraged. Even he hadn't been happy to get up out of bed this morning. In fact, no one could blame anyone else for not being able to make it out of bed this morning. It was the day after America had fallen. Everyone remained cocooned in their bedsheets as they tried to escape this grim new reality. He couldn't reprimand anyone for that today. George Baton looked up at the white ceiling and let out a sigh.

It had been almost three years since Baton and his teammates from the backup team had been stationed here. During that time, there had been no worrying accidents or incidents to speak of. They were also the closest to Bridges HQ, so there hadn't been any trouble from any radical separatists, either. They had maintained the facility on a skeleton crew, and although it was sometimes hard work, they had enjoyed an issue-free three years.

Three years after Bridges I departed, Bridges II had also left Central Knot City in the east and were heading west, equipped with a Q-pid. The development of the Q-pid tech had progressed smoothly and the new team to transport it across America had assembled without any problems. The expedition should have been deployed on schedule.

But now there had been a drastic change in circumstances. Central Knot City, home to Bridges HQ, had been completely and utterly decimated by a voidout.

The news had left everyone at the waystation speechless. After Baton had delivered the message, no one even had the energy to ask any questions. In the end, all he could do was dish out some smart drugs and tell the team to get some rest. Baton doubted that any of them would have been able to get a good night's sleep, though. They had waited here for three long years. Now, Bridges II was supposed to come along and connect them with HQ, along with other sites down the line. But would they still be coming? It felt like the station and everyone in it had been left to float untethered into the void.

Even if they were to scream out as loud as they could, there would be no one to hear.

Yesterday, Baton hadn't been able to look another person in the eye. They were all in mourning.

A few members of staff appeared in the meeting room the next morning, subdued and sporting vacant expressions. The air purifier appeared to be running normally, but a foul odor had begun to permeate the room, nonetheless. "What are we supposed to do now?" someone asked to no one in particular.

The next day, a member of staff turned up in the meeting room with swollen eyelids and bloodstained cheeks, demanding oxytocin. Another member of staff asked for the same. When Baton asked the two of them what had happened, they admitted to coming to blows. The foul smell began to spread from the meeting room into the rest of the waystation. He recognized the odor: it was the same stench of death given off by the Beach. So, the end was coming for this place, too? Just when Baton was convinced the end was near, he awoke to some good news. A radio communication from HQ. The message came through in pieces and was drowned out by a lot of static, but it was good news.

<Bridges II has departed. The plan to rebuild America lives on.>

Some people cried, some shouted. Others hugged. The team had been brought back from the brink of despair.

"This is Waystation UCA-01-155. All systems and team members are raring to go. We are all awaiting the new team," George Baton shouted into the transceiver with glee.

The Q-pid around Sam's neck made a clacking noise as he walked. He pressed down on the six metal shards from over the top of his uniform. It felt like they were floating under there. Sam knew that it was all just in his head.

Suddenly, Sam felt like he was being watched. When he looked around all he could see were the low, trapezoid-shaped mountain range of exposed rock and the dark gray sky.

There was not a bird among the clouds, or indeed any signs of any other beast on the land. Sam let out a deep sigh and continued walking.

In the distance, Sam could faintly see the outline of a building with a sphere affixed to its roof. It was the waystation, and the first sign of human activity that Sam had seen since he set out from Capital Knot City.

He had finally reached the first "Knot" that he was to connect. This wasn't the first time he had seen a facility like this, though. Sam had been working as a porter for ten years, and in that time he had seen his fair share of Bridges facilities, although he had always kept his distance.

—*Sam, please.*

He suddenly heard Bridget's plea inside his head. He also thought he could feel the BB moving around inside its pod. Sam shook his head to rid himself of Bridget's voice. He pressed down on his chest, reassuring himself that the Q-pid was still there. When he touched it, he could feel the weight of responsibility that had been placed on his shoulders. There was no turning back now. All he could do was continue to push westwards, lightening the load little by little as he went. He would look after the BB. He would reconnect America. He would find Amelie.

And then, when everything was connected again, he would finally be able to liberate himself from the detestable Q-pid and the American nightmare.

Every step he took was a step closer to that goal.

To reach the waystation that he'd spied between the gaps in the hills, he had to climb a slope, slowly and carefully making his way up the unsteady rockface. When he misjudged where to place a foot, he began to lose his balance. The ground underneath was loose scree and several rocks tumbled down the hillside. Now there were traces that he had been here. If someone else happened to travel through here, the signs were faint, but they would be able to tell that he had come in this direction.

Eventually, the bare rockfaces turned to grassland and the waystation began to loom overhead.

An invisible wave washed over his body. The Bridges ID strand around Sam's waist and the cargo on his back were scanned, and Sam was permitted to enter the waystation area. As he looked around, Sam could see that two sensor poles had been erected an even space apart. Most of the facilities scattered across the land were equipped with those kinds of sensors. Every visitor and piece of cargo was assigned an ID, which was transmitted to the waystation so they would always know when a Bridges-approved porter had arrived.

Sam climbed up the stairs that led to the delivery area and stood in the square in front of the entrance.

The concrete under his feet was dried out and riddled with cracks. There was a particularly large fissure in the center, which had turned white. This place had been built by Bridges I three years ago. But it had already aged decades. The waystation itself was in no better condition. Sam had heard that the surface of the building had been treated with some anti-timefall coating, but it didn't look like it had been very effective. Even if he did get the whole Chiral Network up and running, if the timefall destroyed all the facilities then the connection would surely just be severed again.

Sam sighed and looked up.

The south side of the elevated station was on the edge of a steep cliff face above a coursing river. He could hear the roar of the waters all the way from where he was standing. Sam speculated that the river probably hadn't even existed before the Death Stranding. He didn't have any proof or anything, but that's what he would have guessed.

The river was not the only strange new thing. The world had become a primeval wilderness. The continent wasn't dotted with rounded boulders smoothed by millennia of exposure to rain and snow, but jagged rocks of hardened magma that had violently erupted forth from the Earth's crust. Even the riverbanks were roughly hewn, yet to be tamed by the currents of the water. It was like the Earth had been torn to pieces and smashed back together, with the water simply forging its own path through the cracks left behind. The river was neither tranquil nor meandering, but rather impatient and impulsive.

This land was young and wild. And humans couldn't adapt to that youth. Still, the timefall was attempting to propel this world quickly from youth to adulthood, and drive an elderly and decrepit humanity all the more quickly to the brink of death.

Sam stared at the cracks in the concrete beneath his feet.

The water would flow through here, too, eventually splitting the concrete in half. Everything that humans could make was already obsolete. It didn't matter how hi-tech the invention was, it was dwarfed by the scale and force of the natural world.

Sam found himself sighing. He was by no means an old man, but sometimes he sure felt like it. He smiled wryly and entered the delivery area.

CAPITAL KNOT CITY // WEST // WAYSTATION

George Baton watched the porter arrive on the monitor in the basement cargo collection area. It showed a man in a blue Bridges uniform looking around the entrance to the delivery area.

When the alarm had sounded to notify them of an arrival, Baton could hardly contain himself, knowing that Bridges II had finally arrived. But when he looked at the monitor, it seemed like he had jumped the gun a little. The porter didn't belong to any kind of caravan. In fact, he was all alone. It was unusual to see lone porters even for normal deliveries. Baton supposed that they must have been short-staffed after the tragedy in Central Knot City.

But still, he was grateful. They had run out of oxytocin, and even though the staff had rejoiced when they heard about the departure of Bridges II, they were still worried about that. Baton couldn't thank this man enough.

Once the porter had entered the delivery area, he operated the cuff link on his wrist and requested access to the delivery terminal. The tags on the ID strand around his

waist and on his cargo were scanned more rigorously than
when he had first entered the facility. A cylindrical delivery
terminal that had been concealed in the floor appeared.
The porter's data flashed up in one corner of the projected
monitor, and Baton tilted his head in puzzlement.

It must be a system error.

The man's name was Sam Porter Bridges. He was a
porter from Bridges and the sole member of Bridges II.

There was no way there could only be one member of
Bridges II. The monitor showed Sam unloading his baggage
to complete the delivery. The goods were scanned for
damage and freshness, and whether they were carrying any
bacteria or contained any explosives, before being sent to
the back room. When they took one of the containers and
looked inside, the goods were in perfect condition. There
was hardly any damage at all.

George Baton booted up the hologram equipment and
began to speak to the porter.

"Sam Porter Bridges. You made it."

Sam looked in the direction of George's voice. In front of
Sam was a low-resolution hologram of George Baton. Direct
contact between external porters and the facility staff was
prohibited. No matter how many layers of protection you
had, there was always the risk of viral infection or an attack
by someone with malicious intent. At first glance, those were
the main reasons why such a rule might be required, but in

reality there was another underlying reason. They were actually kept apart because once people became used to only maintaining human relationships with the others who had been isolated with them, the introduction of someone new could cause incredible stress.

"Thank you, Sam. These smart drugs that you have brought us are gonna help us feel back to normal." George Baton's mannerisms seemed a little exaggerated. It must have been stressful to meet with someone unfamiliar to him, but he was managing to communicate with Sam well enough so far.

"By the way, there's something else I would like you to tell me. When is Bridges II coming?" George asked.

Sam grimaced uncomfortably on the monitor. He fingered something near his chest and took it out from underneath his uniform. It was several shards of metal.

Maybe the monitor was acting up.

"Does this mean that you're…?"

Sam nodded and held up the six shards of metal on their chain.

"You're really all alone? Are you going to connect this whole damn continent up by yourself?"

Baton's voice was shrill with excitement. On the monitor, Sam waved the metal shards to try and move the conversation along.

"Alright, I know. Then get us all linked up with that Q-pid you've got there."

Sam nodded. Baton bit his lip. Before he knew it, tears were running down his face. Even if he tried to wipe them away, they kept coming. He had been waiting for this moment for three years and he couldn't hold back his suppressed tears any longer.

"Alright, link us up."

The hologram of George Baton bowed its head.

Sam took the Q-pid from around his neck and inserted it into the port on the device. The metal pieces floated as if they had forgotten their own weight and emitted a dim light. The light grew brighter, engulfing both Sam and the device. He felt himself begin to float. It was a similar sensation to that which he had experienced when he connected to the BB. It wasn't uncomfortable per se, but it wasn't pleasant either. It felt like he was drifting away from the world of the living and being reeled in by the world of the dead. The haziness stretched out over Sam's sense of reality and brought him both unease and a feeling of liberation. The BB let out a soft laugh.

Sam was being torn away from something and reconnected to something else. Undone and reforged.

"Thank you so much, Sam Bridges." The low-resolution hologram that looked like it had been made from children's toy blocks sharpened into a more realistic 3D image. It was a byproduct of activating the Chiral Network with the Q-pid. Now he could see more detail, Sam noticed the tears rolling down Baton's face.

Sam felt a twinge in his chest and lightly slapped at his face with both hands, trying to knock some sense into himself.

"So, you really are Bridges II." Baton's voice was still trembling a little. Sam silently nodded. His own composure was threatened upon seeing the hologram's tears and hearing the other man's trembling voice.

Sam had been thanked countless times after successfully delivering goods. One or two of his clients had even shed tears. But he had never felt so moved by such a reaction.

"Connection to Capital Knot City confirmed. We've connected to the UCA. We're a part of America. I don't know what to tell you, Sam. We were scared. We were lonely. We haven't been able to go anywhere. But this... This is a huge relief for all of us."

He didn't need to be that grateful. All Sam had done was pick up a pack and carry it here. Sam was feeling every bit as awkward as Baton was joyous. He wasn't heading west to reconnect America. He was doing it for Amelie's sake. He was doing it so that he didn't need to abandon this BB to decommission. And he was doing it so that he could liberate himself from the heavy profile that he had been conned into carrying. Once he reached the West Coast and fulfilled his promise to Bridget, he would be free. He was in this for himself.

That's why he felt so guilty to be thanked like this. Sam tried to depart before his composure crumbled. "Hold on a second, Sam Bridges." George Baton's voice stopped him in his tracks. "You're headed for the distro center west of here next, right?"

That was indeed what Die-Hardman had instructed him to do. Sam turned around and nodded.

"In that case, could you take these with you?"

An order was displayed on the monitor of the delivery terminal. It showed the client, the delivery address, and the cargo. The same screen he had seen countless times before as a freelance porter.

It made sense. He couldn't just turn up at the next location empty-handed. He actually felt better about heading west as a porter. Even if he acknowledged that it was a lie.

Sam fiddled with the terminal and accepted the order.

A shelf appeared from the floor, holding a tidy row of cases full of cargo. Materials for use with a chiral printer. According to Die-Hardman, any high-functioning 3D printer connected to the Chiral Network could produce copies of any remote object. But to do that, they needed materials to print with. Several types of material—like heavy metals, light metals, and ceramics—were therefore stored separately in each case. Was Baton asking Sam to take all this with him, though? It looked ridiculously heavy.

Yet it wasn't impossible. Sam took a deep breath and hoisted the cargo up onto his shoulders.

"Thanks, Sam. I know I probably don't need to tell you this, but there are MULEs up ahead."

By MULEs, Baton meant porters who had been consumed by their irrational obsession with their deliveries. Known as Porter Syndrome, MULEs felt compelled to steal the cargo from other porters, even turning aggressive, stopping just short of murder in their hunger for new packages.

Sam knew. He turned toward the hologram of George Baton and raised his left hand.

"Take care, Sam—"

Baton began to say more, but Sam couldn't quite hear him. As he left the delivery area, Sam looked up at the faintly cloudy sky and sighed.

His cuff link vibrated and the melody it beeped told Sam that Die-Hardman was trying to make contact.

<I knew you had it in you, Sam.>

As Sam looked at the map that was displayed, he replied bluntly, "I guess I do feel better about being a porter."

<Well, people with your skills are in high demand. Now, let's go over the next part of the plan.>

Die-Hardman didn't appear concerned whether it was currently convenient for Sam or not, and launched straight into the briefing.

<The first thing we want you to do is head for Port Knot City, and connect them to Capital Knot City and HQ via the Chiral Network. The thing is,

they can't be directly linked, so you'll need to
connect them by way of the Bridges facilities
dotted between us. You've already connected the
waystation, so the next facility that you're going
to connect is a distro center.>

As Sam let Die-Hardman carry on talking, he left the
area surrounding the waystation and began his descent
down the hill. The straps of his backpack dug into his
shoulders with every step.

Carrying close to his maximum weight, Sam was already
beginning to sweat.

<Port Knot City is a Knot that was built adjacent
to Ground Zero, the scene of the first voidout in
this country.>

In all likelihood, there were multiple ground zeros all
over the world. Bridget had talked about them once a long
time ago. (*You were still so small.*) Back then, multiple mysterious
explosions struck the world simultaneously. It wasn't just in
America, but all over Europe, Asia, and South America too.
Even on this continent, explosions occurred at the same time
in different locations. On the East Coast, the West Coast, in
the South, even along the border with what had once been
called Canada. But the most powerful explosion of all had
left a huge crater right in the middle of America.

Vast quantities of water had flooded in to form an
enormous lake. Someone, somewhere, had named it Lake

Ground Zero. With a hole in the bottom of America, there were some who said it was a sure sign that the country was going to sink. (*I won't let that happen to you.*)

<Are you listening, Sam?> The director sounded annoyed. <The damage around Ground Zero is particularly bad even compared to the other sites. The government at the time couldn't do anything. People had to rely on private couriers to deliver aid and supplies to them. There are a lot of people in that area who can't tear themselves away from the high of being the saviors who deliver.>

"If you're talking about MULEs, then I'm already aware of them."

Those were Sam's first words in the entire conversation, and they seemed to encourage Die-Hardman to become even more talkative.

<I guess you probably know more about it than I do. Man has always had issues with the division of resources and imbalances in their distribution.>

The director kept talking.

<Listen, Sam. The resources that we need to survive, like fuel and food, haven't just disappeared into thin air. I can't definitely say that we have enough to go around, but going by the number of us left, there should be. One of the problems that we have is that these resources aren't getting to the

places that need them. We need to optimize our resources. It's all an issue of delivery.>

"So that's why we ended up with people like MULEs."

Sam took note of where the director was headed with his lecture and came to his conclusion for him. Die-Hardman cleared his throat and started again.

<That's right, Sam. Watch out for those MULEs and make sure that none of your cargo gets taken.>

White noise interrupted the codec call. He had finally left the area covered by the Chiral Network. Now Sam would have to rely on normal radio communications. Unfortunately, the reception here wasn't very stable either, thanks to the chiral clouds filled with timefall rain. The fluctuations in atmospheric chiral density made long-distance communications pretty much impossible. The state of radio communications had rolled back so far that they were as bad as they were a century ago.

What little landline infrastructure remained intact wasn't reliable enough to connect the disparate facilities and cities. Constant exposure to the timefall degraded the lines, and they were vulnerable to disruptions caused by separatists and extremists.

The only exception was the old-generation network that ran from the East to the West Coast, and even across Lake Ground Zero. A patchwork of landline and wireless systems that Bridges I had managed to throw together as they headed west. No one knew how long it would last. Their advance westward was rejected by separatists, who called it a regressive westward expansion based on old, narrow-minded America-first ideology. To them it was an act of terrorism hidden behind a façade of benevolent reconstruction.

But none of their criticism ever amounted to much. At least, their disruptions had never managed to sever the link completely. It was like the separatists were just sitting around waiting for the end of the world.

Bridget and Die-Hardman had once strongly argued for the reconstruction of America on that very point. A younger Sam had agreed with them.

Once a transcendental system like the Chiral Network was completed, everything would be solved. Once connected, they could work together to find a logical explanation for the Beach and a realistic way of dealing with it.

Once we understand the Beach then we'll be saved. That's what Sam had once believed. That "we" was Amelie and Sam, who lived constantly with the shadow of the Beach looming over their heads.

Sam reached the bottom of the hill and continued to walk onward, watching out for the rapids on his left, and soon noticed trampled grass and muddy footprints. His intuition as a porter flared in warning. George Baton had told him at the waystation that MULEs were active around here. He was almost certainly looking at their tracks.

Sam had encountered them plenty of times before. They worried porters for different reasons than the BTs. MULEs had once been porters, but had become addicted to the high of delivering the goods that would rebuild society. They had become so dependent on that high that they resorted to stealing deliveries from other porters. It didn't matter what the content or destination of the cargo was. They would just take it.

And once they had taken this cargo, it wasn't as if they would do anything with it. They didn't consume it. Nor did they try and trade it with other groups or use it for provisions. They just hoarded it away like squirrels. Just like the wealthy classes of the past, they simply aimed to amass as many resources as possible and keep them all for themselves.

This area was a delivery route between the waystation and the station that was Sam's destination. The MULEs had probably been attracted to that.

Sam could see shadows on the opposite side of the river. Maybe a small group of two or three people. Luckily, they were separated not only by the rapids, but also by a fair distance. There was no need for Sam to panic, but he couldn't be careless either. He was carrying a lot of cargo and there was nothing he could hide behind.

To avoid them he would have to climb back up the slope he had just come down, and then pass over the hills to the right. Sam sighed and pressed on.

The footing on the slope was even worse than Sam had expected, and every time he stumbled, several stones came loose and tumbled down the hillside.

It was taking an enormous amount of effort for Sam to keep his balance because of the weight on his back. He had to thrust his hands out onto the ground to stop himself from falling on more than one occasion.

After putting some distance between himself and the MULEs and climbing dozens of meters, Sam paused for a breather. They probably wouldn't bother chasing him all the way up here. But when he looked back he saw that the small group of MULEs had already crossed over the river. All of them were clad in the exact same clothing from head to toe. They looked like little chrysalises that had sprouted arms and legs. Their direct and relentless running form and speed was uniform too. In fact, this uniformity was a trait of the MULEs. Their aims, means, and methods were also identical.

That's why they were also named Homo gestalts. Their social structure was based on the division of duties and was much closer to that of ants and bees.

The MULE at the head of the pack was booting up some search equipment. It fired an ultra-high-frequency sensor that could immediately identify what Sam was carrying. Now he only had two options. He could either drop some of the cargo he was carrying and let them take it, or prepare for battle and try to make a getaway. Rationally, Sam knew that he should pick the first option. That's what he had always done before.

But he couldn't decide. He couldn't stop thinking about George Baton's tears. Why had he cried like that? What had made him so happy?

Sam's cargo had been entrusted to him by Baton. He couldn't just get rid of it. He would never be forgiven. Sam cursed Baton's tears and put all of his strength into climbing farther up the slope.

As he struggled with the climb, he felt something graze his ear. He glanced to the side to see a spear jutting from the cliff face. One of the MULEs had thrown it. As Sam struggled to decide whether he should just cast off the rest of his baggage and face them, another spear came flying past.

Sam didn't possess any projectiles. All he could do now was run.

Then he heard a grizzle from the pod.

The BB had its hands up against the window of the pod and was gazing up at Sam. BBs were transferred to their pods around seven months after conception, so its eyesight shouldn't have been very developed. Despite this, Sam felt like the baby had made eye contact with him. He could sense how anxious it was.

The air current changed and brought a rust-like stench with it. When Sam looked up at the westward sky, he could see muddy-colored clouds loosely swirling into a vortex. It felt like he was witnessing the birth of some gigantic creature, something stupendous that would be depicted in legends. The clouds that brought the timefall didn't blow in on the breeze. They formed and rumbled according to their own laws and dynamics.

There was a flash of light in the center of the vortex, followed by a clap of thunder as loud as a dragon's roar. An upside-down rainbow spanned the sky. The BB trembled with fright and the Odradek on Sam's shoulder sprang to life. There was no mistaking it. These were signs that BTs were coming. The MULEs who had almost caught up to him turned back in a panic. The BTs were a threat to them, too. A moment later, Sam felt cold raindrops against his cheeks, and the timefall began to pour down like a waterfall. The BB cried out and the Odradek spun around wildly.

Sam felt dazed, like he was intoxicated. The sound of the raindrops pattering against the hood covering his head grew intermittently louder then quieter. The world twisted itself into the perspective of an abstract painting. The worlds of the living and the dead were converging and Sam was stripped of his senses. He couldn't tell where he ended and the world around him began.

He closed his eyes tightly and took a deep breath to try and regain some control. He tried listening for the beating of his heart over the sound of the thunder and the rain. He centered himself. Sam reopened his eyes. There was no more fluctuation in his consciousness or vision, and everything appeared back to normal.

Come on, BB. Sam stroked the pod as he muttered encouragement. The Odradek formed itself into a cross shape as it found something. Warning that a BT was creeping up on Sam from behind. He had to get out of here. Deciding on a course of action, he got down low and covered his mouth with his right hand. He held his breath. He could feel the back of his neck burning. It was urging his cowardly self to look back.

You're afraid because you can't see it. Turn around and see how far away the BT is! You connected to the BB so that you don't have to fear the unknown. If you can see it, then you'll be able to make a calm judgment. But he just couldn't do it. If he moved so much as a muscle, the BT would sense him and attack.

The dead couldn't see people either. They just blindly waved their invisible arms around, attempting to snatch up the living and fulfil their sole desire of returning to the world of the living.

That's why the trick was to hold his breath as long as he could and get down low to hide his presence.

You can repatriate. You shouldn't be scared of a voidout, should you? But then again, one mistake and you'll end up drilling another crater into this country. Who knows how many would die? You're so conceited. How could someone who can't die possibly know the fear that BTs bring? That's what was driven into Sam when he still worked for Bridges.

That instructor whose name and face Sam had long forgotten hadn't died. But Sam had. As a repatriate, he had come to know the repulsiveness that drifted in the space between life and death. That was something that Sam couldn't tell anyone. They would never understand.

Long ago, he had wanted to be understood, but now he accepted that he wouldn't be.

From the corner of his eye, Sam saw the ground sink silently. Even that slight rotation of his eyeball was enough to attract one of the BTs. The outline of a large handprint appeared in his direction. The handprints moved closer, right hand over left as if probing for him. It took all of Sam's willpower not to surrender as his lungs begged for air. The sweat on his brow and the tears from the antigen-antibody reaction ran together and merged with the droplets of timefall.

The handprints were almost at Sam's kneecaps. It felt like time had stopped. He was in a stand-off with their invisible owner.

Sam continued to hold his breath, but he was already at his limit. His vision was tinged the color of blood and he felt like his head was about to burst. His body was crying out for air. Without thinking, he bit down harder on his lip. He tasted blood in his mouth. It began to drip down from his chin.

Sam sensed that the BT was confused and it began to back away. Moving in the opposite direction, the BT backed up farther and farther and left.

Sam was finally able to release his hand from his mouth and take a gasp of air. The oxygen coursed through his body and reawakened his brain. The timefall was letting up slightly and the faintest trace of light was now coming back to the sky.

The danger had passed for now.

The second breath that he breathed out was a sigh of relief. As he attempted to stand, he felt the full weight of the cargo on his back. At the same time, pain radiated throughout his body. It was proof that he was still alive and standing there.

As Sam got ready to depart, he got a feeling that something was off and stopped. Something was missing. It felt like a perfect cog had broken somewhere in the system. He found the answer to his confusion on his chest.

Sam called out to the BB and rapped his knuckles lightly on the pod.

But the pod window was dark and there was no response.

The BB was silent again. *Come on, BB, you saved both our necks again. Answer me, BB. Come on.*

The baby's hands moved slightly. But it didn't look like a planned movement, more like a spasm.

Igor entrusted you to me. I saved you at the incinerator. Deadman fine-tuned you so that we could set out across the continent together, and put off your decommission for me. One of the reasons I even agreed to go west in the first place was to keep you alive.

It was only the vibration of the cuff link that broke his train of thought.

<Are you alright, Sam?>

The voice belonged to Deadman.

"I'm not sure. The BB isn't moving anymore," Sam answered, looking down at the pod to find the BB floating in the amniotic fluid looking dead.

<It's alright.>

Deadman's voice sounded calm.

<It may have stopped functioning temporarily, but you can fix it. You can do some maintenance on it using the equipment at the distro center. You need to hurry.>

He spoke about BB as if it was some machine that had simply malfunctioned. He dealt with it like it was just some object. Sam couldn't stand that kind of attitude, and cut off communication.

CAPITAL KNOT CITY // WEST // DISTRIBUTION CENTER

Sam could see the majesty of the distribution center on the opposite side of the river.

It had been three days since he had left the waystation and George Baton behind. He booted up the Odradek's sensors and scanned the riverbed.

Sam found a relatively flat and shallow part of the river and crossed.

There was a well-worn path that seemed to follow the course of the river. It was a primitive trail worn into the greenery and it exposed rough patches of earth as it curved up steadily toward the entrance. Many people must have walked this path over the years, judging by how the earth was so compacted. If truth be told, Sam was more relieved to stumble upon this simple trail than when he saw the big, artificial buildings like the stations and centers erected in the midst of the wilderness.

Such signs of all the human life that had passed through here, and the layers of time they depicted, eased Sam's feelings of solitude.

Sam wondered how someone like him, with his aphenphosmphobia—who couldn't even join hands with those right in front of him—could still feel somehow connected to those who had come before him.

—*Hey, Sam. Can you join hands with me?*

Sam was scanned by the sensors and entered the distro center territory.

The hard soles of his boots echoed on the floor. As he descended the lonely slope into the distro center, Sam and his cargo were cleansed by equipment to remove any contamination. Before Sam's eyes could adjust to the darkness of the cargo collection area, a cylindrical delivery terminal that had detected Sam rose through a hatch in the floor. Impatient for the delivery process to begin, Sam unloaded the cargo from his back onto the counter. It felt like he had been released as all of the weight and pressure on his back and shoulders disappeared, but a seed of worry soon began to grow in his chest.

The BB was still just drifting in the amniotic fluid of the pod.

The monitor projected into the air in front of Sam was keeping track of the progress of the inspection of the delivered goods. Eventually, a hologram of one of the staff operating in the back room appeared before him.

"Thanks, Sam." The 3D hologram was low resolution. But even though Sam couldn't make out the particulars of his face, he could still recognize the happiness and excitement exuding from him.

"So, you're the one-man expedition, huh? I can't thank you enough for all this cargo that you've brought us."

The inspection concluded without a problem and instructions prompting Sam to insert the Q-pid flashed up on the screen. It seemed like the staff member still had more to say, but Sam wasn't really paying attention.

"We're finally going to be connected to the Chiral Network. Do your thing."

Sam was assailed by a sensation like his feet were floating. The worlds of the living and the dead had converged and Sam existed in the space in between them. The antigen-antibody reaction was causing tears in his eyes. When this had happened at the waystation, the BB had laughed softly, but this time it showed no reaction at all.

Once Sam had regained the feeling in the bottom of his feet, he accessed the terminal and requested a private room in the basement to rest the BB.

The floor was adorned with a huge Bridges logo and it began to quietly sink, with Sam standing in the middle of it.

The building visible from the ground was only part of the distro center. The majority of it was actually buried underground.

A light vibration indicated that Sam had reached his destination. When the doors opened and he stepped out, he found himself in a private room reserved for porters. It was usually a place where a porter could rest and prepare for the next part of their journey, but this time Sam had other priorities.

"What do I do, Deadman?" Sam booted up the communications function on the cuff link and spoke aloud.

\<Sam, first you need to remove the pod and connect it to an incubator.\> Deadman's calm voice replied. There was a toilet and a shower booth opposite the door. To the left, there was a bed, and opposite that, a storage space for equipment that resembled some sort of display cabinet. The medical equipment next to it must have been the incubator.

Just as Deadman had instructed, Sam removed the pod and tried to look inside. The BB on the other side of the smoky glass didn't move. Sam connected the pod to the incubator, praying for a miracle.

"Like that."

A voice suddenly rang out from beside him. When he looked around, Sam found himself standing face-to-face with Deadman, who was looking at the incubator. Now that this facility was connected to the Chiral Network, they too could receive chiral holograms. Deadman looked Sam in the eye. Sam could almost believe Deadman was actually in the room beside him.

"A temporary excess of stress. It's triggering autotoxemia. Easily addressed if we return it to its mother's womb." Deadman quietly sighed and nodded. "She's located in the Capital Knot City ICU." Deadman looked back toward the incubator and pointed at the pod. "Braindead, of course."

"So, she's a stillmother," Sam muttered. He had heard of those.

"Correct. A stillmother's womb facilitates a connection between the world of the dead and the BB. And you, in turn, connect yourself to a BB, granting you the ability to sense BTs."

Sam had heard this story before. It was because BBs connected people to the world of the dead that their use was not recommended for people with DOOMS. But he had never heard why they had that kind of ability in the first place.

"These pods were designed to simulate the conditions inside a stillmother's womb. BBs need to believe they're in one at all times to function properly."

Deadman's arm slipped through the incubator partition and then through the window of the pod. Sam could see him twist his wrist and operate his cuff link.

"However, we can only maintain this deception for so long, which is why we must periodically update the environmental data by synchronizing it with a stillmother via the Chiral Network."

Deadman's hand continued to work away as he spoke, making adjustments to the pod remotely.

"Previously, we had to connect the pod to the mother with a wire to get them to synchronize. But if you're inside an area with the Chiral Network, there's no need to do that. Luckily, you just linked this area up to the network."

Light began to fill the interior of the pod and spill from the incubator. As soon as Sam felt something weird in the depths of his nose, his eyes began to well up. Deadman's form began to warp unnaturally, and an upside-down rainbow straddled the room. The Chiral Network had connected the BB to its mother in Capital Knot City.

"I'm reconfiguring the settings based on the latest data. The autotoxemia will be taken care of by returning the BB to the womb of its mother. If this was a real baby, it still wouldn't be able to survive outside of the mother yet."

So that means the anti-BT sensor system that uses BBs was formed by tricking them, huh? You still haven't been born. You're still in your mother's belly, connected to her. They were trying to protect the world of the living based on a lie. What was the point if they were going to do something like that? Sam sighed and stared at the BB pod.

That said, there was still no way that Sam could abandon the BB.

He tapped on the pod with his fingertips. As soon as he touched the glass, the BB opened its eyes and laughed faintly. Sam couldn't help but break into a smile himself. Then he remembered that Deadman was standing next to him and restrained himself.

"Looks like it's back," Deadman commented.

Sam nodded silently.

"I'll try adjusting the oxytocin dosage. Autotoxemia should set in much slower from now on."

The BB wriggled around in its pod. It held out its tiny hands on the other side of the window. Sam placed his hand on top as if it attracted to the BB's hand like a magnet. He didn't care what Deadman thought. The kid had been saved.

"You should remember that BBs are just equipment. Try not to get attached. Each one has been physically removed from its stillmother's womb, a process that renders them unpredictable and prone to failure. All the pod is doing is providing an approximation of their real environment."

Deadman sounded like a tutor admonishing a student.

"No BB on record has remained in service for over a year. It may need to be retired before this expedition is over."

"And then?"

Decommissioned. Deadman ignored Sam's question and went to leave the room.

"You saying there's no way to keep my BB alive?" Sam asked.

"You must understand, there is still a great deal we don't know about BBs. As we expand the Chiral Network and recover more past data, perhaps we'll find our answers," Deadman lightly shrugged his shoulders and muttered. The latter part of his answer didn't seem addressed to anyone, it was more like something he was pondering himself.

Deadman waved his finger in Sam's direction. "Anyway, get some rest. Now that your BB is sorted, it's time for you to recover. You must be exhausted. Your next destination is Port Knot City, and it's going to be one long walk, so rest up and get your strength back. Good night, Sam."

Deadman disappeared without a sound, leaving only a smile.

Sam woke in a room alone—no, together with just his **BB**.

It seemed like he had fallen asleep face down on the bed. Even he didn't know how much time had passed. But his hair was untied and still wet, so it couldn't have been for that long. Yet the biological monitoring equipment set up beside his bed told him that his blood had already been taken using the cuff link. They hadn't wasted any time.

Every time he slept or showered, every time he went to the damn toilet, they were always taking something away to analyze, whether that was blood, sweat, or any kind of waste. It had been explained to him when he first departed Capital Knot City. It was mostly for the benefit of managing Sam's health as he traveled, but its other purpose was to observe and study the unique makeup of a repatriate.

If everything went to plan then they might be able to use that analysis to see how this world, the Seam, the Beach, and the world of the dead were all connected.

Someone named Heartman had informed him of this plan. Sam remembered the startlingly intelligent light he had glimpsed in that pair of eyes set deep behind a pair of spectacles. It coexisted with a curious sense of resignation, like they had witnessed the end of the world. Sam had only interacted with the man as a relatively low-res hologram— although he had apparently been by Bridget's bedside as a hologram when she died—but Sam at least remembered that much about him.

It was why Heartman had given him such an uneasy feeling. It felt like he could see into a part of Sam that Sam didn't even know himself. Something dormant, deep inside. Something that would spill over to the surface through countless blood vessels and pores before it wrapped itself around Sam's body, bound him, and rendered him immobile. Like a venomous spider caught in its own web, killed with its own poison. Sam found it increasingly difficult to breathe just thinking about it.

Before Sam knew it, he found himself clutching at the dreamcatcher around his neck. (*That's what I gave you. A talisman to turn all your nightmares into peaceful dreams.*)

The lights in the ceiling flickered out all at once, but by the time Sam looked back up, they had all already turned back to normal.

London Bridge is falling down, falling down.

Sam thought he could hear humming, and looked back to where he was staring before.

Amelie was stood there.

"Can you see me, Sam?" Amelie reached out, squinting her eyes as though looking at something bright. Sam loosened his grip on the dreamcatcher and held his own arms out. (Could you join hands with me?)

Sam knew his arms would just pass straight through. This was just a hologram of Amelie. An exact copy, but still just a hologram.

According to Die-Hardman, Bridges I left behind local data to recreate Amelie at each Bridges facility as they proceeded west. It had originally been intended for use when Amelie was giving instructions as a commander, but before long the staff were just using it to admire Amelie as a symbol. In any case, that was how they could reproduce Amelie in hologram form from Edge Knot City, which wasn't connected to the Chiral Network yet.

"How're things over there?" asked Sam.

After a slight time-lag, Amelie made a face as if she was examining her surroundings before she answered.

"Still not under guard, still not chained up... still can't leave. But if you keep making connections, if you can get to me... we can go back east. Back home."

Amelie looked Sam in the eye.

"Humans aren't made for living alone. They're supposed to come together—to help one another. And if we as a people can't do that—if we can't reconnect..."

Amelie looked away into the distance as if she was searching for something. Or maybe she was wavering about something. He couldn't stand the silence, but there was nothing that Sam could do about it. All he could do was stare blankly at the gold necklace hanging around Amelie's neck. Strings extended out from the main body of the necklace, swaying around Amelie's chest like the rays of a rising sun. It resembled a *quipu*, a recording device made of knots used by the ancient Incas.

"It's like Bridget said. 'Extinction,'" Amelie finished.

"Rebuilding America isn't gonna get rid of the BTs. Long as they're still around, there's no escaping it."

It was a fair argument, but Amelie simply smiled.

"But at least we'll have hope. Sam, I'll be waiting. Waiting for you. Come and find me."

The EKG was shrieking. It was flatlining. Die-Hardman stood next to the bed, glaring at Sam. He was late. The president was dead. Sam was shocked into silence as a door opened behind him and Deadman came rushing in. What have you done? This is all your fault.

That's not true! As he tried to protest, a man and a woman appeared flanking Die-Hardman's left and right sides. It was Heartman and Mama. You have to atone for it. We want you to atone for it.

Bridget died because you kept running away. Sam, you have to take responsibility.

He closed his eyes to try to suppress the dizziness.

Are you going to run away again?

He heard Bridget's voice and opened his eyes. He had clapped his hands over his mouth and was desperately holding on to prevent himself from screaming. Everyone was wearing masks like Die-Hardman. Even the bedridden Bridget.

You didn't do anything wrong. I'll be waiting for you.

He could hear Amelie's voice from the direction of the door. Let's run away. Let's get away from this place and this nightmare. When he turned around, Amelie was standing there. But then he heard the shriek of the machines again.

Come on, Sam. I'll be there to get you.

Amelie put the same mask back on.

The shriek was deafening. He had only just realized that it was coming from him.

When Sam woke up he was clutching the dreamcatcher so tightly that his right hand had gone numb.

EAST OF THE UNITED STATES OF AMERICA

The southern sky glowed red in the middle of the night.

Someone had said it was because the city had been burning down there for over a week.

Viktor wondered if he would be able to get warm if he got close to the burning city.

As he rubbed his fingers to try and bring back some of the sensation stolen by the cold, and tried to imagine toasting them beside the inferno, he heard a small groan from his little brother, whose head was nuzzled against his chest below his armpit. Igor must have been having a nightmare. His little brother's eyes were shut tightly as he clung onto a small astronaut figure hung around his neck.

Viktor had the same figure. It was a hero to them both.

The astronaut was the main character from the brothers' favorite game, a knight of the universe called Ludens.

Instead of a blanket, an adult's coat was drawn up to his

chin. Their noses were assaulted by the stench of rotting blood and flesh. It was a coat they had stolen yesterday from a dying man who was no longer able to move.

In the bathroom behind the gas station, both the door and the toilet were broken and there was no water to be found. The smell of mixed urine and feces kept everybody away. That's why it was the perfect place for two young brothers who were all alone in the world. He wondered how long it would be until morning came. That was all that Viktor Frank could think about as he ground his teeth to try and keep the cold at bay. Viktor was six years old, his brother, Igor, four, and to them the night seemed to go on forever.

Once morning came, Viktor dragged a grumbling Igor east. If they went east and reached the coast, then they would manage somehow or other. Viktor had heard someone say so.

He didn't really understand why or what "they would manage" really meant, though.

It was easy to tell which direction was east in the mornings. All they had to do was aim for the sun.

Their breath still came out white even though the sun was rising, as its warmth couldn't penetrate the thin cloud cover and reach the land below.

This had been their life since that day. Adults would call it "that day," but Viktor wasn't sure what day they meant. They were probably referring to the day when the Internet was cut off and the TV stopped airing. Viktor wasn't happy about how he was no longer able to play his games or watch his favorite movies. His mother and father were no longer able to watch the news and no one could connect to social media. Everyone just complained about how they didn't understand what was going on.

Within days his parents were at each other's throats.

Viktor's little brother was only four years old, so he would get scared and cry when his parents began yelling at each other. Viktor began to despise his parents for it. Now he understood why they argued. They were scared.

There had been explosions all over America and no one was sure what had caused them. All branches of the government had been completely disabled. The USA was tearing at the seams and breaking apart.

Strange rumors and unverifiable information permeated through the cities at astonishing speed. Citizens grew increasingly suspicious of one another and were overcome with anxiety.

First, they claimed the explosions were part of an attack by some country. Then they said that a natural disaster had struck, affecting the entire planet. Then it was the wrath of God. Revenge of the dead. Then the rumors spoke of how the dead must be incinerated or we would be overrun by them. They said this place would eventually belong to the dead.

The number of suicides increased. Then the number of

killings along with it. Neighbor killed neighbor, and those that didn't have the heart to kill their fellow man were left with the choice of either killing themselves or getting away.

It wasn't long before Viktor's father drunk himself into a stupor and hung himself.

Igor was the one who discovered his father's body in the bathroom.

Their half-crazed mother had to cut the body down, lay it in the bathtub, and cover it with gasoline. Then she doused her own body and set both herself and her husband ablaze right in front of their children.

Viktor could still smell the stench of burning hair and flesh in his nose.

The flames that engulfed his mother and father burned through the bathtub and eventually claimed their entire home.

The newly orphaned brothers held hands as they wandered through the city streets at night, until they eventually left the concrete of the suburbs and found themselves following a muddy trail. Viktor couldn't even remember how many days they walked or how they managed to stave off the starvation. And when every other person the boys came across looked like a killer, it was only natural that they had ended up walking out of town.

After departing the gas station, the brothers found their route east flanked by rows of wilted cornfields. The sun had reached as high as it would go in the winter sky, but the temperature hadn't improved one bit. Rising black smoke caught Viktor's eye from the other side of the field.

Viktor felt the grip on his hand loosen and the brothers stopped. Igor freed his hand and crouched down. His shoelaces had come untied.

"Maybe we should rest here for a while," Viktor suggested as he sat down next to Igor. A terrible smell immediately entered his nostrils. The smell of burning flesh. Startled, Viktor sniffed at his little brother.

But all he could smell was a mix of mud, sweat, and urine.

A strong wind blew, and the smell grew stronger. It was the same smell as back then. The same smell as his mother's and father's burning corpses. Viktor stood on his tiptoes and looked upwind. The black smoke must have been coming from a burning body. Once he realized that, the tears came. He felt deathly scared.

Viktor gripped Igor's hand. They had to go back the way they came.

His feet hurt so much that he couldn't stand it. The soles of his shoes were torn to shreds and every step was difficult.

Neither of the brothers said a word, they just kept walking. It was only once the smell of burning had disappeared that they allowed themselves to sit down by the side of the road. They should have been walking toward the sun as it rose, but now they chased it as it sank. They would end up back in town at this rate. They could feel the cold in the soles of their feet. Night was approaching. As Viktor thought about where they could go to shelter from the cold, they heard the sound of an engine from behind them. It was coming from the cornfield. He didn't know what to do.

As soon as he made a grab for Igor's hand and tried to run away, he slipped over. His ankle felt strangely twisted. Having fallen face first into the muddy ground, Viktor could taste dust inside his mouth. The car's headlights swooped down on the two brothers. And that's all he remembered.

When Viktor woke up, the pair weren't wrapped in some foul-smelling coat, but a thin, musty blanket. It wasn't cold anymore. A fire was crackling away in a metal drum that had been placed in the center of an auditorium-like room. Behind it was an altar. They were in a church.

When Viktor tried to get up out of the hard, wooden chair he had been lying in, a pain surged through his ankle. He took a closer look and found it wrapped in a white bandage.

"Oh, you're awake."

It was a rough voice, but its calmness helped put Viktor at ease. When the boy looked up, he found himself looking at a face surrounded by unkempt hair and hidden behind a shaggy beard. The man reminded him of a bear. He spotted the Federal Express logo on the man's dusty overalls.

"How are you feeling? Are you hungry?" the man asked, holding out a hand. It completely engulfed Viktor's.

Now that Viktor had some time to look around, he could

see all kinds of people wrapped in the same blankets as he and Igor, taking refuge in this holy sanctuary. Now that the government was no longer functioning and people had been left to fend for themselves, this was one of the few places where they could gather to help each other.

It was this very church that ensured the young lives of Viktor and Igor Frank got to continue.

PORT KNOT CITY

Viktor was shouting down the communications terminal to the person on the other end, asking them to repeat what they'd just said. There was so much noise and static that he thought he must have misheard. But the same reply came through.

<Central Knot City has been destroyed in a voidout.>

Viktor was speechless. Central was where Bridges was headquartered. That meant that everything vital to the plan to build the UCA had been wiped out. The voice on the other end suggested that the voidout might have been the result of an act of terrorism. It warned that all Bridges facilities and Knot Cities should be on their guard.

He couldn't believe it. What was the point in volunteering for the expedition and guarding this place now?

Had the life that he had dedicated to the rebuilding of

America after he and Igor were saved by the church come to an end as well? His fears were soon alleviated.

<We may have lost Central, but our headquarters had already moved to Capital. Don't worry, the president has ordered the departure of Bridges II.>

The voice was almost drowned out by the noise, but Viktor didn't ask for a repeat this time. He didn't want anyone to refute what he had just heard.

The communication ended and Viktor sighed with relief. It looked like he would be able to meet a certain someone again for the first time in three years.

It had been around half a year ago when he last received word from his little brother, Igor, who had long been involved in the thankless work of corpse disposal.

"Viktor, I was picked for the expedition, too. Did you hear about what we're going to do? We're going to use a Q-pid to reconnect the whole continent. We're going to visit your place, too. I got hit pretty bad by the timefall, so I probably look even older than you now. Promise not to laugh, when you see me? We're going to restore America to its glory days."

Viktor could hear the pride in Igor's voice in his own head as he remembered.

That's right. America's not going down without a fight.

Viktor conjured a map of the continent in his head. He wondered how long it would take Bridges II to reach Port Knot City if they left right then. As long as there was no change in route, they would probably head to the waystation first, then to the distro center and then to Port Knot City. He knew there were multiple BT-occupied territories between here and there, though. And even if they managed to avoid all of them, they'd probably have issues where the MULEs were active. And then, if they made it through all of that, they would have to get through the wasteland. It was unlikely they would arrive in Port Knot City without any casualties.

Viktor wanted nothing more than for Igor to turn up safe and unharmed, but he knew better than to pray for anything. Viktor continued to daydream about the reunion with his little brother. But this wasn't the time for that. He couldn't just think about this small bone of happiness that had been thrown to him, he had to think about the bigger picture, and the bigger prize that lay farther ahead.

Viktor put a hand to the Bridges logo that adorned his blue uniform and remembered the Federal Express logo on the uniform of that bear who had saved them all those years ago.

CAPITAL KNOT CITY // WEST // DISTRIBUTION CENTER

When Sam opened his right hand, the weave of the rope had left a clear mark on his skin from clutching the dreamcatcher so tightly.

As he lay down on the bed in his private room, Sam

stared at the amulet that the indigenous people of this land had once used. Amelie had told him that it would turn his nightmares into peaceful dreams, but Sam wasn't sure how effective it was.

He felt like lately, all he saw was nightmares. Sometimes he felt he was still dreaming. Everything felt like a dream, as though he was a fetus dozing in its mother's womb. Some things—Amelie, burning Bridget's corpse, and his cargo-laden journey west—he wished were all dreams. He wished he could reject reality.

<Sam!>

Die-Hardman's voice broke the silence. Now Sam had connected the distribution center to the Chiral Network, the director's voice sounded clear as day, almost like he was in the room. He could even hear the breathing behind the man's mask.

<Did you get some rest?> Die-Hardman was most likely monitoring Sam's vitals back at HQ, so it's not like he needed to ask. <From here, we want you to go to Port Knot City> the director continued without waiting for Sam's reply.

A map was displayed on the monitor on the wall. The route Sam had taken from Capital Knot City in the far east, through to the waystation and the distribution center, was precisely tracked. From there, a straight line stretched westward into the interior of the continent and toward a large lake. All the way to Port Knot City, a city nestled right next to the enormous body of water known as Ground Zero.

Sam wouldn't be able to travel in such a straight line. He would have to work his way around all the areas that he wouldn't be able to traverse on foot, all the BT territory, and all the areas that he knew to be infested with MULEs. He had no idea how long it was going to take.

<Alright, Sam. Once you get them online, you'll start to see how this Chiral Network is going to look. We aren't just connecting point to point in one long line. They'll form more of a net, expanding the operational area of the network outwards. Once that's in place, we won't just be able to exchange information, we'll also be able to physically "gram" objects using chiral printers, allowing us to remotely copy inorganic objects. We'll be able to send you useful equipment and apparatus as you continue west, too.>

That was one of the main reasons for getting the Chiral Network up and running, and why it was so significant to the rebuilding of America.

Once the director had finished explaining, he cut off the communication.

Sam got into his shower booth. His body had never been perfect and he was always sporting some kind of injury somewhere. But he never complained about it as he carried his cargo. Never had done, never planned to. The hot water hit his shoulders, ran down his back, and pooled at his feet. A dull pain radiated from the big toe on his right foot. The nail was hanging off, so Sam bent forward and ripped it away. The blood that trickled out disappeared down the drain along with the toenail.

Once he had gotten out of the shower, Sam treated it with a hemostatic spray. He put his uniform on over his undershirt and prepared to set out.

Inside the incubator, the BB was drifting around with its eyes closed inside the pod. The baby squirmed as Sam disconnected the pod and removed it, before carefully attaching it to his chest unit so as not to wake the BB. He caressed the pod gently to cause as little stress as possible and to put the BB at ease.

Then he left the room and took the elevator back up to the surface.

Feeling the vibration of the floor as it rose, Sam connected himself to the BB pod via the cord.

Immediately, he felt lightheaded. In his mind, he could hear the intolerable sound of metal scraping on metal and his field of vision narrowed.

He couldn't feel his body, it was like his spine had been ripped out. The sensation should have died down after a few seconds.

But it didn't.

His field of vision grew more and more narrow and the color drained from the world, before blacking out entirely. Sam thought that he might have fainted, but that didn't appear to be the case. He was still conscious and, not only that, his mind was racing. Pitch black dominated Sam's world. His body had dissolved into that black and now he existed as pure consciousness.

—*BB.*

He could hear soft whispers. He tried to ask who was there, but his mouth would not open.

Light drenched him as if a curtain covering the entire world had opened up.

—*BB.*

He heard that voice again. It was a man's voice. The man was looking at Sam.

—*I'm your papa, BB.*

The light went out. Sam's field of vision was cloaked by the man's hand. He wanted to get away. But he still couldn't feel his body. He couldn't do anything. He couldn't close his eyes, he couldn't run away, he couldn't do a damn thing. The hand belonging to the mystery man bore down on him. It would seize everything and steal it all away. *Please don't.* He hated this. All he could do was feel how much he hated it.

The BB cried out for him.

The BB was scared of the hand and was screeching.

—*I'll protect you, BB. I won't let anyone take you away from me.*

That urge to protect the BB restored Sam's physical senses. Blurred outlines felt crisp again and color was returning to the world.

"It's okay, BB," Sam said reassuringly, having come back to his senses.

The elevator arrived at the surface and the BB stopped crying.

Not only was Sam now carrying even more weight on his back than before, but the inexplicable vision that Sam had when he connected to his BB also weighed on his mind. *Who was that man? What did he mean by "papa"? Was it because of my DOOMS that I saw that vision?*

On his back, Sam was carrying aid intended for Port Knot City and some anti-BT weaponry. It was all packed away in his bags. According to the director, its value far exceeded even its weight. Most of the aid consisted of preserved sperm and eggs. No one was really moving between the cities anymore and they needed to expand the gene pool. If they didn't, then even children born among the same generation would end up with similar genetics and all diversity would be lost, weakening mankind as a species. The aid in this cargo was the very future of the human race.

But more important than even that was the inclusion of anti-BT weapons.

These weapons used blood and fluids harvested from Sam's body. Heartman was supposedly the one who had developed the theoretical backbone, which had subsequently been engineered into weapons and brought to life by Mama. Mama was a key member of Bridges and had been a part of Bridges I. An expert in theoretical physics, she was the woman behind the development of the Q-pid and the Chiral Network. Sam had heard she was now working in a lab on the outskirts of South Knot City, in the center of the continent and to the west of Ground Zero.

He remembered the director showing him a picture of her before he left. She wore her hair in a ponytail and sported thin-rimmed glasses and a tank top.

There was speculation that Sam's unique constitution as a repatriate could have some kind of effect on BTs, who themselves were "special among the dead." These weapons were going to test that theory. Sam wasn't exactly skeptical of the idea going by his recent experiences, so he had accepted the experiment without argument. He remembered the time he encountered that BT with Igor, the incinerator where he burned Bridget's body and the blood from his bitten lip. There had been other instances before which had given Sam cause to believe that the BTs avoided his bodily fluids.

But it was still just conjecture. Sam thought it was jumping the gun a little to deliver weapons that hadn't even been tested yet. Where had he heard that before? Sam had to do things that no one else had ever experienced. It was true of the Chiral Network, and it was true of the countermeasures against the BTs as well. His journey west was a grand experiment in itself.

In a sense, Sam's body was a tool. The tool that would be used to accomplish the mission. That's how Bridges must have thought of him, anyway. But before Sam was even aware of the mission, his body had already adapted for his purpose. His stride grew longer, the blisters that covered his feet had burst and hardened, and his soles were now thick and tough like leather. Any energy he consumed was used as fuel for walking before it could even be converted into fat or muscle.

Sam was seized by the thought that his body had become their machine. Bridges probably felt the same way about the BB, maybe that was why Deadman always referred to it as "equipment."

The wind caressed Sam's face. He closed his eyes at how pleasant it felt. He thought he heard the BB laugh as well. The outlines of the mountain ridges towering in the distance were unusually clear. The mountains themselves blocked Sam's path up ahead, but in that moment all he could think about was how majestic and beautiful they looked. They exuded a majesty that human hands would never be able to capture.

Sam wondered if holding such contradictory feelings in his head could be considered proof that he was indeed human after all. And the fact that the BB, too, could laugh, become scared and suffer from the effects of autotoxemia if put under too much stress, meant it wasn't a piece of equipment either. It was human, too.

Sam thought back to a fact once recited to him by one of his porter pals. They claimed that the reason most porters failed in their line of duty was not because of any kind of physical injury, but for psychological reasons. Walking hundreds of kilometers in silence had broken a lot of their colleagues. If a porter sustained an injury they could always receive treatment, so long as it wasn't life-threatening. But most people found their spirit broke long before their body did. It was because of this proclivity that porters were recommended to work in pairs or teams. Lone porters like Sam were in an extreme minority.

Sam's cuff link began to vibrate, letting him know that he had a codec call incoming from Deadman.

<How is the BB doing?>

This area was covered by the Chiral Network, so his voice came through clear as day.

"I have something I need you to answer for me," Sam said, looking down at the BB attached to his chest. "I saw something when I connected to the BB. It was someone's face. And they were talking to me. They said that they were my papa."

A theatrical sigh came from the other end of the line.

<Didn't I tell you before? You're seeing the BB's memories. It's showing them to you in flashbacks. Listen. BBs are extracted from their mothers' wombs

at around the twenty-eight-week mark, and transferred straight into pods before they can be born into life. They stop developing at that stage.>

The BB looked up at Sam and their eyes met for a moment. They stopped developing? Sam had difficulty believing that.

<But by that point their main senses, like sight and hearing, are more or less formed. All the BB is doing is regurgitating the memories of the sensations and information it received at that time into your head. That's my best guess.>

"So then who was that guy I saw?"

<He could have been one of our medical staff or on the production team. The BB has been used as a piece of equipment several times over. It has been in contact with lots of people, so it would be difficult to identify a specific individual.>

"Come on, don't you know shit?" Sam hadn't realized how severe his tone had begun to sound.

<I'm sorry, but by the time I arrived here, BB-28 was already at Bridges. Research into BBs supposedly began quite a while ago, but it's been sealed away for quite some time now. They said it was dangerous to use them in the field. In any case, the content of a BB's head is basically a black box. For the moment, anyway.>

Deadman explained quickly, but Sam had heard it all before. If you worked as a porter you heard all kinds of crazy things. Sam had once heard that some separatist extremists had uncovered some long-buried records held by a former government think tank, and had a crack at reproducing BB technology themselves. Apparently, Bridges hadn't been happy about it and stolen the technology back. Still, Sam had never heard of any BB tech talk himself when he was working there proper.

`<I've been researching what I can, but there aren't very many records left.>` Deadman sounded genuine. `<I'll keep looking into BBs. I'll let you know if I find anything.>`

The BB had been taken from its mother's womb before it even had a chance to become alive. Deadman tried to ignore his own relationship to the dead. And Sam was a repatriate. There was something that linked the three of them. None of them were truly members of the living.

Once Sam crossed over the hills, his view expanded and he could see the silhouette of something man-made in the distance. Sam had almost made it to Port Knot City on the banks of Ground Zero. The city was encircled by a wall that closed it off and discouraged contact with outsiders. Unlike him and the company he currently kept, the people residing within those walls were the real living.

Sam let out a deep sigh and continued walking.

PORT KNOT CITY

It was just like a space station.

The distribution center on the edge of town always gave Viktor Frank that impression.

Life in the closed-off interior of the city couldn't honestly be called comfortable, but people could live their lives. Only those with the special key could venture outside of the facility. The physical distance separating Port Knot City from other cities and stations made it difficult to facilitate any kind of interaction with the outside world. This isolation was what reminded Viktor of a space station.

Obviously, he had never been to space himself, but he knew all about it from the movies and TV shows that he used to watch as a kid. The astronauts from the fictional worlds he loved were all heroes, emboldened by a pioneer spirit as they expanded the frontier and undertook important missions. When he had joined Bridges I, Viktor felt like he himself had become an astronaut in much the same way.

Once upon a time, their ancestors had pushed the frontier of this land from east to west. Once they had finally reached the west coast and the frontier vanished, they had set their sights beyond this land. This time it wasn't a simple walk across the ground, but upwards into the sky. They had set their sights on space. After the Death Stranding, when mankind was cut off from the stars, the frontier spirit had once again shifted back to the journey westward.

But what was decidedly different to before was the fact that it was no longer about expanding territory but the process of reclamation and reconstruction. In other words, it was a movement to create a future. That was the spirit of the UCA rebuilding plan that President Bridget and Bridges had proposed.

A young Viktor and Igor had got their first taste of how cool space was from a TV series that was broadcast through the clouds. When Viktor thought back to that time, he now realized that people had already begun to shut themselves away. All kinds of stories and access to any information that they wanted lay at their fingertips without them even having to step foot out of the door. They could even interact with other people from their own homes via social media. They didn't even need to go out to shop, because they could just buy everything they needed and more online.

But the Death Stranding destroyed all that.

Compared to before, humans were now confined to the limits of their bodies. Hands that had previously been able to reach out digitally and connect with others across great distances could now only connect in person. To travel, they could only go as far as their legs could carry them. The only thing that would be able to resurrect these decaying bodies that could no longer move was spirit.

The plan to rebuild the UCA was going to enable this, but

until the Chiral Network that would once again transcend the physical limitations of an emasculated mankind was brought online, it was the porters who were responsible for keeping this wasteland connected. The porter system may have been small and fragile, and could only offer arms and legs that looked like they might snap at any moment, but it was also a life-support system that prevented those who couldn't move on their own from simply decaying into nothing. The bear-like man who had saved Viktor and his brother had been a porter for one of the companies in America.

Becoming a member of Bridges and being entrusted to carry part of the American spirit had reignited the dreams of the brothers' youth, and had allowed them to reconnect some of the lives that had been severed.

The electronic beeps of the monitor interrupted Viktor's train of thought. The distribution center sensors alerted him to the fact that someone had entered the vicinity. But it wasn't a warning sign. Its tone was far more welcoming and forgiving of this intrusion. A porter from Bridges was here. The monitor displayed the porter's attributes. His name was Sam Porter Bridges. He belonged to—Viktor couldn't believe what he was seeing.

He was with Bridges II. They had only sent one person. How could they be so stupid? Either that, or the second expedition had dwindled down to the very last man on its way here. That would mean they had been all but wiped out before they had even reached the halfway point, and the plan to rebuild America was in dire straits. And what about Igor?

As Viktor worried, Sam Bridges passed through the entrance to the center and activated the delivery terminal. Now he was unloading his cargo bag by bag into the collection area.

As Viktor looked at the total weight of the cargo on the monitor in the basement, he couldn't believe that a single porter had managed to carry it all. It included hard-to-get construction materials, medicine, and frozen sperm and eggs. All of it was essential aid to maintain the city. As Viktor checked the inspection result, he noticed some cargo that he wasn't familiar with. The screen displayed the name, "Anti-BT Weaponry." He had never heard of anything like that. Going by the name, he supposed it must be some kind of weapon that was effective against BTs. He had no idea that they were even developing anything like that. He would have to ask either Sam or HQ about it. Everything else he had heard of.

Viktor opened a line to the ground floor and saw a hologram of Sam on the screen in front of him. Simultaneously, Viktor's hologram appeared in front of Sam.

He cleared his throat in preparation for expressing his gratitude.

The hologram of Sam looked like a ghoul. Most of the hair that he had gathered at the back of his head had come loose, and disheveled bangs hid half of his face. There was some gray hair mixed in with the brown now. His stubbled cheeks were streaked with gray, too. His eyes were sunken, but there was an intelligence within them. Although he had different features, Sam reminded Viktor of the porter who had saved him and Igor all those years ago. His blue uniform was dirty and dotted with what looked like bloodstains. If Viktor hadn't been looking at a hologram, he probably would have smelled something akin to a wild beast.

If this man was the sole survivor of the second expedition, then maybe a miracle could still happen. Viktor had to hear what this man had to say. He bit his lip and stared back at the tattered Sam.

"What's that?" Viktor blurted without thinking.

"What's what?" Sam appeared taken aback.

Viktor pointed at the BB pod on Sam's chest. Sam looked puzzled as he stared down at it.

"That figure…"

Viktor fumbled around in his pants pocket and pulled out a figure. He held it up in the air for Sam to see. It was the figure of Ludens, the astronaut.

"Same as mine! Where the hell'd you get it?" Viktor asked incredulously.

Sam squinted and looked back and forth between Viktor's Ludens and the Ludens hanging off the pod.

"Yeah, I can't really say… but the little guy, he came with the pod, if you gotta know."

"And who'd you get the pod from?" Viktor pressed.

Sam looked around awkwardly and frowned. "Igor from Corpse Disposal," he answered eventually.

"My little brother."

Viktor noticed how Sam didn't say "from the expedition." It must mean that Viktor's little brother had died as a member of the Corpse Disposal Team. He must have been caught up in the voidout that wiped out Central Knot City, and now that the original second expedition had been destroyed, it had been reformed into the one-man expedition that was Sam Porter Bridges.

"I was there with him. At the end." Sam began to speak slowly as if he was choosing each word carefully. "We were moving a body. Things went to shit. There were BTs everywhere. And one of 'em grabbed him. He put up a fight right until the end. He even tried to sacrifice himself first, so there was no voidout. He told me to take it and run."

Viktor realized that he was gripping his Ludens tightly and shaking. He began to speak slowly, so that his voice didn't waver.

"That right…"

Sam's silence was confirmation. He would never see his little brother again.

"Guess it can't be helped," Viktor muttered as his trembling faded like it had been washed away by a wave. But it hadn't disappeared completely. Viktor knew that it would be back in due time. And he also knew that he should let himself feel sorrow, mourn, and grieve when that time came.

"So what's your story?" Viktor asked Sam. "You live through a catastrophe like that only to keep on doin' the same work?"

Viktor was confronted by a man who, despite the fact that he had witnessed a voidout, had still walked all the way to Port Knot City in the name of the expedition. That in itself was a miracle.

Viktor had heard of this man, the repatriate, Sam Porter Bridges. Everyone had pinned their hopes on him at Bridges to put the plan to rebuild the UCA into action, but he had left ten years ago.

If Sam Porter Bridges was back, then Viktor was certain that this expedition could bring forth a miracle, even if it was only one man.

Oblivious to the thoughts in Viktor's head, Sam silently held up the necklace around his neck. Six shards of metal were floating above Sam's hand. It was the Q-pid. Viktor knew what it was immediately and began to operate the equipment.

"Okay... Been a long time coming, I suppose. They even completed that thing. Well, time to get us connected to the rest of the UCA and up on the Chiral Network."

Viktor wondered how many times he had dreamt of this moment. He wondered if they could hear his voice in the control tower. This place, floating in the middle of the void, would finally be connected to his hometown. And just as the name of the city suggested, they would finally become a knot. Sam was no ordinary porter. He was an astronaut who had conquered this frontier.

"You take good care of that little guy. He belongs with the expedition. With you."

It might have been his imagination, but Viktor could have sworn that he saw a hint of a smile on Sam's face. That was enough for Viktor. Sam took Ludens from where he was dangling on the pod and placed it in his hand. "Alright," he answered. As Sam spoke, Viktor thought that his voice no longer sounded like it belonged to a tortured soul dragged up from the depths of hell, but more like a seraph who bestowed blessings from above. However, the angelic voice that Viktor heard was no illusion.

<Sam, you've done it.>

Viktor had never forgotten how her voice sounded like music drifting out of heaven. It belonged to the woman who had led Viktor and the rest of the first expedition. It belonged to Amelie.

Sam looked up at Amelie's hologram. Edge Knot City, where she was currently held, and here were still not connected via the Chiral Network. That meant he was still looking at a vision of Amelie made up of rebooted signals that had been patched through various wireless and land lines all the way from the West Coast, and rejigged based on the data kept locally at the distribution center. The hologram was interspersed with noise and sometimes the image faltered or the voice became scrambled. But her mannerisms and cadence were unmistakably those of the Amelie who Sam remembered.

<Port Knot City is back on the grid. It doesn't need to stand alone anymore. It can reap the benefits of the Chiral Network and all that the UCA has to offer. We know that any city that joins the UCA becomes a bigger target for the Homo Demens, but we have to accept the dangers and press on, no matter what. If we remain divided all that awaits us is ruin and extinction, but if we're connected there is still hope for the future. Even if we have to sacrifice the present, there is still a future that we have to build.>

As Sam listened to Amelie's voice, he could feel a distance between them that he needed to close. And he didn't just mean physically heading west.

<The rest of America is waiting, Sam. Waiting for you to take the first step and connect them to the Chiral Network.>

By the time Sam realized why the hologram felt so weird,

the communication had already been cut. Amelie disappeared. He couldn't help but notice that throughout the entire short communication, Amelie had never said the word, "I," only, "we."

Sam thought he could hear thunder in the distance and looked back. He was already halfway under the ground, so he couldn't see outside very well, but it didn't seem like the timefall was falling in the city.

Setting aside his worries, Sam headed for a private room in the basement. As he descended, he was overcome by an intense sleepiness.

The feeling of waking back up was like rising from the seabed. It was the opposite of when he returned from the Seam. When he was brought back, he was desperately groping toward a vision of his body trapped on the ocean floor. The mechanism of consciousness that went into the process of waking up and returning to reality was a real mystery. The Beach was tied to an individual's consciousness. Just as there was a feeling of rising when waking up, there was a feeling of falling when being repatriated. The Beach and unconsciousness. The two states stood back-to-back and intertwined like a Klein bottle.

As Sam woke up in his private room, he felt a slight headache and a little nausea.

The vitals that his cuff link was measuring were in a
normal range. The sickness that Sam felt must have been
within the range of error. Luckily, the all-encompassing
pain and exhaustion that Sam had felt before he fell asleep
were mostly gone.

Sam didn't even remember falling asleep. He must have
dozed off as he sat on the bed listening to Viktor's status report.

He hadn't had any bad dreams this time. In fact, he had
slept deeply. Maybe the headache and nausea were caused
by all the filth that had clung to him. He could smell the
stink of his own body.

As Sam headed for the shower booth, he checked in on
the pod in the incubator. The BB was still sleeping soundly.

The hot water washed everything away down the drain.
The dirt, the blood and sweat, even all the trimmings from
his beard. The BTs hated all of it. Sam assumed that his
blood had been drawn as he slept like usual. It was his blood
that was being used in the anti-BT weapons he had brought
here. According to Viktor, once the weapons had reached
Port Knot City, the plan was to have them turned over to
Sam. Their usefulness was yet to be verified, so unless they
tested them, they were pointless. If they were ineffective,
they would just be scrapped.

But Viktor seemed to have great hopes for them. He
told Sam how he was counting on him, the "one man who
bore the duty of the entire second expedition," to realize

his dream. How they would probably now even be able to restart the boat crossings across Ground Zero that had been suspended. About how the city was no longer a lone satellite, but a knot that connected the Earth and outer space. Viktor had continued to chatter excitedly as Sam drifted off to sleep.

Sam dried his hair as he remembered their conversation, before putting on his undershirt and sticking his arms through the sleeves of his uniform. Sam felt much more positive about his journey when he felt like he had been entrusted with the dreams of people like Viktor, rather than just burdened with Die-Hardman's instructions. Sam hadn't taken on any jobs with a greater purpose in his work as a porter, only individual requests, for a while.

Sam strapped his backpack on and removed the pod from the incubator. Then he left the room and took the elevator to the upper floor.

Roars of thunder awaited Sam. Because of the structure of this level, which led to the outside world up a slope, the low rumble of thunder shook the floor and walls and jolted Sam's body in its tight grip. Sam's spine tingled and he felt a spark in his brain. He could feel his gastric juices in his throat as his mouth filled with an acidic taste and tears spilled out of his eyes.

Knot cities were built in areas that didn't experience the timefall. That was why the incinerators were built at a distance, like satellites that emitted chiralium pollution. But none of that seemed to apply anymore as the skies poured with time-stealing rain.

Despite the strangeness of the situation, there were no alarms warning of danger or codec calls instructing anyone to be alert. It looked like everyone had fled from the anomaly and shut themselves up somewhere safe.

Gusts of wind penetrated the room from the slope, and Sam immediately grabbed for one of the pillars. The pallets that were used for accepting cargo had been left out and the wind had slammed them against the wall. It startled the BB, who began to cry. This storm wasn't natural. This wind and thunder that were bearing down on Sam were full of malice. He didn't know why he felt that way, but it was some kind of intuition. The Odradek was spinning around wildly. But neither of them could detect the source nor identify the owner of this ill will. The place had turned into the belly of a whale. Sam had been swallowed up and was going to dissolve into nothing in its strong stomach acid. He had to get out of here.

He stood his ground against the gale and inched his way up the slope.

The BB was wailing. It was desperately trying to show Sam how scared it was. Sam cradled the pod with both arms when the BB flipped itself around, seemingly in response to something. The kid was angry and directed its hostility at this mysterious source of malice. Sam ran up the hill as fast as he could.

There was no one outside. Just the howling wind and darkness. The lightning tore the black asunder. The air was filled with evil. The winds, the darkness, and the lightning all served it. When he raised his head, all he saw was a pitch-black sky. The clouds were undulating like a stormy sea. The waves bore flashes of lightning that felt like they were ricocheting and exploding within Sam's skull in the depths behind his eyes, and the world went red. It was sucking him up. Sam was engulfed and began to drown in the sky.

He could see a rainbow. It was upside-down. An upside-down bridge that linked this world and the next. The ocean parted together with the sky.

Torrential rain poured forth. In an instant, the ground that had been pounded by the timefall transformed into a sticky, tarlike substance. Sam couldn't stop the tears.

Sam's vision warped and he saw a beach littered with the remains of crabs and coral. Before he knew it, he was in BT territory. One of the inky dead bodies was clinging to his leg. It was over. Sam readied himself. That dead being was a BT. It was the same as what happened last time with Igor. Once he was caught, all it would take was one swallow before it was game over: a voidout.

Memories of Viktor's face and voice swam into Sam's

mind. Sam was so sorry. He hadn't been able to save Igor and now he was unable to save his big brother either. So now it was Port Knot's turn. How many cities was Sam going to do this to?

It wasn't the time to rebuild America. Sam had told them that enough times. Sam saw the faces of Amelie, Deadman, Die-Hardman, and Bridget before each faded away. It wasn't something that Sam was ever going to be able to accomplish. *Goodbye, America.*

The BB wailed. It howled like a beast and brought Sam back to his senses. His leg was still sinking into the quagmire, but the force that was pulling him down had disappeared. Sam strained his eyes, and through the dark could see the sheeting rain beating against a silhouette. The shape of a man that was the source of this malice. The master of this space.

"The name's Higgs." The man opened his mouth. Rocks and the carcasses of marine animals were suspended in the air all around him. Fish on their backs, crustaceans, coral…

"The particle of God that permeates all existence." His voice penetrated all. It filled the entire space. It wasn't dulled by the golden mask that covered its master's face and mouth.

Sam had heard of this "Higgs." He had a stronghold around the central region of the country, and together with his band of separatist extremists was responsible for much death and destruction. He was a terrorist and he showed absolutely no mercy.

Higgs appeared to defy the laws of gravity as he strode across the tar toward Sam. Masses of rocks jutted up out of the sticky, black substance and Higgs stepped between them. As he walked, he glared at Sam. It was like being pierced by the cold stare of a ruthless emperor. As the glare hit him, Sam held his breath. But Higgs was the first to look away. A second shadow had appeared on top of the rain-battered distribution center. Higgs glowered as another flash of lightning revealed who it belonged to. Her golden hair had been whipped up into a frenzy by the wind and her asymmetrical umbrella looked as if it was about to get blown away. The jet-black bodysuit that she wore from the neck down made her glisten like the skin of an amphibian. Spikes protruded from her shoulders.

It was her. It was the woman who had ambushed Sam in that cave. It was Fragile.

"Ah, so it was you that dragged him into all this?" Higgs asked Fragile.

Sam wasn't sure what it was supposed to mean. Higgs's voice was laced with rage.

Higgs held up a finger and waved it toward Fragile as a gust finally blew away her umbrella. The rain beat down mercilessly on her face, and in the next second, Fragile was gone.

"Heh. Bloodied but unbowed."

Sam could suddenly hear Higgs's voice right next to his

ear, so when he turned he was face-to-face with the man in the golden mask.

Behind it, he saw a nose twitch.

"What's that? Bridget Strand is dead?"

A stinging pain shot through Sam's eyes. Tears kept rolling out. He was having an intense antigen-antibody reaction. He tried to get away from Higgs, but his body wouldn't listen. It was like it no longer even belonged to him.

"America's last president. Dead and burned." Higgs brought his face closer, as if he was enjoying Sam's reaction.

"Oh, and now the girl's been chosen to take Mommy's place…" Higgs goaded.

Sam's tears would not stop falling. All his stiff body could do was tremble faintly in response to Higgs's voice.

"Well, that won't wash. She's not cut out for politics, is she?"

Suddenly Sam's body was free and Higgs had disappeared.

"Oh, but don't worry. I'll find her. I'll keep her real safe."

Higgs appeared in front of Sam. His mobility had once again been snatched away and all he could do was bite his lip and glare at the golden mask. Higgs passed by Sam's shoulder, sneering at the state of him.

"You see, I've come to understand the truth of the Death Stranding. Oh, there's so much you people don't know," he snarled.

Sam could hear Higgs's voice behind him, but he still couldn't move a muscle.

"The girl, for instance—she's not like you or me. DOOMS ain't her thing. She's more into destruction on a worldwide scale. An Extinction Entity."

An extinction entity? It was the first time Sam had ever heard such a term. Is that supposed to mean that she precipitates extinction?

Those who carried out the most erratic and extreme acts of violence of all terrorists were known as the deranged Homo Demens. Higgs was their leader. They thought and acted in the opposite way to however Homo Sapiens would. Sam wondered if that really was how Higgs viewed Amelie. How ridiculous. Higgs was wrong. This was nothing more than one of the Demens' delusions. Sam struggled with all his might to shake off what Higgs had just said.

Higgs suddenly appeared back in front of Sam. He reached out with both hands clad in black gloves toward a motionless Sam. Flames erupted from Higgs's fingers and engulfed his entire hand.

"Oh, it's so hard to form connections when you can't shake hands…"

The flames blazed and burned right through Higgs's gloves. But there was nothing underneath.

There was nothing below Higgs's wrists.

"Fortunately, I've got a good connection to the other side," Higgs continued.

The space was warped by an invisible force and black

particles burst forth from Higgs's wrists. The particles clumped together and knitted themselves into several cords. As Higgs let out a deep breath, the cords came to life and shot toward the surface of the tar.

"Now you? You're no bridge."

When he pulled on the cords that had been swallowed up by the tar, the inky sea undulated like Higgs was tearing up some sort of carpet.

The BB was sobbing and the Odradek was rotating so violently that it looked like it was going to take off. Sam felt the same fear the BB was experiencing and grew nauseous.

"But me? I'm bound to all of it—this world, that world, and our sweet little angel of death."

The swelling ocean surface broke. A passage to the world beyond had opened up, just as Higgs had declared. A gigantic serpent-like animal reared four ugly heads. The tar dripped from its jowls like the saliva of a hungry beast. The dead that crawled forth from that world were groping into the dark clouds in search of the living. "You're on the menu!" screamed Higgs as the true form of the dead appeared. It breached like a whale and writhed like a snake as the rest of what was lurking below was also dragged forth. What had at first appeared to be sea serpents were in fact numerous tentacles attached to the main body of this dead creature. Its loud cry constricted Sam's organs. This was like no other BT that Sam had ever had to face before. In the center of the enormous knot of waving tentacles, a grotesque mass that looked like an amalgamation of every evolutionary step of every sea creature that had ever drawn breath. Its hide was a tangle of scales, flagellum, and shell that squirmed unevenly.

It was an abomination born from the imagination of Demens that had no place on this earth.

"All it'll take is one itty-bitty voidout to blow us all to kingdom come!"

As Higgs swung a hand down toward Sam, the ties that bound Sam came undone and he could finally move again. Sam lunged forward, but a wave of tar loomed over him, forming a wall, and when it collapsed, Higgs was no longer anywhere to be seen.

Instead, the monster's tentacles came plowing through the rain toward Sam. He stooped low to dodge but was hit by another, square in the back, knocking him to the ground. A sharp pain ran up his spinal cord like a flash of lightning. It felt like his blood was boiling. The BB cried out louder to warn Sam of the next danger. It took all of Sam's strength, but he managed to get up and dodge the incoming appendage.

The BB's shrieks grew even more ear-piercing. Sam looked up, guided by its screams, to see the BT move in for the kill with sprays of black tar bursting forth all around it.

—*Run!*

Sam heard the scream inside his head. The voice belonged

to Igor. The man who had fought to his dying breath to protect Central Knot City. He had tried so desperately to avoid a voidout that he was willing to give his own life, never to join Bridges II or see his big brother ever again. He had sacrificed all by attempting to save everyone else.

The BB wasn't all that Sam had been entrusted with back then. It was now his duty to carry the dream that Igor never got to realize. Sam's gaze fell on the figure of Ludens hanging from the pod.

He grabbed a grenade from his backpack.

It was one of the anti-BT weapons he had been tasked to deliver. They still hadn't been tested and no one was quite sure what effect they would have. As he released the safety device, a pain shot through his right wrist. The cuff link was biting into it. Needles built into the interior of the ring were pricking him all at once. As they sucked up his blood, the grenade changed color.

It felt like it had an iron grip on his heart. It was going to rain Sam's blood down on the monster. It was going to hit the monster over the head with the very life-force of a repatriate. It had to hurt it somehow. Such faith was unfounded, but he knew it was the end for him if he didn't at least try.

The monster's cries threatened to split Sam's eardrums as he turned and lobbed the grenade. There was a bang and a flash. The malice and bitterness of the dead descended into a wail. Destroying a BT meant severing whatever lingering attachment the wandering dead had to this world and sending them back where they belonged. Sam knew this.

This world was no place for them. The dead needed to be with the dead just as the living belonged with the living.

Sam had to unravel this entangled thread and restore the world to its natural order. But where did he belong? Sam would never die in the conventional sense.

The aftershock of the explosion subsided.

But the dead thing remained in this world. The BT howled. It sounded like the warped cries of children who couldn't find their way home. It seemed that the anti-BT weapons were nothing more than a theory after all. Nothing more than hope and delusion based on the peculiarity of repatriates. Sam's disappointment in the weapon mixed with feelings of pity and sympathy for the BT. They were one and the same, both exiled from the place where they were supposed to be.

The BT howled again, as if appealing to Sam to put it out of its misery. It wasn't so different to us.

He grabbed a fresh grenade out of his pack.

Sam had to steer the dead back to where they belonged. If this BT had been summoned by Higgs, then it wasn't here through any fault of its own. If Higgs was going to exploit their bitterness and delusions, then Sam would have to be the one to purify them. Sam felt almost righteous as he grabbed the grenade.

His heart was pounding as he let the grenade fill with his blood. It sucked out so much it was almost like he was holding another heart in the palm of his hand. Sam's vision narrowed as the dizziness from the loss of blood began to set in. Having filled it to bursting point, Sam prayed as the grenade left his grip. Goodbye and rest in peace. The dead belonged in the land of the dead. The BT swallowed up Sam's extra heart and began to chew.

In an instant, a dull light shone from inside the BT. Sam's blood had penetrated its insides and was exorcising it. The BT's tentacles waved around frantically as if it was desperately trying to cling to this world as it shrieked in agony. Eventually, its extremities began to break down into fine particles. Multiple holes opened up all over the main body and the monster began to collapse in on itself.

Ripples formed and disappeared on the surface of the tar as the BT broke down, and the area slowly turned back into the wilderness they were all used to.

The incessant rain lost its vigor and the darkness retreated.

Now free of their BT cages, the dead had returned home.

The world was still, and no sound could be heard. Sam understood that the stillness was a manifestation of fear as he stood there motionless.

<Sam!>

It was a communication from Viktor that first broke the silence and put Sam at ease.

<What was that?! You killed that thing!>

Viktor's words swallowed Sam up like a flood. Normally he wouldn't be able to stand being talked at like that and would have just cut the codec call there and then, but right now that chattiness made him feel a lot more comfortable. Voices were what filled the cracks that had opened up all across this world. The voices of the living plugged the gaps and stopped the dead from getting through.

<If you could beat that thing, then you'll have no problem crossing the lake and connecting the rest of us. Igor's sacrifice wasn't in vain. Now that Port Knot City is a hub on the Chiral Network, we can help reconnect the west.>

Sam sat down among the rubble and listened to Viktor go on and on. The BB slept as if relieved, and Sam flicked Ludens with his finger.

<Thank you, Sam. Thank you, Sam Porter Bridges—>

Viktor was choking up and was finally unable to hold back his sobs any longer.

<Are you listening, Sam?>

Viktor's voice was replaced by one that Sam didn't recognize.

<It's Heartman.>

The device projected the figure of a man. Sam remembered him. They had conversed in his private room once.

<Just as we'd hoped. A repatriate's blood does affect BTs. That's been proven now.>

Heartman's picture was smiling, but the eyes behind his glasses weren't. They held a light that felt as if it was gazing at something far away. It made Sam uncomfortable for some reason. The projection was but a portrait of the man contained within his cuff link. It was nothing more than an icon to show him who was calling, but it was still somehow unnerving.

<But we're not entirely sure why it does.>

Heartman's voice was being transmitted from an area not yet covered by the Chiral Network, so it broke up intermittently and was hard to understand.

<As you know, the Death Stranding is named after the fact that the phenomenon stranded the dead in this world. The dead take on a disposition similar to that of antimatter, and it's been well documented that being touched by the dead causes a voidout. However, based on past reports and observations, the act of touching alone does not induce a voidout. In fact, a voidout only occurs once a human has been consumed by a Beached Thing. We believe it's likely that your unique *ha* forces the BTs back to the other side.>

An electronic beep interrupted Heartman's voice. An electronic, almost artificial, voice came soon after, but Sam couldn't hear what it said because of the static.

<Excuse me, Sam. I'm out of time. Let's pick this up again later.>

Heartman cut the call with the same abruptness with which he had started it.

What the hell was that all about?

Sam let out a deep sigh. Only then did he realize that his body ached all over.

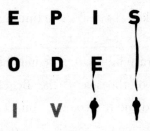

EPISODE IV

FRAGILE

Sam couldn't believe it was a lake.

Even though it had been several hours since the boat had left the port at Port Knot City, he was still having trouble digesting his surprise.

All he could see from the deck of the transport ship crossing Ground Zero was the horizon. This place was an enormous hole bored into ground; a gigantic crack that symbolized the division of America. Sam still couldn't get his head around the fact that it was now a lake. Nor how it was formed in one fell swoop by the huge explosion that marked the beginning of the Death Stranding. He wondered how many people had been wiped out that day. How much energy had been spent?

All that was left was the vast crack that was etched into this land.

Someone had once called it a sea.

Bridget had talked about it a long time ago. (*Hey, that was me.*)

This land embraced a sea at its center. The dead crossed from the depths of the sea to the Beach and became stranded. This land and this country connected to the world of the dead at their center. (*Someone said something about it. They had said that it was a real-life Dirac Sea.*)

If the land was surrounded by sea, we could just build breakwaters or something to keep any potential intruders out. But, Sam, this sea is connected to the center of this world. And the Beach that connects to it lies at the center of us. If we're not careful, we'll be swallowed up by our own sea. That's why we can't protect ourselves with breakwaters. We need to build a bridge to cross this sea, not walls. Do you understand, Sam? Everyone holds on another's hands so that no one drowns and so that we can rescue those that have.

"We'll arrive at the west bank tomorrow."

Fragile had appeared beside Sam. Her black-gloved hands gripped the handrail that ran along the deck.

She was the one who had arranged this ship. All the ships belonging to Port Knot City had been destroyed due to escalating terrorism in the region. The only ships still in service belonged to her company, Fragile Express. The crew was made up of Fragile's people, but Bridges had promised to provide resources like fuel to get the ship running. Deals were no longer cut using economic principles. Ever since the government had fallen, people were no longer motivated by money.

Money may have connected people as a sort of lingua franca, but it also relied on a collective backbone. Once that had gone, connections reverted back to a more primitive form: people and resources. Things you could see. Things you could touch. That's how people began to trade again. However, even though primitive forms of trade and economics were taking place, people couldn't stop being human.

"Snack?"

Fragile offered Sam a cryptobiote. A bug that resembled a rhinoceros beetle larva was squirming between her fingertips. It was just like back in that cave.

Sam sighed and shook his head. Fragile popped the bug into her mouth with a smile.

Fragile had turned up again at the Port Knot City dock after she had evaded the blow from Higgs. Her expression seemed to say that she knew Sam would be able to kill the BT.

Sam couldn't understand Fragile's actions and intentions, but he had her arrange a boat anyway. He still didn't know if he could trust her or if she was just using him.

"You saw that asshole too, right?" Fragile asked.

It was obvious to Sam that Higgs and Fragile shared some kind of connection.

"Higgs. He's the leader of a separatist group," Fragile continued.

"Seemed to me like he was controlling that BT." As far as

Sam knew, there wasn't a person alive with that kind of ability.

"That's a level seven for you. Higher, maybe." Fragile looked up at Sam. He couldn't stand that kind of meaningful stare, so he moved away from the handrail.

"Used to work together." Fragile's voice followed Sam. "Guess you could say we had a contract."

"You did business with terrorists? Whoever pays, huh?" Sam couldn't keep the sharp tone out of his voice.

"He wasn't like that back then," Fragile replied.

"So what's your angle? You wanna save the world? Or you wanna fuck it all up like him?"

Fragile gasped and Sam immediately felt bad for being so harsh.

"I wish I—I just wish things were different, alright?" Fragile's voice was stiff and quiet, yet it was not extinguished and her tone almost sounded like she was trying to convince herself. Sam didn't have any right to pry into whether there was anything between Fragile and Higgs right now. He removed his backpack and sat down on the rusty bench that was fixed to the deck.

He had forgotten the weariness and pain. The scars left by the impact of the BT's tentacles, the aches in his toes where the nails had been ripped off—it soon all flooded back. Sam loosened the laces on his boots and removed the BB pod. He undid the fastenings on his suit and untied his hair. He wanted to get a little more comfortable.

"I told you before, Sam. The past just won't let go."
Fragile peered at Sam and held a scrap of paper aloft.

It was a picture of three people. Bridget was in the center
and still in good health. She was standing between a stiff-
faced Sam and another woman. Sam wondered when he
had dropped it. It had happened in the cave with Fragile
before, too.

He gave Fragile a look of appreciation and took the
picture from her.

The face of the woman to the left side of Bridget had
faded after it had been exposed to the timefall, but Sam
could still recall it vividly in his mind's eye. Yet he still
couldn't bring himself to look at the woman's swollen
abdomen. Nor could he look at the handwritten signature in
the corner made up of "Strand" and "Bridget."

Why didn't the timefall do me a favor and erase that instead?

—I told you before, Sam. The past just won't let go.

"Listen, I have something to ask of you." He could hear
Fragile's voice, but couldn't tear himself away from the
picture. "It has to do with that asshole, Higgs."

A strong wind blew, ruffling Sam's hair. Fragile's
umbrella spun gently in the breeze.

—Can you hear me, Sam?

Sam heard a clatter against the wood of the deck and
opened his eyes. It looked like he'd fallen asleep.

He wiped away some tears that he had shed for some

unknown reason and looked up. A vivid red flooded his vision.

"Sam."

Amelie was stood in front of the bench, clad in red. She smiled and stared at him as if to block any doubts or questions. In her hand, she held the photo Sam had dropped.

The skies had turned cloudy and gray and the surface of the lake was reflecting a muddy light. In a world in which all color seemed to have seeped away, Amelie in her bright red dress looked like the only thing alive.

"Sam," she whispered once more. As if entranced by her voice, Sam stood up and walked over to the handrail on deck. A pod of whales followed the side of the ship as golden sparks were scattered by them.

It was a dream.

The ship was still headed for the shore. But this was not Ground Zero.

If the ship kept on like this, it would get stranded on the Beach.

"Do you remember?" Amelie pointed toward the shore. Dozens of whales and dolphins were lying on their backs where the waves broke. Lying next to them was the small figure of a person face-down in the sand. It was a little boy. It was Sam. The grown-up Sam was looking at his younger self collapsed on the Beach. No, wait, he was remembering something about Amelie and his younger self.

"It's almost time to go, Sam."

The little Sam woke up when Amelie called him.

Since he had fallen asleep on the Beach, half of his face was covered in grains of sand. Amelie took Sam by the arms and picked him up. He could feel Amelie's warmth through his back, and realized for the first time that he was shivering from the cold and the loneliness that threatened to overflow from his small body.

Amelie hugged Sam as he trembled.

"It's so warm." Sam couldn't help but blurt it out. Amelie smiled and wrapped her arms around him more tightly.

"I had no idea until you told me…" Amelie whispered into Sam's ear. He was close enough to catch the scent of her hair as he looked out to sea. The Fragile Express ship had disappeared somewhere, but this small Sam wasn't worried.

"No idea that I was alive. Living is no different from being dead if you're all alone."

Sam couldn't hold back his tears. Her words scared him. They were going to be sorted into either the living or the dead. He was struck by the feeling that he had to get out of here.

"I don't wanna go home," Sam pleaded with no one in particular. His falling tears mixed with the sand on his face, creating muddy patches. He shook off Amelie's hands as she tried to wipe his tears away, and ran toward the sea.

"I don't wanna go home!" His words were swallowed up by the ocean as the waves drowned out his faint voice.

Amelie came after him and crouched down beside him.

As she stared into Sam's eyes, he noticed she was holding something in her right hand.

"Here. It's a dreamcatcher." Amelie hung the dreamcatcher around Sam's neck. It was a decorative piece made up of parts that resembled a spider's web, or maybe even a star shape. When Sam touched it, he felt strangely comforted.

"Wear it when you sleep, and I'll keep the nightmares away. I'll always be with you." Amelie held Sam's hand that was clutching the dreamcatcher. The dreamcatcher started to grow bigger in his hand and poke out through his grip. The mesh began to cover Sam's hand, then Amelie's hand, before eventually their entire bodies were covered with it. They were inside a cocoon, and inside Sam and Amelie melted into each other, completely protected from all evil. Inside the mother's womb, they were neither alive nor dead. He was filled with the sweet sensation that he had become one with the world.

"Did you forget how to go home?" Amelie's voice cut through this sweet world. It was a line that separated the worlds of the living and the dead. The crouching Amelie stood up and pulled Sam by the hand. He had to go back. He had to leave this space between life and death and return to the world of the living.

"Come on. I'll take you halfway. And then you can do the rest by yourself."

Sam looked up at Amelie and began to walk.

"Better now?" she asked.

Sam nodded assuredly and Amelie readjusted her grip on his hand.

"I'll be waiting for you on the Beach. Come and find me."

The pair walked on toward the sea. Then they parted and Sam returned alone.

Amelie was left all by herself on the Beach.

Sam had no idea how many times he had been through this with her. Just as a shoreline that distinctly separates the sea from the land didn't exist, the line between the child Sam and the present Sam was also blurred.

That's why he was no longer on the deck of Fragile's cargo ship. That was why he was on the Beach.

"We used to play together a lot in this place," Amelie muttered as she watched their younger selves disappear into the waves.

"You brought me here. I couldn't make the trip on my own," Sam muttered back.

"So long as you have a body to return to, you can't come and go as you please..." Amelie replied.

On the other hand, Amelie spent most of her life on this beach, in this space that had been liberated from the constraints of the real world. In a certain sense, this beach was like an embodiment of Amelie's character.

"So, you can't just come back east through here?" Sam asked.

Amelie shook her head. "Not until you make us whole again, Sam."

Amelie's body was suddenly enveloped in a black shadow. A whale breached through the water's surface behind her. As it soared through the sky, it tried to swallow Amelie up. Sam stretched out his arms to try and save her but simply passed straight through her. The shadow became blacker and blacker until all was dark, and the only bit of color that Sam could see was the red of Amelie's dress.

"I'll be waiting for you on the Beach." Her voice was drowned out by the song of the whale. Its enormous body sank back into the ocean and the shadow cast over Amelie disappeared. The surface of the ocean heaved and rained down on her. Amelie's hair, her clothes, and the whole of her body was drenched as she shed a tear.

The ocean's surface surged once more like there was a mountain erupting underneath, and the whale's head reappeared. But it wasn't the whale. Fragile Express's cargo ship was trying to run itself aground. As it tore through the waves, it made a beeline for Amelie.

"Come and find me."

Amelie!

Sam's scream didn't reach her. His arms didn't reach her. All that Sam could touch was empty darkness.

✝

LAKE KNOT CITY

Sam was thrown out of the dark and awoke.

The vibrations of the ship traveled through the deck. Sam's back was stiff after falling asleep on the bench. He cracked his spine and stretched, then got up. The ship had already crossed Ground Zero and had arrived at port. He could hear the sound of people's voices and heavy machinery below him. They were probably unloading the cargo. Sam wiped away the tears he had shed during his sleep. Then he scowled at the weird smell that had invaded his nostrils. It was the smell of chiral matter.

Sam felt strange. *Where am I?*

"I don't know how you sleep."

He remembered that he was on Fragile's ship.

Fragile looked amazed as she stared at his barely awake face and offered him a cryptobiote.

"Need a pick-me-up?"

Sam shook his head, feeling a little relieved. Fragile understood and ate the cryptobiote herself. This familiar exchange brought him back down to earth.

"Welcome to Lake Knot City." Fragile smiled. They had finally made it. Sam stamped his boots to make sure that he was no longer in a dream world or back on Amelie's beach. He didn't remember putting them back on, though.

Sam felt the stiffness of his pack against his back. *When did I put that back on?*

Perhaps he had put everything back on in a trance, now that it had all become so routine. He groped around his chest, but the photo he always kept concealed there was gone. It was the same photo that he had dropped and Fragile had recovered. The past that he couldn't escape. It had vanished. He searched the pockets of his uniform and had a look around the deck, but it was nowhere to be found.

"What?" Fragile asked.

Sam wanted to break away from his past, but he knew that parting with that photo would make him feel uneasy. He was fully aware that it was somewhat of a childish sentiment to have, and that was part of the reason why he didn't want Fragile to pick up on it.

Sam simply muttered a, "Nothin'," and kept on walking.

"Let's go." Fragile opened her umbrella and led the way. As he stared absentmindedly at her back, he realized that it was smaller and more delicate than he had first thought. He wondered if her delicate frame had something to do with her name.

"This cargo's from Port Knot City, bound for Lake Knot. I'll leave these up to you. The dispatch terminal is up ahead."

The containers that had been unloaded from the cargo ship were arranged neatly in a line.

"In the meantime, I've got some business to attend to. Later, alligator." Fragile walked away, playfully spinning her umbrella as she went. Sam turned back toward the cargo to check the contents.

"Thank you, Sam." The hologram of Amelie that the delivery terminal projected flickered.

Even though he had now crossed Ground Zero and progressed much further west, Amelie's image was still fuzzy and unstable.

"It'll only get harder from here, though. When we first came through, it was different. Peaceful," she warned.

The static echoed loudly around the cargo collection area. Sam couldn't help but cover his ears and close his eyes tightly. When he opened them again, he was all alone. Amelie had disappeared.

"The three cities out there—Lake, Middle, and South Knot—were all on board with our plans for reconstruction."

He could still hear Amelie's voice but her hologram had been replaced with a 2D projection of a simplified map of America. To Sam's right was a hole that represented Ground Zero, the lake that he had just crossed. On the left-hand side, on what would have been the lake's west bank, was Lake Knot City. Middle Knot City was displayed to the northwest, and south of that city lay South Knot City.

"Once these three cities and some surrounding facilities are activated using the Q-pid and connected to the Chiral

Network, transmissions between the central region will begin to stabilize. At least, that's the plan."

The terrain flipped over, revealing a new map.

One of the cities that had been shown on the map, Middle Knot City, had disappeared and was now marked with a black spot.

It was like a brand-new miniature version of Ground Zero had been added to the map. When Sam looked more closely, he could see that several other smaller black spots had been added, too. They all marked areas where acts of terrorism or actions to obstruct the reconstruction of the UCA had taken place.

At this rate, these black spots would multiply until they swallowed up the entire continent.

"Then the separatists began to get in the way."

Sam couldn't be sure if it was the instability of the transmission or if Amelie's voice was trembling.

"First, they took out Middle Knot City. They detonated nukes from the old days. They sneaked them in with the goods brought into the city." Amelie's voice began to sound even more depressed and the static seemed to whine in sympathy.

"And it didn't end there. Or rather, we couldn't stop it there. Next, they attacked South Knot City. Luckily, it wasn't completely destroyed, but a lot of people still lost their lives that day."

The entire area was motheaten with holes. Sure, if Sam connected the infrastructure left behind by Bridges I using the Q-pid then he could activate the Chiral Network, but what would be the point if the cities and facilities had already been destroyed? Sam didn't have the means or the resources to fix any of them, and neither did Bridges. But there was no way that Bridges would have just left things as they were. The dots spread across the map were clusters of black holes. They connected to form an ominous-looking constellation in the shape of a monster that threatened to swallow the entire world. Sam remembered the cold laugh that rang out from behind Higgs's golden mask.

"Fragile Express used to help us with deliveries in this area."

The map lit up with white spots in response.

"Fragile and the others were already taking on orders in this region, so we signed a contract with them and had them move our cargo, too. It was actually Fragile Express who established the distribution systems in this area, which is why a lot of people don't even think that we need a country like the UCA if we just want to survive. Those people are isolationists. We call them 'preppers.'"

Sam, of course, knew what preppers were. In fact, as a porter, he was very well acquainted with them. For freelance porters, it never mattered whether jobs were coming from preppers or some kind of organization. It was only really Bridges that still cared about the concept of nations, while the separatists who opposed it formed the other side of the coin. They were the only two parties concerned by it. The preppers had cut themselves off entirely.

Although, maybe not completely entirely. They relied on lifelines from organizations like Fragile Express and other freelance porters. Perhaps "isolationists" wasn't the most accurate word to describe them.

"In this state, even if you were to bring all the Bridges facilities online, the Chiral Network wouldn't be able to cover this area," Amelie admitted.

"What do you need me to do?" Sam asked the hologram, which had taken its place back from the map.

Just a little while ago, Sam would have probably said they should quit and there was no forcing it. Even if they couldn't turn a blind eye to terrorism, there were still those who would simply take exception to the rebuilding of "America." Was there really such a need to reconnect people who showed such resistance? Destruction and restoration. Even though they existed in completely opposite vectors, it was always those two major forces that were vying to change the state of this world. Sam still had mixed feelings in the back of his mind.

"I can't go back unless you connect all the way up to here."

The whole reason that Sam had taken the Q-pid and headed west was because of Amelie.

"We need to secure the support of everyone—even those who want nothing to do with the UCA, impossible as that may seem."

The gold necklace that hung on Amelie's chest glinted in

the light. Strangely, that light was the only vivid part of the hologram.

"But—" Sam was unable to finish his sentence, as the transmission was cut abruptly and Amelie's hologram disappeared. The words he had been about to utter never had a chance to reach Amelie's ears.

"It's just as you heard, Sam." It was Die-Hardman. Amelie's hologram had been replaced by the director in his black iron mask.

"The destruction of Middle Knot in particular forced us to adopt a new strategy. It's like Amelie said. We don't have the time or resources to construct another knot on that scale. That's why we've taken to cutting deals with preppers and the like. Our only recourse is to utilize their shelters to bolster the strength of the network."

"Takes a special kinda person to live out here on their own. The kind that'll tell us to fuck off if we ask 'em to join the UCA," Sam retorted.

"Oh, we know. No one's expecting them to say yes up front. Most of the preppers around there have contracts with Fragile Express. If a porter like you from Bridges were to try and enter a shelter, you would probably get stopped by security."

Die-Hardman's hologram disappeared and was replaced by a map like Amelie's before him. The white spots marked where the preppers had shelters.

"We have always held a collaborative relationship with Fragile Express. It doesn't matter how the preppers feel, because we co-own that delivery system. Bridges I also updated the delivery terminals in the shelters to make them compatible with the Q-pid, based on how things worked when the Chiral Network was up before. People are human, so they inevitably die someday. It doesn't matter what principles or ideals they hold, if their bodies aren't properly disposed of, they become BTs. I would love nothing more than for them to join the UCA, but I want at least to be able to know about and manage any deaths that do occur. This is a measure for that as well."

Sam touched the cuff link on his right wrist. It was the same. Death connected everyone. With the exception of the Homo Demens, all humans shared the fear of death, repugnance for the BTs and the threat of voidouts. The system provided by the UCA was established based on death.

The director and others at Bridges (*maybe even Amelie?*) used this primitive and instinctive feeling to achieve their goals. Connecting people may have offered hope, but it also formed shackles.

The cuff link was a communication tool, as was the UCA system, but both shackled people as much as they joined them.

"Fragile has already pledged her cooperation in any case." The director's voice sounded confident.

"And in exchange, she gets?" Sam asked.

"Nothing really. A chance to get back at Higgs, I suppose. I can't blame her for wanting one. He took everything from her and then some. Time heals some wounds, but not hers."

Revenge? I wonder if I wouldn't mind some of that, too?

Sam averted his eyes from Die-Hardman and stared at the ceiling. His emotions were a mix of sharp, lance-like feelings and slow-burning magma. For now, they meant nothing. He may have been harboring negative feelings, but they were the kind of feelings that needed to be directed at someone. He didn't have anyone like that. Sure, he had some regrets, but they were because he had been torn away from someone.

He wasn't connected to anyone anymore. He was a porter. His job was to connect people to each other, not forge connections for himself.

Once Sam was no longer lost in thought, he found himself alone in the room. The director's hologram had disappeared. He could no longer hear the noise of the staff or the ebb of the waves.

He felt a vibration through his feet. He pressed a button in the lift and felt the floor sink as it carried him toward his private room.

The sound of the waves carried Sam off to sleep and back toward the Beach.

—*Hey, Sam.*

All life on this earth came from the sea, and all life will

eventually return to it. That means that the sea is where the memories of this planet go to sleep. And the sea cocoons and protects the life of this planet that those memories form. The water's edge is the line that separates life and death. For those who dwell in the sea, beyond that line is the land of the dead, but for those who live on land, the land of the dead lies back beyond the Beach.

—*Hey, look, Sam.*

Bodies littered the Beach in rows. Whales, dolphins, crabs. Even the carcasses of small fish that Sam couldn't identify. All had been washed up from the sea. Even the sand itself was made up of the remains of shells, coral, and other small creatures. Amelie had told him so long ago.

The sound of the waves woke Sam up. He wiped away the sand (*you mean the decay?*) that was stuck to his face and body, and stood up. He could see another corpse in the distance. The corpse of a human child.

It had been carried here by the waves and washed up on the shore. It was the memory of his past. His past was stranded. It was a phenomenon that was all too possible on the Beach.

The child's body rose and the memory stood up and opened its mouth.

"Here." Sam looked up at Amelie and held out both hands. In them was something that appeared to be a gold necklace. Amelie squinted as she looked at it, almost like she was blinded by it.

"For me?" she asked.

A golden charm was situated in the center of a golden chain. It was a primitively designed necklace from which finely woven golden cords dangled.

"It's called a *quipu*. It means 'knot' in old words. You can also use it to count stuff. I add a knot when I make a friend," young Sam explained.

"Okay. Then, how about I add another knot every time I see you?"

Sam let out a shout of joy and hung the necklace around Amelie's neck as she crouched to accept it. Her eyes were glistening. She was crying. Sam had never noticed that back when he was a kid.

"This must be very important to you, if you were able to bring it here. Very special," she noted.

"It is special. I made it for you." Sam jumped up, pointing at the *quipu*.

"I'll treasure it, Sam." Amelie hugged him. *Thank you, Sam.*

Amelie held her face close to little Sam's cheek and looked up. Then she looked straight at the present Sam.

The past pierced the future. Sam felt like someone had grabbed hold of his heart and he couldn't breathe.

He let go of the dreamcatcher that he was holding tightly to his chest instead, but the pain didn't go away.

This is something that often happens on the Beach.

"Hey, Sam."

Fragile woke Sam up. Sam's left hand was clutching the dreamcatcher and bent unnaturally toward his left breast. He took a deep breath and sat up. His undergarments were drenched in sweat and clung to his back. He slapped his face with both hands to try and wake himself up properly.

"Something to eat?"

As usual, it was a cryptobiote being dangled in front of Sam's face, and as usual, he shook his head to refuse.

"Why are you here?" he asked.

Sam was in a private room in the basement of the distribution center. Fragile must have let herself in while he was asleep.

"Ask your boss man," she replied.

Sam was more annoyed at Die-Hardman for letting her in than at Fragile herself. Once again, it seemed like Bridges had no concept of the word "privacy."

"Got a delivery for a porter." Fragile seemed to have guessed how irritated he was, and smiled as she opened her hand. "You're gonna need this on the road ahead."

It was a misanga bracelet woven from red and white fibers.

"This will ID you as an associate of Fragile Express. It's woven from my blood and chiral crystals," Fragile explained.

It was a Fragile Express ID, a pass that contained a porter's biological information. All sorts of porters went back and forth with deliveries, and left unchecked anyone could easily sneak something dangerous into a shelter. This

ID was a necessary countermeasure. *But won't that mean that I'll be lying to them about my identity?* It gave Sam pause.

"We were the only people making deliveries out here," Fragile went on.

As if hurt by the fact that Sam didn't immediately reach for the misanga bracelet, Fragile sat down next to him. She was so close that Sam could feel her body heat.

"This was our territory. Until Higgs fucked it all up. Me, the Express, our reputation—all of it." Fragile's anger wasn't directed toward Sam at all, but toward Higgs.

"And now you want to fuck him back?" Sam asked.

He thought back to the revenge the director had mentioned. Was she really planning to offer up the reputation of Fragile Express as collateral to work with Bridges? Yielding her ID to give him access to the preppers seemed fundamentally different from the "collaborative" relationship they had maintained until now.

Sam's mission here wasn't to deliver goods to the preppers, but to seek their cooperation in the plan to rebuild America. That proposal had the potential to completely rewrite the entire foundation of the preppers' existence. These were the very people that had come to rely on Fragile Express. What Fragile was about to do was akin to throwing the principles of her organization out of the window.

The only thing that Fragile could do to avoid that was to seek revenge by herself. Whatever she did, she would still end up betraying her organization, but Sam couldn't possible see what she was hoping to get out of Bridges by doing this.

"On your own?" Sam asked.

Fragile shook her head slightly and said, "I'm not on my own. The cave. Port Knot City. Next to your bed. So far apart, yet somehow we keep meeting? All that BT country in between, where I should've been caught in a voidout..." Her umbrella opened above her head like magic. "Yet here I am."

The umbrella floated softly.

Then Fragile disappeared and all that was left was an umbrella floating in the air.

"Here I am again."

Sam heard a voice from behind him. It was only a short distance, but Fragile had teleported. There was only one other person who had that ability. Amelie. She had the extraordinary ability to freely come and go to her own Beach.

"I have a Beach. You've got yours, I've got mine." Only Fragile's smile remained. "I use it to jump across space."

Fragile appeared back in front of Sam, umbrella in hand.

"I can't conjure up BTs the way Higgs can, but I can go after him. Chase him to the Beach."

Fragile bit down on another cryptobiote and swallowed. The color somehow seemed to have drained from her face.

"The jumps take a lot out of me. It doesn't matter the physical distance. They suck my blood dry. So, I have to top up with these."

It sounded like Fragile's ability consumed her blood, or at least something within her blood. Sam had never seen anything like that happen to Amelie, so their abilities must have also been different in some way. It was pointless to question why. Just like it was pointless to ask why Amelie was born on the Beach, and why Sam could repatriate. Why did his blood affect the BTs? Sometimes Sam felt like this world was just a huge pile of whys.

But this was a world where people had to prioritize survival over the great mysteries.

Mankind hadn't survived by striking back or preventing the blows. They had only managed to hold out by avoiding dealing with their situation entirely. That's why they had built so many cities surrounded by great high walls to hide within.

"You're going to Edge Knot City, right? Place is full of terrorists. But if you're dead set on it, then you're gonna have to deal with Higgs sooner or later," said Fragile.

"Look, I make deliveries. Killing monsters and terrorists, that's not what I do."

"What if we did it together? I could use my power to help you. We don't have to want the same thing to be on the same side."

Sam couldn't say yes just like that. Neither could he reject her offer so easily.

"I could 'send' you. Across my Beach. To any place the

chiralium's thick enough. Any place connected to the Chiral Network."

"And what do you expect in return?" Sam asked.

Fragile closed her umbrella and sat down next to him. She was close enough that their shoulders were almost touching. Sam tried to squirm away instinctively, but she looked right at him. It was like she was silently telling him not to run.

"I expect you to think it over," she stated.

Sam had no choice but to accept the misanga bracelet that she offered him.

"Here. Call it an incentive. And call me if you need me. This will keep us connected."

Fragile stood up, moved toward the wall, and began to open her umbrella.

"See you when I see you."

Then she disappeared again, leaving behind only the echo of her voice and the smile on her lips.

The terminal that Sam had booted up on the upper floor was displaying a map. Beyond it, he could hear the heavy mechanical clanging of the conveyor belt and the sorter that were funneling cases both big and small toward him.

There was much more cargo than he had anticipated, and he knew that it would take a lot of work to transport it all in one go. He shouldn't have been too surprised, though. He was supposed to be doing a round of three shelters from here.

The points where the shelters were located were lit up on the map. The names "Engineer," "Craftsman," and "Elder" were displayed next to each point. They were codenames rather than official names. Sam had been making deliveries to preppers up until fairly recently, so he was familiar with the practice.

There was a reason why things had become this way. In the months and years since the Death Stranding, everything made by human hands had gradually decayed into dust because of the timefall. The land changed completely as it reverted back to wilderness, and the preppers no longer had a use for addresses. People may not have completely ceased interaction with those who were geographically distant from them, but face-to-face communication had become extremely rare, and as they had adapted to this, places had begun to adopt symbolic avatars based on the traits of their residents, rather than their official names. Sam had heard some people compare it to how people had communicated online back in the days of the Internet, but he didn't have much idea of what that had been like.

Sam stacked the boxes in his backpack, trying to strike a balance between size and weight, and hauled it onto his back. The shoulder straps dug in and the entire weight of the pack rested on his lower back. He felt a stabbing pain run through his nail-less toes. This pain and the weight of the cargo reminded Sam that he was more than just an avatar, even if that was how everyone saw him. People were waiting for his cargo, not for him. To them, he was just a porter-shaped token. But that was fine with Sam—in fact, he liked it that way.

Once Sam had left the Lake Knot City distribution center and walked a little way, he began to see traces of past destruction. Abandoned EVs and bikes lay there with their engines ripped out and transportation trucks lay on their sides, exposing their charred underbellies. The paved road was lined with deep cracks, even reduced to rubble in some areas, as it stretched out toward the southern hills. The ruins of a gas station from a previous life stood by the side of the road. A signboard in the shape of a seashell was covered in reddish-brown rust. This region had originally been quite arid and had been left untouched by the timefall. That's why Sam could see both the destruction left behind in the early stages of the Death Stranding and traces of destruction from just a few months ago. It was the separatists who had destroyed the bikes and trucks, but they still didn't understand the truth of the Death Stranding that had destroyed the world as it once was.

The reason so many preppers lived in this area was also because of the absence of the timefall. BTs had never shown up here either, so as long as they could maintain supply lines, it wasn't so difficult to survive. Even so, the ever-increasing acts of terror made it impossible for them to let their guard down. As the number of destructive incidents racked up, so did the tally of the dead. Then the dead turned into BTs and that brought the timefall. The actions of the separatists irreversibly transformed this whole area. The last remnants of the old world that had once been preserved here, like the road and the gas station, were now at the mercy of the timefall and doomed to rot and crumble away.

Sam followed the path and found his view open up completely as soon as he reached the top of the hill. He could look out over the entire west.

To the northeast, he could see large, abandoned ruins. It was the remains of Middle Knot City, which had been destroyed by a smuggled nuclear bomb. Masses of dark clouds floated in the skies above.

The codec on Sam's cuff link activated. <Hey, Sam.>

The call came from Heartman. His location was only connected by a regular line, so the call was full of noise.

<Middle Knot City was obliterated in an instant by a nuke. I'll bet you can see it from there, can't you? That's right, HQ knows where you are. You're still in an area covered by the Chiral Network. That's how I found out, too.> Heartman continued talking without waiting for a response. <Most people were burned to a crisp in the blast. That's why they were

able to go to the other side without having to wander on the Beach. Unfortunately, and this might sound callous, there were some people that didn't die so perfectly. Their bodies were broken, but they weren't burnt, so they became BTs. The black clouds above the city represent the citizens who became BTs. It's more than likely that you would find high levels of chiralium in the ruins, and timefall probably falls there intermittently. Eventually, the ruins will disappear too and turn back to wilderness. Anyway, as long as people don't approach, then the BTs won't appear. And if the BTs don't appear, then there won't be any voidouts–> The static flared and Sam covered his ears.

<Did you get that, Sam?> The voice was breaking up and Sam couldn't catch almost anything of what Heartman was saying.

<–Got it? Five, four, three–>

Instead, all he could hear was a mechanical beeping. Heartman's panicked voice broke through. <Sorry, Sam. Got to run.>

That was the last Sam heard before an electronic beep and the codec cut out.

Sam fiddled with the cuff link to try and get the line with Heartman back, but it was no good.

He had to make sure that whatever happened, he didn't

approach Middle Knot City. He looked back at the ruins and the dark clouds and nodded.

As he descended the hill, Sam found that the paved road was gradually covered in more and more sand until it disappeared entirely, together with the remnants of the old world that he had found himself wandering. All traces of humanity disappeared with it. As he walked onward, the sand transformed into more rugged, rocky terrain. He started to feel like he was becoming more and more separate from the human world.

An object that looked like a whale brain rolled past.

It was called Earth coral, and much like Fragile's beloved cryptobiotes, it hadn't existed before the Death Stranding. Just like the Beach, just like the timefall, and just like the chiral clouds that rained the timefall down on the land. They were all part of this new Earth and their purpose was to eliminate any organism that couldn't adapt. The people born with special abilities like Sam were the result. He had been forced to sit and listen to that theory so many times. All the main members of Bridges were required to have DOOMS. They were the ones entrusted to lead mankind out of the darkness as they rebuilt America.

Sam had naively believed in that mission before. He longed to be that innocent again.

Mankind's time was coming to a close. The people with DOOMS were the flowers that bore no fruit. They were just there to make humanity bloom one last time.

Sam had accepted the fact before he had even realized. Back when he was trying to overcome his aphenphosmphobia, there was a time when he too had been a member of Bridges and had devoted his life to American reconstructionism. But that youthful enthusiasm had gone now. All he carried now was feelings of resignation as he simply walked from person to person. Over and over again. He would keep walking until all of humanity had disappeared from the Earth. Eventually, his body would wear down, and once he had delivered the last piece of cargo to the last human being, maybe then he would finally be able to rest in peace.

It was all just a step toward the death he longed for.

He finally neared the preppers' shelter.

CENTRAL UNITED STATES

A flame flickered before the Elder's eyes.

In an ashtray, a passport, social security ID, and a credit card were burning. The documents twisted and writhed like a small creature that had been set aflame. He positioned his face closer and lit his cigarette, the first one he had smoked in two years. It made him feel dizzy, just like the first time he had taken a puff at the tender age of fourteen.

There was no point worrying over his health any longer.

Besides, it was unlikely that he would even get his hands on cigarettes ever again after this.

The flames died down, leaving only ash behind. He dropped the ashes onto the floor of the ruins. Even if he opened the window to let the smoke out, he would just find the smell of something burning outside wandering back in.

The southern night sky was glowing red. A city was burning somewhere. He wondered how many days it would go on for. A dark whirlwind of smoke snaked up into the sky. Below it raged the flames that would end America.

Beyond that inferno and beyond the borders of this country lived his elderly parents, but before disaster had even had a chance to strike, he had already known that he would never see them again.

America had closed off his path back home. His parents had placed all their hope in this country and had crossed the border to come here and have him, but they were never granted citizenship. The American child and non-American parents had subsequently been torn apart.

He wondered when the fire would stop raging, but he was about to get his answer as the skies parted and rain poured down like a flood. It extinguished the fire that was burning through the city in an instant, and made quick work of rotting away everything underneath. It was the timefall, and the beginning of the cataclysm that would come to be known as the Death Stranding.

✦

The Elder looked up at the clouds and lit his cigarette.

Years had passed since that night when he had burned his passport and cards, and all without a single clear sky.

He had believed that it would likely have been his last cigarette, but he had never once imagined that he would never see a clear sky again. He never thought that he would live to an age older than his parents, and he certainly never expected to survive the disaster.

The monitor mounted in the basement of the shelter reported that a porter was approaching. He answered with his cigarette still in his mouth and unlocked the entrance. The sound of the footsteps descending the stairs was accompanied by a bearded man. He was well acquainted with this porter. He was the leader of Fragile Express.

He was the only person he ever got to speak to. His last friend in the world.

The man frowned and wafted his arm to chase away the tobacco smoke. He did it every single time.

The man then picked up a medium-sized case from inside the backpack that had been dropped on the floor, and set it on the table.

"Isn't it time you quit smoking those? You're the oldest elder in these parts," the porter commented.

The Elder pretended not to notice and continued to

examine inside the case. It contained boxes of cigarettes, smart drugs for stress relief, and packets of preserved food. It was more or less the same amount as usual.

"It's getting harder to swing by here." The grizzled porter laughed, lighting the smoke that he was offered. "What were you thinking, building a shelter on a cliff like this? Everyone hates it. They never want to come here."

"Gets me personal service from the leader, though," the Elder reasoned.

"Yeah, well, I doubt any of them would want to run a job to a sourpuss like you even if they did live close by."

The Elder turned toward the storehouse, dragging his right leg behind him. He brought back a bottle of Aqua Vitae and a glass. "Got any news for me?"

"Yeah. Two things." The porter picked up the glass and downed the drink in one gulp. The Elder took a sip of his own drink as he refilled the empty glass. The scent of a potato-based spirit wafted through the air.

"It looks like Bridget Strand is getting serious about rebuilding America," the porter stated.

The alcohol left on the Elder's tongue suddenly tasted bitter. Decades after that disaster and she still hadn't given up? She was a megalomaniacal leader who continued to call herself the last American president.

"I heard that she formed an organization called 'Bridges.' They're supposed to be the ones who'll rebuild this country.

There used to be a team directly under the control of the president, who were tasked with putting an end to the chaos after the Death Stranding. It's just rumor, but I heard they didn't exactly balk at stuff like assassinations or causing any other trouble. Eventually, they ended up going into research and countermeasures to help us get past the disaster. Haven't heard much in the way of them coming up with anything useful yet, though. Someone told me they recently started researching people who have these special abilities called DOOMS. They're supposedly more in tune with the Beach and death than normal people, and Bridges is interested in how they can sense BTs," explained the grizzled porter.

"We build too many walls and not enough bridges."

"You going all philosophical on me now?" The porter filled his glass.

"I just heard it somewhere before. America used to love walls. All to keep the people like me out. Split me and my parents up for good. I probably mentioned this to you before, but America wasn't anything special in the first place."

"Bridget reckons she formed Bridges to make bridges. Clever, right?" the porter said sarcastically.

"Amazing wordplay. But building a bridge is no good if you don't let anyone cross it. Besides, we have all the bridges that we need in you boys." The Elder pointed at the Fragile Express symbol on the porter's chest. It showed a small box, cradled by skeletal hands.

"It's one hell of a brittle bridge, though. If something were to happen to us, then you'd be on your own."

"You are the ones who always helped us, ever since the start of all this. It didn't matter if we were immigrants, travelers, poor... You helped us all equally. All the army ever knew was war, and all the police ever did was crack down on us. As soon as the chain of command was wiped out they were both useless."

"I wouldn't call America any old country. They allowed you to take up arms against your own nation, if you needed to. They guaranteed you the right to live, to freedom and hope, not just to depend," the porter reasoned.

"Yeah, the Second Amendment. It was thanks to that so many citizens were able to slaughter each other."

The porter took the packing rope that hung by his waist into his hand and wrapped it around his right wrist. Then he quickly tied it to the Elder's left wrist.

"You and I are connected." He pulled the Elder's arm toward him. "If that leg of yours gets any worse and you can no longer walk, I'll be the first to know, and the first to come help you out. If someone comes and attacks you, I'll be there to protect you. But you're going to be stuck walking with me."

"Man is born free and everywhere he is in chains. One thinks himself the master of others, and still remains a greater slave than they."

The porter shrugged and untied the rope. "And who's the one who said that?" he asked.

"Ever heard of a guy called Rousseau?" The Elder poured some of the dwindling alcohol into the porter's glass.

"Haven't heard of any preppers called that." The porter laughed, bringing the glass to his lips. "Can I tell you something else?"

The Elder put another cigarette to his lips instead of answering.

"I won't be coming back here for a while. I'm gonna be a dad." The porter took another sip of alcohol, as if he was trying to put off what he was about to broach next. "And, well, because how things have turned out, I'm gonna be the one who has to raise her. I know this puts you in a bind," he continued sheepishly.

"Congratulations," the Elder smiled, "and don't worry about it. As long as I have this, I'll be fine." The Elder poured the rest of the Aqua Vitae into the pair's empty glasses and made a toast.

"Thanks, she's a girl. Gonna name her Fragile."

LAKE KNOT CITY OUTSKIRTS // ELDER'S SHELTER

The sensor read the biological data contained within the misanga bracelet on Sam's right wrist and permitted him entry.

The entrance was already open. The design concept was pretty much the same as the Bridges facilities. External parties like porters were only allowed into the entrance to drop cargo off, and the living quarters were concealed in the basement to make it difficult for them to penetrate if they happened to be so inclined. It was rare for the residents to come to the surface.

Once he had cleared the other sensor that had been placed at the entrance, the delivery terminal appeared.

After a few minutes the terminal activated, and the hologram of a resident popped up. The man was referred to as the Elder, and was leaning to one side as though his legs weren't what they used to be.

"So, you're the guy that Fragile sent? Sam Bridges from Bridges, right?"

The man's face and voice looked and sounded completely worn out, but Sam was surprised that the man already knew Fragile had sent him. Wasn't he supposed to be living in isolation?

"Look, can you just drop the cargo and walk right back out that door? I don't have a grudge against you or anything. In fact, I'm grateful that you came all the way up that cliff. If you were just any old porter then things might be different, but…"

Sam dropped his backpack onto the floor and removed the cargo addressed to the Elder. He had some household medicine for him. There had been no deliveries up here for a while and it looked like the man's stock was almost completely depleted. The delivery was likely a matter of life or death for the man.

"Bet you brought that Q-pid thing here, didn't you? All to rebuild America. And let me guess, you want to add this shelter on your little Chiral Network? Is the medicine you've brought supposed to butter me up? What are you gonna do if I flat out refuse you? Threaten to take it all back?"

Sam would never be able to do such a thing. Doing so would mean admitting that he was nothing more than a Bridges puppet. He was a porter. So, Sam silently placed the cargo on the shelf.

"You got that? You know I'm not connecting to no Chiral Network and you can forget about me joining the UCA, alright?" the Elder asked, sounding surprised. Sam simply hoisted his backpack back on. He couldn't force someone to support the movement if they didn't want to. Sam just left the cargo behind and exited the building without saying a single word to the man. The directors and everyone else back at HQ would probably find out what had happened soon, but Sam was a porter, he wasn't suited to being a mindless Bridges drone. They probably wouldn't let this go. Sam himself was literally handcuffed to his mission to reconnect America using the Chiral Network and to save Amelie. And right now, he didn't feel like he had the right to persuade this old man to join them and shackle himself to the big UCA ball and chain as well.

LAKE KNOT CITY OUTSKIRTS // ENGINEER'S SHELTER

After leaving the Elder's shelter, Sam made his way down the cliff and headed in the direction of the next one. This prepper was known as the Engineer.

According to the information detailed in the briefing, the Engineer was a second-generation prepper who had been living in the shelter since birth. In other words, that small shelter was all he had ever known. Sam passed through the entrance and waited for the terminal to activate. Once he had finished the delivery procedures, the hologram of a young man appeared.

"You don't look like Fragile." He had a calm, mild-mannered voice, but Sam could still pick up notes of distrust. His expression was stiff, too. It shouldn't have come as much of a surprise for Sam, though, since he was wearing a Bridges uniform while brandishing a Fragile Express ID.

"Oh, right, are you the porter she sent in her stead?"

It sounded like the man had cottoned on before Sam had even had time to explain. Sam was glad he didn't have to go through the trouble of getting the man up to speed, but the Engineer's lack of vigilance was alarming, especially when you considered the rising numbers of terrorist attacks and other incidents lately.

"I trust you. And Fragile. She told me you were coming, you see. She and the others said that a porter from Bridges would be dropping by with some new tech that was still under development. I said that if you let me have a go on it, then I might consider Bridges' request. So how about? Do we have ourselves a deal?" The hologram of the Engineer was opening the case that Sam had brought. As he discarded all the layers of packaging, a look of sheer joy washed over his face.

"Don't you have something else to be getting on with?" The man's tone was more high-pitched. There was a low start-up sound from the terminal.

"You brought the Q-pid, right? Well, that's how you're going to activate the Chiral Network. Isn't that the goal?"

It was almost an anticlimax to find out how easy it was to convince the Engineer to join the UCA.

"You look surprised. I heard the Elder said no. That guy is a dyed-in-the-wool prepper. But second-generation preppers like me aren't so hung up on it. We never knew what America was like before. Did you?" The hologram disappeared and Sam could only hear his voice, meaning the man had left the range of the scanner.

"Man, I was so excited to hear about the concept behind the Chiral Network. High-capacity instantaneous communications. That's no ordinary communications infrastructure. It goes through the Beach, right? That means that we'll be able to access all the data from the past, too, like chiral printers and chiral computers. I don't really get everything, but it's still amazing. I heard they're researching how to take fragments of information from the past and reconstruct its timeline to reproduce things in their entirety. The prototype you just delivered is going to help with that. It's called an evo-devo unit. They're letting me do the testing, so I'd love to try connecting to it with a Q-pid. What do you say, Sam?"

The hologram reappeared with a flushed face as the Engineer prattled on. He had probably gone off to install the evo-devo unit, or whatever it was, into the printer. There was no mistaking the fact that after being cooped up inside this little shelter all his life, the Engineer was overflowing with immeasurable curiosity about the wider world that the Chiral Network was about to show him. Having experienced the wilderness of this land and illogical domains like the Beach and the Seam, Sam thought the Engineer's curiosity dangerous, but he decided against saying anything. Sam was more surprised that all it had taken was one little bargaining chip from Bridges to get the Engineer to join the UCA. It meant the man wasn't isolating himself based on some bull-headed ideology.

Sam took the Q-pid from around his neck and held it out over the terminal's receptor.

"Thanks, Sam! Now this place is a part of America, too. I have no doubt that America will be the bridgehead that connects the whole world. Now we can connect to the past, we can connect to a wider world, too."

That was the bright side of America. It was the future

that a more optimistic Sam had once looked forward to.

"Can I tell you something?" the Engineer asked. "It's about Fragile Express. There's a rumor going around that Fragile and the others have been helping terrorists. People are saying it was Fragile who planned the nuclear bomb attack on Middle Knot City, and the failed attack on South Knot City. That she messed around with the cargo tags and ID and slipped in the bomb. Some say she transported it into the city herself. But it's all bullshit. I just know it. Why would an organization that's helping Bridges rebuild America get involved with terrorism?"

Sam thought the Engineer was probably right. From the conversations he'd had with Fragile and with the director, he found it hard to believe that Fragile would get involved with terrorists. Yet he still didn't believe her to be whiter than white.

LAKE KNOT CITY OUTSKIRTS // CRAFTSMAN'S SHELTER

The rumors Sam heard at the Craftsman's shelter only reinforced his gut feeling about Fragile.

"No one thinks that Fragile is innocent," noted the Craftsman, who claimed to be a non-lethal weapons maker. "Fragile Express went too far. Apparently, they even made use of her DOOMS. Didn't you hear? I thought Bridges would be all over that? Fragile was the ringleader who brought the bomb into South Knot City. She got caught red-handed on camera at the distro center. When people hear her name they think of terrorists now. I heard some people say that they haven't seen her around these parts since. Sounds like she's on the run to me. Care to tell me I'm wrong?

"Frankly, we shouldn't even have weapons capable of killing people like that in this world to begin with. Sure, MULEs and terrorists are a danger and a nuisance, but why do we need lethal weapons specifically to oppose them? Isn't it enough to just have weapons and tools that can stop them from doing anything wrong in the first place? We need to rid the world of weapons. We can't help accidents and disease, they'll carry on killing no matter what we do. But we have to rid ourselves of sudden death by violence. That's why I've been sat out here, developing tools that can be used for self-defense without killing anyone."

Eventually, after rattling on about this and that, the Craftsman got down to business and refused to join the UCA, but he did agree to allow them to use his shelter as a Chiral Network node.

The Craftsman may have called himself an isolationist, but he was still working to develop non-lethal weapons. If he thought he needed them, then it seemed like he knew all too well that he couldn't completely alienate himself from the rest of the world forever. It would catch up with him someday. It was probably also why he was so interested in the allegations against Fragile.

After leaving the Craftsman's shelter, Sam heard the cuff link emit a quiet electronic noise to tell him that he had a message. It was from the Lake Knot City distribution center. They had a delivery request for Sam from the Elder.

LAKE KNOT CITY OUTSKIRTS // ELDER'S SHELTER

Sam had once again climbed the cliff and reached the Elder's shelter at the top. As the terminal gradually rose from the ground, the Elder's hologram immediately appeared alongside, as if he had been waiting for Sam.

"Thank you, Sam Bridges." The Elder looked at Sam standing there with his empty backpack and grinned. It was surprising how youthful his smile was.

The Elder wanted Sam to pick up an item from the shelter and take it to a designated location. There was no fixed timeframe. The Elder's only instruction in that regard was to drop it off promptly when the time came. There were other conditions, too. He had to connect the shelter to the Chiral Network before he came to pick the item up. He wasn't allowed to ask about the date. And this was a job only for Sam.

It had already been more than a week since Sam had departed Lake Knot City to call on the preppers. Apart from the night when he had found a communal safe house, he had been camping. Not only had the injuries Sam had incurred during his encounter with the BT that Higgs had conjured still not healed, but the toenail he had torn off still hadn't grown back either. It was sheer luck that he wasn't near BT territory and hadn't come face to face with any MULEs—although once he had finished his deliveries and run out of cargo at the Craftsman's place, it was unlikely they would have attacked him anyway.

If Sam could finish this new job, then he would probably be allowed to finally rest up a bit.

"I had this dream," the Elder said. "Not once, but over and over again. Recurring every single night... You know, I remember hearing something once. That guys with DOOMS like you dream about extinction. Well, my dream was slightly different. It was about me specifically going extinct."

Sam thought he saw the Elder grimace. He was acting like he was trying to avoid something.

"I've already lived long enough. I've seen America alive and strong, and I've lived through the hell left behind after it vanished without a trace. I reckon it's about time for me to depart this world. Don't get me wrong, I don't want you to hasten my departure, I'll go naturally, but it won't be much longer now. And I was thinking about what I would leave behind when my time comes, so now I have a favor to ask of you, Sam. Will you listen to this old coot reflect on the past? After that, you can go ahead and connect this shelter up to the Chiral Network."

The Elder began to talk.

He spoke about Bridges I.

LAKE KNOT CITY OUTSKIRTS // ELDER'S SHELTER

"Hold up there!" the Elder shouted toward the figure. The emaciated man in a Fragile Express uniform who was trying to exit the shelter stopped. The logo of the skeletal hands cradling a box on his back had faded. Ever since the grizzled leader of Fragile Express had died, the organization had changed dramatically. "Won't you please tell me what happened?"

Word had reached the Elder about a huge explosion in the north. A nuclear bomb had wiped out Middle Knot City.

He had heard the bare bones of the story through the preppers' communication networks. When Bridges I had visited, they built lots of infrastructure around Lake Knot City, which had made it easier to hear about what was happening on the outside. They had become able to send more precise delivery requests to Fragile Express. But the Elder also began to feel a worry that he had never felt before. While the amount of information that he heard had increased, he hadn't failed to notice that the information itself was but fragments, mixed in with plenty of bullshit, rumors, and gossip.

"Is it true about what happened in South Knot City?" he asked falteringly. The man from Fragile Express stood with his back to him, still as a statue. That was enough for the Elder.

"So it was a nuke? And your boss was the one who smuggled it in?"

The man turned around. "It's all lies. We were tricked and used. Me, my boss, every one of us."

"But she did smuggle it into the city?" pressed the Elder.

"We don't know exactly who planned it, but it had to be separatists. We didn't even notice them slip it into the cargo."

The Elder tried to read the face of the man on the monitor. It didn't look like he was lying. He just looked angry. He looked like he was furious but just didn't know where to target it. The Elder took a deep breath and stared at the console. That piece of equipment, too, had been brought to him by Bridges. And he had accepted it.

Ever since those guys from Bridges I had swarmed through, there had been skirmishes with the separatists. At first they just stole things from the Bridges caravan, but eventually, they went on to attack the delivery units. They originally thought it was MULEs, but when one of their facilities on the outskirts of the city was blown up, the series of events was quickly pinned on the separatists.

If we all just sit and do nothing, then the ties between people and cities will disintegrate altogether and we really will be done for. That's why you need to join us now. That was the usual Bridges spiel told to people to convince them to join the UCA.

The first city they proposed the UCA concept to was a city called Bonneville, which was right next to Ground Zero. Eventually, they threw away that name and it came to be known as Port Knot City. Bridges put infrastructure in place and began to redistribute the supplies that had been getting held up. That was the job of the delivery troops, who used equipment called "Bridge Babies" to avoid the BTs. Then, in the not-so-distant future, they promised to set up communications by way of the Chiral Network, in addition to a whole new delivery network.

That meant a reemergence of the state. It meant the rebirth of America, a country that had not been kind to a younger Elder before the Death Stranding had changed everything.

As Bridges put more and more effort into reconstruction, the terrorist attacks grew worse and worse. It wasn't only the facilities in town and on the outskirts anymore, but the preppers' shelters as well that had become targets for destruction.

Bridges had installed the basic system for the Chiral Network at each shelter in the name of protecting the preppers, and urged them to join the UCA when the time to rebuild finally came. Deliveries from Fragile Express were now getting delayed, and with the interruptions in the already meager information distribution, increasing anxiety had driven the Elder to accept the system. Once the fear had taken root, there had been no way he could completely erase it.

"This area has been troubled ever since Bridges first came."

The Elder averted his eyes from the Bridges logo that was engraved in the console. The porter from Fragile Express nodded back.

"You're right. But they're saying that it's only temporary. Once the Chiral Network is up and running, they think they'll be able to stop the separatists. That they'll be able to prevent a tragedy like in Middle Knot City before it happens. That they'll be able to use the communications network to build a protective wall."

A wall, huh… America tried to build a wall a long time ago. It was because of that wall that the Elder had never been able to go back to where he belonged. That was why he had chosen to live as a prepper.

"Besides, I don't really understand it, but they say that the Chiral Network will allow us to scan information about remote objects and output the information here with a 3D printer. If we can do that, then we won't need to make deliveries anymore while trying not to get killed by MULEs and BTs. Even if it does make us kind of redundant."

Maybe this was some kind of transitional period. Maybe the Chiral Network would turn out be the real deal and produce a country the likes of which had never been seen before. But it would be a long time before that happened. Plenty of time to decide whether it was worth affiliating himself with a new country.

"I'd better head out. Today's shipment should keep you going for a while, right? These cliffs are way too hard going for me to climb too often. I'll see you again. Don't go dying on me in the meantime."

That was the last time the Elder ever saw anyone from Fragile Express.

A few months later, the man was caught up in the bombing of South Knot City and got himself killed.

After finishing his story, the Elder took a deep breath and lit another cigarette. The smoke made the Elder's hologram hazy, like he was standing behind a shimmer of hot air. Hazy like the BTs that wandered the BT territories. Sam thought he heard the BB grizzle in the pod, but when he looked down, it was still fast asleep.

"Fragile Express were the ones who saved me back then. During all that pandemonium after the Death Stranding, the one who built the refuge and supplied people like me with food, medicine, and clothing was their leader. He was Fragile's dad, you know? It wasn't America that saved me, so—"

The Elder burst out in a fit of coughing. After he had

choked and spluttered for a while, he took another puff of his cigarette.

"The leader died very suddenly. Then Fragile took over. She used to come here a lot. This area had calmed down quite a bit at that point. Preppers like me and the people who built the cities lived in our own separate areas. The only ones who connected us were Fragile and the others. But then she changed. After her father died, she was burdened with the organization, his mission, his ideals. She was haunted by the ghost of an America that her father once knew. It was a huge weight on her shoulders.

"She couldn't carry it all alone. That's why she turned to that guy, Higgs. And then do you know what happened? She stopped coming here at all.

"Higgs had arrived here from the west, saying he wanted to create a land where we could all coexist, one that would take the place of America.

"The issue back then wasn't that food and energy resources had run dry, but that they hadn't been shared out properly. He claimed the problem was with unfair distribution and that there were plenty of resources out west. He said he would bring them here and restore this region from the brink of death.

"He said that it was possible to avoid the BTs, that the technology already existed. He said that people with certain abilities also existed, and Bridges had been gathering them all up for themselves. He said that if we could just learn to share fairly, then all our problems would be solved. Fragile believed him. She had extraordinary abilities herself and she believed that she could use them for the good of all mankind.

"But she entrusted control of those abilities to Higgs. It all went well at first. Fragile's DOOMS allowed her to use her own Beach as inexhaustible storage. She and Higgs used to store massive amounts of cargo on it and then retrieve whatever they needed for wherever they were going. The pair still had to traverse the physical distances, but there was no need to carry the goods themselves. It was a delivery revolution.

"It was sometime after this revolution when I first started hearing about a new name in terrorism. History had repeated itself and Higgs had turned. He was no longer about building a new world of coexistence, but one of destruction. It was around that time when he began to hide his face behind that golden mask, too. He wanted a garment fit for his new authority.

"I couldn't tell you what changed his mind suddenly, but soon enough he'd forsaken distribution for monopolization, and we found ourselves left in the dark, not being told a damn thing.

"Next thing I heard, Fragile's DOOMS had been used to nuke Middle Knot City. And sure, they might have escaped total disaster, but her DOOMS did its fair share of damage in South Knot City a little while after as well. It didn't even matter if she meant to or not, just by sheer virtue of having DOOMS she was caught up in it all."

Vengeance. That word swam to the forefront of Sam's mind once again.

Perhaps Fragile's vengeance hadn't been aimed at Higgs. Perhaps it was aimed at her own mistakes, at her DOOMS. Maybe she was trying to punish herself for being born into this world with those abilities. Sam could relate to that feeling.

That's why Sam couldn't proclaim or defend Fragile's innocence. His own DOOMS was being used in this world in a way that Sam didn't exactly want to be involved in, and it made him feel so hopeless that there was nothing he could do about it.

"But, you know, Sam, I'm guilty of the exact same crime. I'm also a nuclear terrorist. I pretended to be an isolationist on the outside while still relying on the state. I installed the Bridges system because I was scared of all the terrorism and the fighting, and that in turn enhanced Fragile and her crew's delivery system. But that just stimulated more deliveries between the preppers and the cities and opened up new holes in security. It was our dependence that destroyed that city. Connections are fragile, but it's no good just making them stronger. They need to be treasured and treated carefully. The old leader of Fragile Express saw that. It's why he named his organization and daughter the way he did. But it looks like I was a little late on the uptake… I think I wanted to get back at America after it took my family away from me. But I was just being childish. I depended on Fragile, I depended on the fact that America had collapsed. Getting back at the state, rejecting the state… that means living and dying alone.

"People can't do that. At least, I can't. Even after I die, I need someone to help incinerate my corpse. That's something else I realized as my death began to creep nearer.

"I was no prepper. I was just a parasite. This is just my attempt at atonement.

"I want you to use this shelter as a point on the Chiral Network. As one of the foundations for your new America."

The Elder began coughing intensely once again. The hologram flickered violently and disappeared, as if wiped away by an invisible hand. Sam lost his voice to the ether as he called out for the Elder.

Sam wiped a tear from his cheek and left the Elder's shelter behind him. It wasn't because of the old man, but his chiral allergy. Once this area was covered by the Chiral Network and became a part of the UCA, the old man's vitals would be monitored constantly. And once he became a part of the system, he would receive its services.

It would also allow the UCA to deal with the old man's death. It would be able to detect the danger of necrosis in advance and prevent the old man from transforming into a BT. It would stop him from becoming an undead human-shaped bomb.

By managing all of that, the UCA could bring more stability back to the world, so it was another of their main objectives.

Guess I'm just the vanguard hired by a company of grim reapers.

Sam looked over his shoulder toward the shelter one last time.

LAKE KNOT CITY

No matter how long he showered in his private room in Lake Knot City, Sam couldn't wash away the weariness that had lodged itself in his back and shoulders. The blood and sweat that had clung to him as he spent days making his way back to the city now ran down his legs and were harvested by the collection equipment in the shower booth, to be processed into anti-BT weaponry. Heartman, Mama, and Die-Hardman would probably be happy. The more that Sam got dirty, the more weapons they would be able to produce.

Even after lying down on the bed, Sam didn't feel sleepy. His back was stiff and it felt like both his legs had fallen off. But still, he closed his eyes and clutched at his dreamcatcher. It was his normal ritual before getting some shut-eye. A drop of water fell into the palm of his hand.

He opened his eyes and gasped. In his hand was the hand of a dried-up, wrinkled old man.

There was no muscle on his bare arms, and his sad-looking skin hung loosely from his bones. Sam tried to get up to retrieve his fallen dreamcatcher, but his legs wouldn't move. He collapsed onto the Beach. Sand filled his mouth and nose.

It made his arms feel like they were going to snap, but Sam used all his might to sit up and spit out the sand. What came out was dark, tarlike blood. Mixed in with the puddle of blood were yellowing teeth. Sam looked up to survey his surroundings when the sky cracked open and torrential rain began to fall.

When he tried to brush away the hair that the rain stuck to his face, white strands fell out, clumping together and tangling around his fingers. As soon as Sam inhaled to scream, he was overcome by a fit of coughing.

Sam could see the figure of a person walking along the water's edge, their form made hazy by the relentless rain. They were dragging their right leg behind them. It was the Elder.

But it couldn't have been. The Elder looked this way. It wasn't him. It was Sam. The face that stared back at him was Sam as an old man.

Sam almost fell off the bed.

He put all his strength into the arms that were clutching the edge to stop him falling off, jolting him back to reality. The rain he had heard must have been the sound of the shower. Sam spied a silhouette on the other side of the misted glass. Sam tensed up and gripped the bedframe harder. The slender silhouette reminded him of the Elder at the water's edge.

Someone had entered his room while he was asleep, but he couldn't guess why. Maybe he was still dreaming. Sam clutched his dreamcatcher to check if he was still awake, and approached the shower booth. It was a woman.

Sam could see a naked back behind the steamed glass. It was the body of an elderly woman, whoever it was. The arms, shoulders, and waist were covered in wrinkles. It was strange, because her frame didn't look like that of an old woman. Her waist and back were straight with a beautiful arch. Then the woman in the shower booth turned around. It was Fragile. Having noticed Sam's gaze, she covered her bare chest with both arms. Deep wrinkles were carved into her limbs, too.

"Sorry. Didn't mean to startle you." Back in her familiar black suit, Fragile sat herself down next to Sam without a hint of embarrassment. She was so close he could feel her warmth.

"I jumped here. You were sleeping when I dropped by. I needed to get all this stuff off. It seems the chiral density on the Beach is even higher than usual."

"Right… Look, I gotta ask. I've been hearing things. About you," Sam began.

It seemed like Fragile had been anticipating this question.

"'She's in bed with terrorists. Don't trust her?' 'She's just another dumbass Higgs fucked over.' 'She's a goddamn hero, that woman'?"

Fragile's face was so close that Sam could feel her breathing. He looked back at her, and for the first time he was afraid. Beneath that smooth, flawless skin was a rumbling, boiling hot chaos. Like a maelstrom of anger, sadness, and regret. It was an emotion Sam couldn't identify. It was so alarming that Sam didn't know what to say.

"The rumors are all true." Fragile wiped a tear from her cheek. Sam could tell that her tears weren't caused by her jump here from the Beach. They weren't a simple physiological response; they were from the heart.

"Tell me, Sam. What does 'America' mean to you?"

Sam couldn't answer. All he could do was shake his head.

"Way my dad made it sound, we were something special. The glue that held it all together. More than a nation. A symbol of freedom and hope. We could bring it all back, if we kept on making deliveries and connecting people… He was sure of it."

Sam thought back to his conversation with the Elder, and how he had spoken about how they could build more bridges, but they would be fragile bridges.

"I was a wreck after he died. That's when Higgs made his pitch. 'Together, we can run packages from sea to shining sea.' Back then, he had a monopoly west of here. We both stood to gain a lot from a partnership. Business was pretty good at first. But then, a year ago, when those fanatics started stirring up trouble… Fuckers hijacked our system. Somehow they got hold of our security passes and used them to sneak into cities. And just like that, we're delivering guns and bombs instead of medicine, and I didn't even know. We were just cogs in a terrorist machine. Higgs was behind it all. And on top of that, he got his hands on an old-school nuke that I ended up carrying right into Middle Knot City. Could've been different if I wasn't so fucking blind... So I did everything in my power to stop South Knot City from getting destroyed. I tried to get the nuke out of the city But Higgs was one step ahead. He took his pound of flesh and then some. Some wounds, they don't heal." Fragile removed a glove. Sam looked back at the palm of his own hand reflexively. "Whatever time I've got left, the rain took."

As she wiped away her tears with an elderly hand, Fragile turned back toward Sam.

"That's why I came to you," Fragile admitted, lowering her voice. Sam still had his suspicions, but he couldn't quite articulate them.

"So. Trust me now? I'll be there for you, Sam. All you have to do is call." Fragile disappeared in an instant.

Sam found that he could no longer sleep, now the room was empty again.

Before he could depart Lake Knot City, Sam encountered a slight problem.

Just as he had finished climbing all the way up the slope

of the distribution center, the sensor went off. He didn't have all the cargo. Sam tutted and turned around, to find the staff by the terminal carrying containers and bowing their heads in apology.

A man wearing the blue uniform of the delivery team waved a signal at Sam to prevent him from descending back down, and ran up to him with the cargo in his arms.

"Sorry about that. Looks like a system error. The cargo was recorded but it looks like it wasn't properly forwarded to you." As the man tried to get his breath back, he stopped Sam from lowering his backpack.

"This cargo is apparently bound for South Knot City. It's been tagged as 'fragile,' but just let me get it on you there." The man loaded the additional container onto Sam's back with experienced hands.

"I might not be the Man Who Delivers, but I used to be a porter, too. At least leave the packing to me. No matter how smooth the trip goes, it'll take several weeks to reach South Knot City. As long as you're in an area covered by the Chiral Network, we can support you. You can also take shelter in safe houses along the way. Maintenance of that BB shouldn't be an issue, either. And hey, if the mood strikes you, you can even use the chiral printers at the shelters of all those new UCA citizens to print out new equipment. The problems come after that. There are BT-occupied territories and MULEs and terrorists galore. We may seem like we're much better off now in Lake Knot City, thanks to all those anti-BT weapons and support supplies that you brought us, but it's still touch and go. We mustn't underestimate Higgs. That guy gets off on destruction. He isn't the porter he used to be. But I do have a little good news for you, too, Sam.

"The preppers who joined the UCA—the Elder and the Engineer—have been spreading the news about how convenient everything has gotten. The Elder especially has been nagging other preppers to join and calling them all parasites for depending on the delivery systems too much.

"Those guys originally shut themselves away in those shelters to live as long as they could. But now the terrorists are kicking off and their way of life is being threatened, they've started to think it might make more sense to band together and ride all of this out as one. Must feel frustrating for Higgs. Here he is trying to bring down the UCA with terrorism, and all he's actually doing is making it stronger. Anyway, you activate the Chiral Network at all the preppers' places and Bridges sites along the way while you carry all that stuff down to South Knot City. We're depending on you," the man said, lightly clapping on the pack on Sam's back.

"Take care, Sam Porter Bridges. Make sure to get this to South Knot City nice and safe for us."

Sam nodded and stepped away. All of a sudden, a strong wind blew, almost knocking him off his feet.

"You okay?" Sam could hear the man's voice from the

bottom of the slope. He turned back and signed that everything was fine.

"Good luck out there!" The man's voice was all that Sam could hear from the darkness.

It had been eleven days since Sam had left Lake Knot City, and he had finally spotted a safe house.

Since all of this area was covered by the Chiral Network, he hadn't run into too much trouble. While he was in this zone it was possible to predict MULE movements and the timefall, so he had managed to avoid those.

Having experienced the benefits of the Chiral Network firsthand, Sam was beginning to realize the meaning in everything he had accomplished until now. He supposed that it wasn't so bad, but he also knew that establishing a communications network wouldn't get rid of the BT issue altogether, either. In fact, it wasn't even a sure thing that they'd be able to eradicate the MULEs and the terrorists.

—*Exactly. That's why we have to build these bridges. Mankind can't continue to just put up walls and endure any longer, we need bridges that allow us to leap over the monsters below.*

As he got nearer the safe house, the terminal recognized Sam and began to activate, and the entrance that led to the underground lobby opened up. This safe house was the operational limit of the Chiral Network.

Sam deposited all his cargo in storage and entered his private room.

He threw off his blue uniform, which was dark with mud and sweat, and worn boots. As they were cleaned, the blood and sweat that had sunk into them would be collected.

Once again, the nail on Sam's big toe on his right foot had been torn off. It had only just begun to grow back. Sam presumed that he probably wouldn't be able to recover completely until he got to Amelie's place. The pain where the nail had once been was a constant companion to him on this trip.

Sam remembered one of his porter buddies telling him a story about another porter that he didn't particularly like. The man had got sick of his nails getting ripped off all the time, so chose to rip them all out himself. Then he used to dip them in acid to stop them growing back at all.

Sam wouldn't be able to get away with something like that now. His body and any waste it produced could be used to send the BTs back to whence they came. Sam wished the hot water pounding his flesh in the shower booth was a strong acid that could dissolve everything away. Or that he could somehow sacrifice this unique body of his to appease the BTs for good. He wondered whether, once his soul lost its body, it would be able to finally transcend the Seam and peacefully depart the Beach for the world of the dead.

When Sam woke, he noticed that the analysis results

from the device displaying his vitals read "enabled." It also said that the BB was now in good condition. Sam swallowed a painkiller and some smart drugs and washed them down with some special water. Then he pulled on his boots over the supporter that would protect his toes, and put on his newly sterilized uniform. Lastly, he hoisted on his backpack, picked up the BB, and sat down on his bed to connect it.

Tears began to leak out of his eyes from his usual allergic reaction.

He closed his eyes to escape his blurring vision and stave off unbalance. But in his head, someone else's eyes had opened.

BB—

You'll have to forgive Papa, I'm getting you out of here.

A face approached and a hand bore down on Sam as the voice asked for forgiveness.

The vision only lasted a brief moment.

It seemed like it was one of the BB's memories, but Sam really didn't feel so good. Perhaps it was more than that. Maybe Sam was experiencing the BB's emotions as an uneasiness had taken hold that made it feel like the floor had fallen away beneath his feet.

Sam wiped away the sweat and tears, and stood up. The BB was still sleeping soundly as if nothing had happened.

†

The next part of the journey went even smoother than expected. Sam detected MULEs a few times, but managed to avoid them completely.

<The Chiral Network uses the Beach as a communications network. The Beach is connected to the realm of the dead. It's full of the memories, information, and traces of creatures that have gone extinct or died. The Chiral Network should be able to connect us to that domain. But with our "connection" right now, we can't penetrate so deeply.> Heartman was explaining to him.

The codec call had come through while Sam was taking a break at a distribution center northeast of South Knot City.

<The work we have entrusted you with isn't simply about restoring America. There's another dimension to it. You might not believe it, but if we manage to activate the entire Chiral Network, we should be able to come to understand the Death Stranding phenomenon, and even learn to control it.>

"Will that understanding include repatriates like me and other people with DOOMS?"

<Yes, we hope so. In fact, I'm sure of it. The Chiral Network was originally devised as a system that would allow us to access the dead and discover the memories and information lost because of the

Death Stranding. It should help us understand people with special constitutions such as yourself, and other people with DOOMS, like me, Die-Hardman, Fragile, and Amelie. When I think about what's going to come, it makes shutting myself away up here almost feel worth it.>

Sam had heard that Heartman's facility was located in quite a rugged spot next to a snowy glacier and an area bubbling with tar.

<Then there's the Big Five. The five mass extinctions that have occurred on this planet. Not only will we be able to see the traces and memories from those times, but we might be able to see exactly what happened afterward. And then what? We might be able to actually do something about the Death Stranding, the sixth supposed mass extinction event.>

An electronic beep interrupted Heartman's voice.

<Sorry, Sam. Time's up, I'm afraid. Let's pick this up again later.>

The codec fell silent. Sam stared blankly at the Bridges logo on the device's monitor. It was a net that extended out over the entire land. Could that net really get to the bottom of all of this? Or would it get tangled up somehow and throw the world into further confusion? Or would it even be like getting trapped in a spider's web, and no longer being able to move?

Sam was getting a vague feeling in the pit of his stomach that each statement was true and yet false at the same time.

SOUTH KNOT CITY

Owen Southwick was in charge of deliveries and was keeping an eye on the monitor. The country was now covered by a net, from the East Coast to the central regions. It meant that those areas were now on the Chiral Network. Ever since Middle Knot City had been wiped out by nuclear terrorism, followed by the destruction of several waystations, staff morale had been at an all-time low. It seemed like reconstruction was just a dream after all. It was impossible. It had been a mistake to join up with Fragile Express, but by the time opinion had swayed, South Knot City had already become the next target for their bombs.

As it later became clear, the plan had been to set several bombs at facilities in and around the city and set them all off at the same time. Luckily, the nuke that had been brought into the center of town had been disposed of in the nick of time. In fact, with the exception of a few facilities in the surrounding area, they had managed to prevent most of the disaster. But the incident did cause a split in opinion between Bridges and the city folk.

Some people claimed that the reason the attack didn't

fully succeed was because Fragile and her crew detected the plan in time. Others believed that Fragile had formulated and tried to execute the plan together with Higgs, but they had failed because of internal divisions. They had proof, too. A security camera had picked up Fragile carrying a package that looked suspiciously like a bomb.

People's opinions of Fragile Express had completely polarized.

But one thing that everyone did agree on was that they needed to protect themselves against the escalating terrorism.

As did the preppers. While they were waiting for Sam Bridges to reach them with the Q-pid, Owen and the others had visited the preppers' shelters and asked them to join an anti-terror cooperation system.

Preppers came from all kinds of backgrounds. Some were families who narrowly escaped the incident in Middle Knot City and had been forced to live in the shelters, some were unaffiliated researchers who were surveying the landscape that had been transformed by the timefall, some were scavengers on the hunt for relics, and some were plain old junkers. So not only were their circumstances different, but the values they held regarding the state differed too, and now more and more of them were second-generation preppers who had never even experienced the concept of a nation.

The only thing that could unite them was their fear and hatred of Higgs and the Homo Demens. *You don't have to join the UCA and a state system if you don't want to. We just need you to let us use your shelters as nodes on the Chiral Network.* That's how they spun it. Once they had laid the groundwork, it was time for Sam to do his thing. And each time he used the Q-pid to activate more of the Chiral Network, the spider's web stretched farther and wider.

Owen saw it as the long-awaited counterattack of a human race that had been driven into a single corner of the world by ruin and despair, and was now ready to fight back.

To him, the name Sam Porter Bridges was synonymous with the word "savior."

Owen Southwick had received a text from Mama. Mama was one of the chief members of Bridges who had spearheaded the development of the Chiral Network and the Q-pid. Her home and lab weren't far from South Knot City. It was a warning. It said that the chiral density in the area had become unstable. It said that she couldn't get any clear values, locations, or ranges, but they should exercise caution.

This area still wasn't connected to the Chiral Network, so they hadn't been able to obtain any accurate readings. Mama's lab was probably having the same issues, but Owen couldn't imagine her sending a warning without reason, so he decided to call the distribution center, which was covered by the network, just in case. But they said there hadn't been any particularly abnormal readings lately.

Owen couldn't shake his worry, and decided to try to get some air outside. He didn't have DOOMS or anything, but maybe he would be able to sense something or smell something different in the air.

Owen boarded the elevator and went up. He could feel the dry breeze. There was a hint of something rotten to its smell. It was the odor that was carried over from the nearby crater lake. It was given off by the tarlike substance that had built up there. It smelled the same as it usually did, but after Mama's warning, he couldn't help but take it as a bad omen.

Owen climbed the slope. He could see the sky now, but it looked just the same as always. He couldn't see the sun, but that was normal. What light did reach the surface had to pass through a thin veil of chiral clouds. He reached the entrance and looked out farther. All he could see was the barren, alien landscape of rock and sand. He tried using the binoculars to see even farther than that, and managed to recognize the speck in the distance that was the distribution center he had just called.

He could see a man emerging from the shadow of a huge boulder that resembled a whale carcass. He was carrying a lot of cargo and walking this way. Owen couldn't make out his face from this distance, but he was sure of who it was. It was Sam Porter Bridges, their savior.

Owen raised his voice and waved his arms in the air to call him over.

But then he gasped and stopped.

Another shadow suddenly appeared right by Sam's side. The figure was smaller than that of Sam, and it looked like they were arguing about something. Owen zoomed in as far as his binoculars would go. It was Fragile. Sam was running and Fragile was chasing him.

What the hell is she doing? She was trying to stop Sam from getting here.

Even though part of the city in the south that Sam had been aiming for had come into view, the queer-shaped rocks that dotted the reddish-brown landscape prevented him from heading directly for it. He would either have to go over them or go around them. What was worse was how the sand was swallowing up his feet with each and every step, and how the air was so dry that his sweat soon evaporated, sucking away his energy with it.

His lips were cracked and blotted with blood. The fickle wind whipped up the sand in a prolonged attempt to stop him from getting anywhere.

It also delivered the stench of rotting meat straight to Sam's nostrils. It certainly didn't smell like the world of the living. Sam cursed and tightened the straps on his pack. A large boulder that looked like a dead whale monopolized Sam's field of vision. It was so enormous that it looked like the stuff of legend. Like a beast that had been slain millennia ago. South Knot City was now completely blocked from view. He would have to limp around the rock, it was far too big to climb.

Sam forced himself to keep track of how far along the whale he was, all the way from its rectum through to its pancreas, stomach, and gullet. In his head, it was like he was being reborn out of the whale's mouth. Once he had reached the top of the head, the entire city came into view. Sam breathed a sigh of relief.

Then the city disappeared like a mirage.

The space in front of him distorted. Tears leaked out. The scent of the Beach pierced his nostrils.

Once the distortion had righted itself, a woman clad in black appeared before him. Fragile.

"Hurry!" She forcibly grabbed Sam's arm. Sam tried to shake himself free, but his entire arm, all way from the wrist to the shoulder, felt like it was on fire. He couldn't endure the burning touch of Fragile's hand.

"Sam, we've gotta get back to the lake. It's the cargo!"

Sam shook himself free of Fragile's grip and steadied himself. All the blood had drained from Fragile's face, leaving her pale as a ghost. She was breathing heavily, most likely because of the jump.

"There's a bomb in the cargo. A nuclear bomb."

Sam couldn't believe his ears. Before he even had a chance to wonder about the wheres and whys, Fragile had grabbed hold of his arm again. This time he didn't attempt to shake her off and just ran.

"There was a query from Lake Knot. They asked if Fragile Express had lost any cargo. But we couldn't have done. We're no longer in any state to go making deliveries," Fragile panted, her explanation punctuated by gasps of air.

"I knew it immediately. This was Higgs's handiwork. Or a message. I knew that a nuke had been planted in some cargo bound for South Knot just like before."

It must have been that porter. Sam tried to remember his face, but he couldn't quite piece it together.

"If everything goes to plan, then he'll be able to make it look like Bridges is responsible for nuclear terrorism. He predicted that I would come to try and save you, in fact, I bet he anticipated that I would. So now, even if it doesn't reach the city, if the bomb explodes while we are together, we'll still look guilty. He'll be able to paint Bridges and Fragile Express as corrupt nuclear terrorists."

"What should we do?" Sam stopped and put down the backpack. It must have been that smaller case that was added on before he left. It was graffitied with a crude skull that looked like it had been painted by a child, almost like it was laughing at the stupid porter. But Sam could have sworn that the mark wasn't there when he had left that morning.

"Throw it in the crater lake. Just like I did."

That tar-filled lake was the source of the stink around here. The water's surface was dark, like all the colors had been boiled down into one. It sucked in all light like a black hole lying on the surface of the land. It was too repulsive to even approach, so Sam had decided to avoid it.

"Jump me there together with the cargo."

Sam remembered about Fragile's DOOMS. But Fragile simply apologized, making an expression that was half-laughing, half-crying.

"I can't. I couldn't back then, either. When I discovered that I had a bomb, I tried dumping it in my Beach storage. But some other power wouldn't let me. It was someone else's DOOMS. It was so strong that it could control my Beach. It suppressed my own power. Still does today."

"Was it Higgs?" Sam asked.

"No, someone different. Or maybe even 'something' different. But it gives him his power."

Fragile grabbed Sam by the arm one more time and tried to take off running. Sam gently rejected her hands and removed the pod from his chest.

"Take care of the kid."

The BB looked up at Sam from Fragile's arms with a

strange expression on its face. Sam grabbed the case and began to run alone.

He could tell that blood was oozing out of his toes. There was a puddle of it already forming in his boots. It ran out into each and every step, leaving a trail of dark-red footprints on the already red sandy soil.

At least it would keep the BTs away. They may have been far from the BT territories, but that offered Sam little relief now that he had left the BB with Fragile. The increasingly pungent stench of rotten meat and the thickness and stagnation of the air signaled that Sam was nearing the crater. As he reached the final steep slope that led up to the lake at the summit, he clenched his teeth and began to climb.

Fear seized him every time it felt like he might drop the case. If Higgs had been watching Sam ever since he first snuck the bomb into the cargo, then he could have blown it up any time he liked. It was probably remotely controlled or contained some kind of timer. Sam needed to get rid of it as soon as possible.

He couldn't help but hear Higgs's cold laughter in his head. Higgs probably knew exactly what would happen. He probably knew everything that had already transpired and what would happen afterward. All thanks to that "something different" that Fragile spoke about.

But Sam couldn't get caught up in all that right now. Whether that thing was involved or not, if this bomb went off then South Knot City and all the Chiral Network sites he had connected up to here would crumble to nothing. There would be no way to get America back. The BB would be lost. Keeping it alive was his self-appointed mission.

This isn't for America. This is for mankind.

Sam roared from the pit of his stomach and wrung out every last drop of strength. He climbed up the crater, his feet now covered in blood.

Then he picked up the bomb with both hands and lobbed it at the jet-black surface of the lake. It flew in a clear arc and sank. The great ripples that undulated across the surface looked like the arms of monsters, feasting on carrion, each vying to be the one to claim the rotten prize. Drawn down by countless arms, the bomb sank right to the bottom of the lake.

The surface of the lake flashed white, followed by a low rumbling sound. Sam could feel the vibrations in the soles of his feet. Then there was nothing. The surface of the lake was back to normal like nothing had ever happened.

"You saved the city and everyone in it." Fragile had caught up and was catching her breath beside Sam. "Hell of a lot more than I ever did."

The BB was staring at Fragile curiously from inside the pod.

"Maybe there was no way of saving Middle Knot. But South Knot's still here because of you and me," Sam reassured Fragile.

Fragile had done the same as him when Higgs tried to

bomb the city before. She had taken the bomb back then and thrown it into the lake. If she hadn't suggested doing that again, Sam had no idea what he would have done instead.

"By the time I realized what Higgs was planning, the nuke was already at South Knot City gates. I followed the delivery truck and somehow managed to carry the bomb to safety. But Higgs had been on to me from the start. He caught me red-handed outside the gates, nuke still cradled in my arms like a child," Fragile explained as she stared at the lake's surface.

She would never be able to forget the sound and smell of the rain, or the color of the sky from back then. Just like she would never be able to get rid of the scars that covered her body.

She had been forced to place her hands behind her head and ordered to kneel. Her well-worn uniform was torn to pieces and Fragile had been left only in her underwear.

Below the eaves that barely jutted out at the South Knot City distribution center entrance, the ritual had begun. The priest was Higgs and the sacrifice was Fragile. Those witnessing the ceremony were their subordinates. With the exception of Fragile, all their faces were hidden.

"Listen up, Fragile! I got a proposition for ya!" Higgs declared. The witnesses raised their guns. They were all aimed at Fragile. Higgs looked up at the sky and the clouds converged, shrouding the area in dusky darkness. Fragile had barely begun to notice the drops of water begin to fall when the timefall suddenly poured down.

"Do you want to live out your days as damaged goods? Or would you rather take damage *for* the goods?"

The case that contained the nuke was placed in front of Fragile. It was a case that she had transported.

"Alright. If all you want is to save yourself, you just have to jump. However, if you want to see this altruistic streak of yours through, then you'll have to carry my nuke to the bottomless pit and toss it in. Then you'll be the city's savior. Simple enough, right?" Higgs said before looking up at the sky again. The timefall was crashing down like a waterfall.

"I don't want to go too easy on you, though. You will have to walk naked through timefall to do it. Trade a lot of your time for a little bit of the city's. Hell, seems like a fair exchange to me."

Higgs removed his mask, and then the gas mask underneath, to reveal his true face.

"You see, the truth is, I don't much care for my face. That's why I hide it. Oh but you... ooh, you just love yours, don't ya? I bet daddy was real proud."

He grabbed Fragile's hair and pulled her closer. A cruel smile broke across his face as Fragile tried to turn her face away from him. He stuck out his tongue and licked her eyeball.

"Oh! No, no, no. Now, don't worry. I won't mess it up.

See, I want your face to be a kind of testament."

Higgs went on, placing his mask over Fragile's face. They had switched places. Now Higgs was showing his bare face, while Fragile's was concealed.

"Why did you do it? Why did you betray me?"

Higgs threw Fragile and her muffled voice a look of pity.

"Because I found someone who completes me. Someone who doesn't need me to wear a mask." He gave orders to his subordinates and forced Fragile onto her feet.

"Word to the wise. Even if you do save South Knot, you'll always be the nutjob who blew up Middle Knot. That pretty face of yours will always be remembered as the face of a terrorist. They'll never stop hunting you. Believe me, I know. Well, they can slap a sticker on you, but you're still gonna break in transit."

The rain kept falling as hard as ever. Fragile could hear the sound of a building collapsing among the ruins somewhere.

"So. What's it gonna be?" Higgs leaned in and whispered in her ear. This time his tongue flicked against her earlobe. Fragile looked up at him and spoke as if to reject the lukewarm sticky feeling on her ear and the curse Higgs had whispered inside it.

"I'll take the damage. And the goods. I don't break that easy." Fragile recited the same words inside her head to purify the curse and keep her spirits up.

I'll take the damage and the goods. I don't break that easy. I'll take the damage and the goods. I don't break that easy.

Fragile picked up the bomb that lay at her feet and ran.

The timefall pounded relentlessly against her shoulders, back, chest, and limbs, stealing away her time without mercy. Her attunement to her own body, that should have been deteriorating at its own rate, was thrown into disarray. It started to age. The woman who took the damage and the goods was beginning to break.

Protected by Higgs's mask, her face didn't age a day, but her body from neck to toe was now covered by the wrinkled skin of an old woman. The only thing grounding the sensation of her torn and broken body in reality was the weight of the bomb. It kept the woman named Fragile running through the rain.

All life in Knot City was resting on her delicate shoulders.

"Well, there it is. You *are* a goddamn hero. You did the right thing," Sam muttered as Fragile finished recounting her story. "It was all true."

As he looked into the crater that had swallowed up the bomb, Sam praised Fragile, but she just shook her head feebly.

"I'm no hero, Sam. That choice I made? I've regretted it ever since. All I had to do was jump, and I could have saved myself."

"But instead you saved a city."

Fragile shook her head once more.

"Well, now there's only one person left for me to 'save.' I'm going to make Higgs regret he ever crossed me."

"By killing him?" Sam asked.

"Can't. He's way more powerful now than he was before. But you could take him. You could. But promise me… Promise me you'll leave him alive. There's something I wanna ask him to his face. I want to know why he betrayed me."

When Sam saw Fragile's face, he thought that she looked hollow, as if she had lost someone very dear to her. A cryptobiote drifted in the space between them. Fragile plucked it out of the air skillfully.

"Do you want it?"

Sam grimaced for a moment, before taking it and popping it into his mouth. It tasted terrible.

He couldn't hide his disgust, and when Fragile saw his face she burst out laughing. Sam laughed, too.

"Promise me, Sam," Fragile said, and vanished.

SOUTH KNOT CITY

After disposing of the nuke in the crater lake and parting with Fragile, Sam picked up the rest of his cargo and eventually arrived at South Knot City.

A man from Bridges named Owen Southwick greeted him excitedly. Even though it was protocol to interact with porters in hologram form from the control room, Owen had made an exception and gone up to the surface especially. This man was their savior!

And he had just received word that Sam and Fragile had disposed of a nuke that the Demens had tried to sneak into the city.

"You gotta give me the whole story later," Owen remarked as he went to lower the cargo that Sam had brought into the basement for inspection. "By the way, Sam, you know Mama, right?"

Sam nodded as he lowered his backpack. He had only ever spoken to her over codec, but she was an important member of Bridges. She was the developer behind the anti-BT weapons and the Q-pid. Once he had rested in South Knot, Sam had been instructed to drop by the satellite lab on the outskirts where she had taken up residence.

"There's been word from her saying that the fluctuations in chiral density in this region have become unstable. We're not sure why that is, but she told us to be careful," Owen reported on his way down to the basement.

Left on his own, Sam finished his delivery and used the Q-pid to activate the Chiral Network. He was assailed by the usual dizziness, but this time it was worse than usual. He felt like his stomach had been turned inside-out. He felt like he was going to puke, like when he repatriated back from the Seam. Maybe it was because he was so worn out.

Sam had walked all the way from Lake Knot with a lot of cargo and hadn't taken a decent break in days. He was acutely aware of all the aches and pains he had forgotten about, like the toe with the nail that had been torn off and the soreness that coursed through his shoulders and back from the weight of the pack. He needed to rest. So he got on the elevator and took it down to his private room.

Then the BB began to cry. It was probably the stress of autotoxemia setting in. Sam hadn't allowed the BB to sync with its stillmother for a while now. While he tried to quell his recurring urge to vomit, he stroked the pod. *It's going to be alright, BB.*

"Thanks, Sam. You've saved South Knot City."

Now that Sam had taken a shower and seen to his wounds, Amelie was praising him from her prison in Edge Knot City.

The movements and sounds from her hologram kept going out of sync, so her image looked kind of fake. Sam had never experienced network disturbances like this before.

"You're halfway there—halfway to making us whole again. Thank you."

The hologram froze and only her voice could be heard. "Listen, there's something I need to tell you."

But Sam covered his ears. A horrible noise like metal scraping on metal blared out.

Amelie disappeared. Sam kept staring into space. He expected her to come back any time now.

The hologram eventually flashed back up and pieced itself together—they had been betrayed.

Under a black hood and golden mask was Higgs.

"Sam—"

But the voice belonged to Amelie. Maybe the network disturbance was causing the voice or image to lag. Or maybe—

Sam stared at Higgs's chest. Hanging around it was the golden *quipu* that Sam had given Amelie.

"Amelie!"

There was another wave of noise. Higgs disappeared, leaving Sam full of worry and suspicion. But then...

"Sam!"

A woman's voice rang out, followed by a hologram. But it wasn't Amelie. It was a slender woman in a tank top with her hair tied back. It was Mama.

"Sam, I'm detecting a chiral spike. Right in your vicinity. These numbers are off the charts."

The BB cried out at the sound of Mama's voice. It sounded like it was scared. But the pod was in the incubator. The BB was synced with its stillmother, it should have felt safe and at peace, but instead it was crying, terrified of something Sam couldn't see. Sam wondered if it could have been because of the chiral spike. He wondered if the unusually bad dizziness he experienced when he used the Q-pid, and the service interruptions, were down to the spikes as well.

"We have no idea what's going on. Please be careful." Mama made a pained expression and clutched a hand to her breast. The other hand looked like it was carrying something, but there was nothing there. Was that down to the network disturbances, too?

A warning alarm shook the room. Mama's hologram disappeared and the BB's crying got louder and louder.

Tears began to spill out of Sam's eyes. He felt goosepimples develop all over his body as chills ran through it. It was an allergic reaction to chiralium, the likes of which Sam had never experienced before.

Higgs had to be behind it. Sam couldn't just wait where he was. He needed to see what was happening outside, or rather, what Higgs was making happen outside. He unplugged the BB and boarded the elevator to go find out.

Something strange was clearly taking place.

When Sam climbed the slope from the upper floor and exited the distribution center, he looked up at the sky.

It was transforming. The center of the sky was being pulled toward the ground, twisting into a spiral. Several layers of surrounding clouds were pulled toward and around the focal point of the spiral, transforming it into a huge disk that covered the entire sky. Writhing like some kind of creature, it was headed this way. It was an enormous supercell that defied the laws of physics.

The surrounding area was cloaked in darkness. The wind instantly turned into a raging gale, making it difficult to even stand.

The BB was still bawling. The Odradek also came to life and immediately formed a cross shape.

Protecting the pod with one arm, Sam used the other to grab on to a nearby pillar. The stones whipped up by the wind pelted Sam. Even the abandoned debris and machines that were being used to repair the city's outer walls had been sucked up into the sky. Sam's arms and legs were already at their limit. He wouldn't be able to stand anything more than this. Rocks as big as a man's fist hit Sam relentlessly. His body was already so numb from the pain that he couldn't even feel them anymore. He barely noticed as his grip on the pillar was torn loose.

The world turned upside-down as Sam was swallowed up into the heart of the supercell.

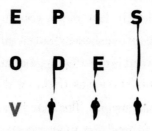

EPISODE VIII

UNGER

Sam could hear the BB crying.

"BB," Sam murmured as he opened his eyes. "Where are you, BB?" The bright white light forced Sam's eyes closed again. *It's crying. The baby is crying. My baby.*

The tears wouldn't stop. A soft creature lay in his arms. It was crying and it wouldn't stop. Sam could hear the harsh voices of men in the distance. The noise was intolerable, like nails on a chalkboard. A group of heavy footsteps was approaching. *Don't come, the kid is scared.* The BB was never going to stop crying at this rate.

There was a wild knocking on the door. Over and over again. They kicked it down. Arguing. Gunshots. Even though it was spilling out of his own body, the blood that leaked out was warmer than his own body heat. He was hit.

He clung to his sides and forced himself onto his feet. The BB was nowhere to be found. He couldn't hear it crying anymore. He was being dragged away somewhere. He no longer had the willpower or strength to walk. The blood pouring out of his chest was trickling down his leg and leaving a smear along the floor. If he could follow the bloodstains, he might be able to return someday. He needed to remember. Even though he had his eyes closed, all he could see was the blood.

The blood flowed and rose. It passed his waist and swallowed up his shoulders until he felt like he was drowning in it.

He was salvaged from the sea of blood by a yank of tremendous strength.

Then he was dragged and pulled forward again by a rope that wound around him. A faint amount of energy returned back to him.

The sea was dark. A black liquid wound its way around him and clung to his body. He let it drip as he was dragged and forced forward. Maybe he was being dragged to the gallows. It reminded him of a man. A savior who had been crucified on the hill of Golgotha. He had no idea why he knew that.

Four skeletons clutched the rope. Their tattered clothing belonged to the US Army. Even though he knew nothing about himself, he knew that. The water became shallower as the shore approached. A dead humpback whale was floating on its back. Whale after whale after whale… He heard the clacking of machine guns. A bomb exploded with a deafening bang. The whale's stomach opened up like a blooming flower and a figure spilled out along with its guts. The figure of a baby covered in black blood.

The skeletal soldiers came to a halt, causing him to trip in the shallows. The metal tags around his neck bumped into each other with a gentle *chink*. They were his. He tried to read the name, but he couldn't. He couldn't understand the letters. It made him feel sad. The waves carried the figure to him. He could hear the baby crying again. It was the BB. It was his kid. *Why isn't it alive?* His sadness turned to anger. His whole body was burning. His skin was on fire, but instead of carbonizing, it became wrapped in army clothing and equipment. The baby kept blinking over and over.

His body was automatically guided by the baby. He moved with an expertise that had been accumulated over years of experience. An enemy appeared. An enemy who was going to take the kid away. He waved his fingers at the skeletal soldiers to give them their instructions. *Spread out.* The rope that he thought was restraining him was actually an umbilical cord. He hadn't been restrained. He had been bound. The umbilical cord wound up back inside his body. In his hand was a rifle, on his head were night-vision goggles.

He was a soldier. He was awake.

Something fell behind him. The gunpowder inside the cast-iron tin exploded and the energy released shook the ground he stood on.

The vibrations traveled all the way through to the top of Sam's head, waking him up. There were explosions and gunshots all around him. He was assailed by masses of screams that no longer sounded human. The smell of the gunpowder made him feel sick, and his head was pounding. In the murky darkness he couldn't see what was going on.

He didn't know where he was. The only things he remembered were leaving the distribution center and getting sucked straight up into that supercell, where he had lost consciousness.

But he knew this was no time to be careless. He wiped the mud away from his cheeks and forced himself up. The BB was crying out of worry. Its body was shaking and it looked like it was drowning in the amniotic fluid.

"Come on!" Sam urged the BB. He was urging himself, too.

An explosion painted the murky sky red, and the next second a thunderous roar shook his body to the core. Where am I? He must have been caught in the firing line somewhere. Sam began to run in an attempt to escape.

Then the Odradek activated. There was a BT somewhere close by. *Was this the world of the dead?* He tried to shake the question out of his mind. As he kept an eye on the reaction of the Odradek and tried to weave through explosions and fire, he was swept off his feet. His leg had gotten caught on something and he had fallen face-down in the mud. He spat the mud out of his mouth and turned back to find someone grabbing onto his leg. But there was nothing past the arm. A disembodied limb was clinging onto Sam. When he tried to kick it away, the arm turned into fragments, then dust, then nothing.

The sound of bullets and shrapnel became louder. The Odradek sensor was now fully open and whizzing around and around. The BB was sobbing like an animal. It looked like they were trapped, unless the sensor was broken somehow. Sam searched for cover so they didn't get taken out by any stray bullets. He could see a trench a little way ahead, so he made a run for it.

As he jumped in, he was greeted by blood- and mud-covered corpses.

Unable to stand the stench, Sam covered his mouth and nose with his hand. He followed the trench, avoiding the corpses along the way, until something fell across his back. He reflexively shook himself free and threw it onto the ground. It was a soldier. His helmet and weapon fell to the floor. But he was still alive. He immediately started ranting and raving to Sam about something in a language that Sam didn't know as he writhed in pain, trying to gather his entrails back into the exploded cavity that was his abdomen.

The soldier stopped moving and looked up. He made eye contact with Sam. Tears of blood trickled from his wide eyes. The soldier tried to talk some more, but Sam couldn't understand. But even if he could speak the same language, Sam doubted he would know what the soldier was talking about. The body disappeared into a mist.

Sam picked up the gun and continued to move forward. *Is there no way out of here? Where the hell am I?* He moved down the trench carefully, unable to see outside. Then a pungent smell hit him. It wasn't the smell of blood. It was the smell of the Beach. Countless tears began to stream down his face. The people here were dead. This was a battlefield where the dead were fighting the dead.

—BB.

He could hear someone's voice inside his head. Then he felt like the nape of his neck was on fire. The Odradek formed a cross. A threat was imminent. But it couldn't tell him where, it just kept spinning around and around.

A bomb was dropped right in front of him. Sam's entire body shook and fragments of earth and rock poured down like rain. They rained relentlessly onto his face, his shoulders, his back... Blood oozed from a wound on his forehead into his eye. He felt dull pain all over his body. Once the fumes that obstructed his vision had thinned, a grotesque soldier appeared in front of him. He wasn't alone. Sam was obstructed by the barrels of several guns. But all the eyes scowling at Sam were hollow cavities. There was no skin or muscle on the hands that pointed the guns. It was the group of four skeletal soldiers from before. Each bony finger pulled the trigger at the same time.

Sam dodged and evaded the firing line. He got back up and fought back. He roared and shot at the skeletons again and again. His bullets shattered their bones, snapped off their arms, and blew away their helmets, turning their skulls into dust. Fragments of bone caught fire and danced in the air like sparks before being carried away by the wind.

—*Where are you, BB?!*

He could hear a voice from far away. It sounded like a voice he had heard in a hallucination before. He couldn't be sure, though. The owner of the voice was summoning them. He felt that if he couldn't find the man who owned it, then he would never make it out of here. The BB gave a loud cry, as if in response to the man. Sam nodded at the BB and spat out the blood that had pooled in his mouth. He looked up and began to walk.

Sam heard an unfamiliar sound. In the depths of his ears he could hear a humming like an insect beating its wings. Then came a loud noise that tore through his eardrum. Something had exploded, but Sam didn't think anything more of it.

The ground began to shake. It was like an earthquake or

a volcanic eruption. Sam couldn't stand up anymore. When he looked up, a huge wave was before him. But it was no wave. The land itself had swelled upward. Countless stones and rocks rained down. The surging wave of land was headed right for him. The posts holding the trench together disassembled, washed away by the advancing earth. It was already too late to escape. Sam turned his back to the wave, grabbed the pod, and curled his body around it. He took a deep breath.

The wave broke over Sam's head.

Once he was consumed by all this sediment, he knew that he wouldn't be able to move anymore and would end up suffocating. But that was not what the wave had in store for Sam.

—*BB*.

The wave simply washed him along and carried him toward the voice's master.

It was that man. The man Sam always saw when he connected to his BB. The only difference was that this time he was wearing a helmet and goggles. The man was looking down at Sam, who was buried waist-deep in earth, and was pointing his gun at him. The gun was almost poking into his forehead.

"Give me back my BB," the man muttered in a low growl. Sam shook his head just as the BB began to cry. The man's face contorted. Sam couldn't read his expression very well with this face hidden behind those goggles, but it looked dismayed. Like he was feeling rejected by the BB's cry.

The man wavered, and in that instant Sam took advantage of the situation to grab the barrel of the gun and get up. But the surprised man soon steadied himself and countered by trying to tackle Sam with all his might. His gun went flying in the ruckus.

The man gave an angry howl and laid his fist right into Sam's stomach, knocking the air out of his lungs. Sam began to black out, and as he faded, the man grabbed onto Sam's arm and aimed a punch straight at Sam's jaw.

Sam managed to block his arm just in time and landed a knee in the man's abdomen, so hard that the man's grip loosened. The two men parted and glared at one another.

"Give me back my BB."

Black tears were pouring out of the man's eyes, leaving streaks down his face.

Sam tried to ask why, but he couldn't. Before he had the chance, the man started to shake his head. Sam's gut was already telling him that he would never be able to converse with this man. Something had inhibited his thinking. Sam may have been overconfident in the fact, but if the man was refusing to be understood, what else could it have been? That idea itself made Sam feel unbearably sad.

"Give me back my BB."

The man stretched out his arms as he said it. Even if Sam

tried to take them, the man would probably be very angry. Sam had a feeling that he would just scream that he didn't want Sam's hands, he wanted the BB. Sam couldn't convey his thoughts to the man. And he knew that he couldn't understand what the man was thinking. They were never going to understand one another. As they were, things would only become tenser and tenser.

"Give me my BB."

He tried to shake Sam's hands away and make a grab for the pod. The man was just repeating, "Give me my BB," like a broken record. Like that was the only line he had been taught to say. But the man's expressions showed more complex emotions. There was no way Sam could read them, though.

"Give me back my BB."

The man raised his voice again, reaching for the pod.

Sam wanted to protect the pod, so he pushed back against the man's chest. Though the force of Sam's push never made contact, there was an explosion. But the explosion didn't give off light or sound. It was an explosion of nothingness. All color was lost from the world, and no outlines remained. All Sam could sense was the BB's crying.

Then Sam was sent flying out of that world and back into the one he had come from.

He was back right next to the South Knot City distribution center.

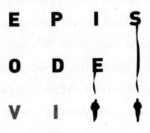

MAMA

A cramp-like pain shot through her chest. Mama was holding a baby that had been crying for some time now as she put her breast to its mouth. The tension and pain in her breast lessened, but the little girl who normally calmed down once she started suckling would not stop crying. And the ache in the depths of her breast lingered. Her body was responding to the unstable fluctuations in chiral density. They had a similar effect on the body to temperature and pressure variations. Ever since the baby had been born, her body had changed. Her sensitivity and abilities as someone with DOOMS became far more enhanced, and now they were telling her that something was wrong.

The changes in chiral density here over the past few hours could not be overlooked. It was continuously fluctuating up and down. She had sent a warning to Owen in South Knot City and urged him to warn Sam at the distribution center.

After that, the chiral density had climbed rapidly and interrupted communications. Mama's daughter continued to cry. She was crying like she was afraid, and that made Mama afraid, too.

She checked the values on the monitor and her fear turned into curiosity. The chiral density had been going up and up, but now it was back to normal. It had fallen so suddenly that it was like someone had just switched it off. It was unbelievable. It hadn't even been one minute since she had lost contact with Sam.

So she's not crying because of the chiral density? Mama wondered if there was something wrong with the equipment. She might have to get maintenance on it later.

It might have been an issue with the sensors that made the vital signs coming from Sam's cuff links cut out for a second. Mama felt frustrated that she couldn't go outside.

She tried calling Sam's cuff links once again.

"Sam, do you read me?" she called out.

\<Yeah. Where am I?\>

The sound quality was clear, but Sam's voice sounded awfully tired on the other end. It wasn't far between Sam's position and the lab, and he should still have been close to the South Knot City distribution center. His reply didn't make any sense.

<What happened to me? I got caught in the storm
and… I was in a war zone…>

Do we have our wires crossed? Maybe the chiral density was
still high. Maybe she was speaking to someone who
happened to sound just like Sam.

"You been daydreaming, Sam? Comms were only down
for a second."

<No, it was much longer than that.>

Sam sounded irritated. He wasn't making sense and that
worried Mama.

<There was this soldier, he tried taking my BB…>

"Sam… it's been less than a minute since we last spoke."

<That can't be right. I was there for… for hours,
it felt like.>

He must just be tired. She was going to tell him so, but
she kept her mouth shut in the end. Sam did sound like he
was completely exhausted. Maybe she was the one who was
tired and getting things wrong.

<Never mind. Coming to you.>

Mama sighed and turned toward her desk. Luckily, this
lab was in an area that was covered by the Chiral Network
that used South Knot City as a node. HQ would most likely
hold a file on Sam's background that she could request. If
she could analyze it, she might find out which battlefield he
was talking about.

After ended the confusing codec call with Mama, Sam walked for a while until a crumbling bridge came into view. It was the ruins of a bridge that had fallen victim to the simultaneous terrorist attacks that had been made against South Knot City.

The data said the bridge had originally been protected as a monument. Sam thought back to the briefing he had received from Die-Hardman just before he set out for South Knot. It was a part of highway that had managed to escape destruction in the period following the Death Stranding, and that had been repaired and preserved as a symbol of revival. It was also very close to South Knot City, and a small colony had formed around it. The heart of this colony was a former large-scale distribution warehouse that had been built right next to the road. The volunteers who would one day go on to form Fragile Express had evacuated goods there that had been left behind in other locations, forming the source of the colony. Mama had first been attracted there by the super-conductive large-scale accelerator that had once been operated there, and all the materials, equipment, and data that had been extracted and preserved from the related facilities to go with it. She had originally been a member of Bridges I and volunteered to stay behind. According to Die-Hardman, one of the main reasons for this was because of the accelerator's principal purpose, which was to observe Higgs particles. It was a treasure trove to a researcher like Mama.

But there was no longer a trace of any of that data left. All that was left now was a pile of concrete wreckage punctuated by the ends of twisted steel bars. It couldn't even be called a temporary shelter. It was nothing more than a shell of what it once was.

Sam couldn't believe that Mama would live somewhere like that, but no matter how many times he checked and rechecked the map, Mama's lab was close. He couldn't see anywhere that looked like it could be an entrance, though.

As he wandered around the perimeter, a security sensor reacted to him. He wasn't carrying any cargo, but it seemed to have sensed the ID strand around his waist and permitted him entry.

A dull sound emanated from a part of the wall that was covered in crushed panels as it opened. The BB grumbled as Sam took a step toward it.

"What is it? It's okay," Sam soothed as he stepped into the murky hallway beyond. The door closed and the hallway became even darker. A low buzzing echoed around the room, indicating that some equipment was up and running nearby. The temperature dropped artificially as if countering the heat of the machinery. Sam's breath hung white in the air. The BB began to cry in a way that seemed a little more fearful than before.

The Odradek activated, and opened and closed nervously as it scanned the surroundings.

He was trapped. This couldn't be Mama's lab. His frozen breath lingered in the air.

He had to go back. But the BB protested. As soon as Sam tried to turn on his heel, the BB cried out loudly as if it was trying to tell him something. It may have been afraid, but the BB wanted Sam to keep on going. Sam did as he was told. As he exited the hallway, Sam found himself in a wide space.

He was surrounded by industrial machines, motorbikes, and other vehicles. He heard a clinking sound from above.

It was a mobile. Plates in the shape of shells, hearts, whales, and dolphins were precariously balanced above him. The BB saw it and stopped crying, but the Odradek was still in warning mode.

As the mobile rattled, the BB laughed. Sam saw a baby softly floating near the large crack that ran along the ceiling. It was dead. Sam instinctively clapped a hand to his mouth. The baby was a BT.

"Don't worry, Sam. She doesn't bite." It was Mama's voice. "Glad you made it."

Like some sort of pantomime, Mama reached out both arms wide into the air and embraced the baby. The minute particles clumped together in her arms. She began to rock it with a smile on her face.

"She's hungry." She was speaking to the baby rather than to Sam. She threw an apologetic look at Sam and then eventually raised her arms back toward the ceiling. The mass of particles in her arms dissolved into the air, but Sam could see a cord made of the same particles stretching out from her abdomen.

"What the…"

Mama ignored Sam and said, "There. She's down."

Mama had her hand to her chest and looked a little embarrassed.

"Even though she can't drink it, my body keeps making it. Going through the motions really helps with the soreness, though." Mama glanced at Sam's chest and laughed. The BB was stirring inside the pod.

"She's my daughter. And I'm her mama. Nice to meet you, Sam."

Mama held out her right hand, but quickly snatched it back as she suddenly remembered Sam's aphenphosmphobia.

One of the rings of the cuff links she had equipped on her arms was dangling down.

"You can see it, right? You're hooked up."

The umbilical cord of particles climbed upward and upward from Mama's abdomen.

"It's okay. She's only connected to me. She's not like the other BTs. She's not after the living."

The BB grizzled as if it understood the meaning of

Mama's words and was trying to say something back, and the Odradek moved slightly and pointed toward the ceiling in response.

"Now you know why I can't leave."

The walls were collapsing in on themselves and the roof was scored with enormous cracks. It hadn't been repaired at all. Much like the exterior, traces of past acts of terror could be seen all over the place. While the room was filled with state-of-the-art machinery, there was also broken medical equipment and hospital beds stashed in the corners.

Mama turned to her desk that was pushed up along the wall.

"So, about the supercell..."

She sighed at the fidgety Odradek. "Do you think the grown-ups could talk for a minute?"

Sam unplugged the umbilical cord on his pod. The pod blacked out and the Odradek stopped moving.

Projected into the air was a graph that showed the fluctuations in chiral density by time.

"This was the chiral density when the supercell appeared. But almost immediately after, it dropped back to normal levels," she explained.

It was just like Mama said, the line on the graph dropped like a cliff face.

"In other words, the storm vanished in less than a second. Then, I was able to establish communications with you again straight after."

Sam's shock must have been plastered all over his face, because Mama simply looked at him, shook her head, and activated her cuff links.

"Okay. Let's pull the data from your cuff links and take a look, then."

A new window opened and the pandemonium of the battlefield was replayed for both to hear. At the same time, the 3D model that visualized the sound data was plotted against a time axis.

"Well, that's all pretty crazy, but at least *you're* not. Timestamps in the logs support your story. I wonder why there was such a difference? Best guess I can muster is you were 'trapped' between two different spacetimes."

The lights in the lab flickered off for a second and then came back. The monitors were full of noise and the images became distorted.

"Just as I suspected," muttered Mama. "There's no doubt that the chiral density has become unstable. I still don't know whether that caused the supercell, or whether the supercell is messing with the chiral density. Did you know that time doesn't flow on the Beach? I'm thinking you were sucked up into a spacetime that was very similar."

Sam shook his head. He had never heard of a Beach like the place he had just visited.

"Although... that's right. You were witnessing a supercell. It even says here that you were picked up by the storm. I've never heard of the Beach encroaching on this world in such a way."

"If it wasn't the Beach, then what was it?" Sam asked.

"HQ is doing a deeper analysis of the data from your cuff links. They should be able to figure out where you were sent."

The sound of a baby crying echoed down from the ceiling. The lights flickered in unison. Sam was disconnected from his own BB, so he couldn't see it, but it sounded like the baby wanted something.

"She's been crying more at night." Mama was looking upward, a radiant look on her face. Tears were streaming down her cheeks, but it didn't seem like it was a reaction to chiralium, otherwise Sam would have been crying, too.

"Chiral density increases in regions connected to the Chiral Network." Mama looked back toward Sam and wiped the tears off her cheek. "But the numbers are way, way higher than I projected."

A chill ran down Sam's spine and the Q-pid that hung around his neck suddenly felt heavy. *Am I doing more harm than good? I wanted to save Amelie and give the BB a life. I had to say yes to Bridges. I know I just turned a blind eye to all the deceit. But in doing that, have I just helped to build a bridge to the world of the dead?*

"I've been concerned ever since the theory was disclosed and practical research got under way. Early on, Bridges did acknowledge this as a potential problem too, so I installed special limiters in the Q-pids to keep the chiral levels in check, even if we had to sacrifice some of the functionality to do so. None of this is tested, mind you."

"Are you saying if I keep extending the network, we might be in for more 'temporal phenomena'?" Sam asked.

"Maybe. Or worse… we cause another Death Stranding."

In that case, they had to stop what they were doing right now. Sam felt for the Q-pid over his uniform. Was it just his imagination, or was it giving off heat? Sam knew that the easiest thing to do right now would be to give up on Amelie and the BB immediately and just go back to being a normal porter. But he couldn't. Even if he could no longer rely on something as risky as the Chiral Network, he still needed to save her. He felt so frustrated at himself for not knowing another way.

"I still haven't tested this yet, either, but I enhanced the limiter that suppresses rises in chiral density. Sure, it might impact the communication function a little, and we might not be able to recreate chiral computers and get back all the things from the past, because logically, it would mean we would have to consider a computational resource like the Beach, that is both timeless and infinite, as something that does still have some limitations. We can only create so strong a connection through our network before the rising chiral density becomes unmanageable. But what's wrong with that? Even if we can't entirely let go of the past, there's no need to be imprisoned by it."

Mama placed a small case on her desk and unlocked it. Inside was a Q-pid that looked exactly like the one that hung around Sam's neck.

Will that fix everything? Sam reached his hand out incredulously, but Mama stopped him.

"That one's not done yet."

It seemed like Mama's hand was going to brush Sam's, but he managed to retract it in time.

"We need to rewrite the software to work with the new hardware," Mama explained.

"Well, then get to it," Sam told her bluntly.

Mama had mostly been in agreement with Sam up to this point, but this time she stopped and shook her head feebly.

"Yeah, um… no can do. I designed the hardware, but the software was written by someone else."

Her gaze seemed to go right through Sam and focused on something behind him. Sam turned to look over his shoulder, but all he found was a hastily reconstructed wall.

"Her name's Lockne. She was a member of Bridges I. You'll have to head to Mountain Knot City," Mama told him.

Mountain Knot City was farther out west than the lab. It was built within a mountain chain that ran from north to south. It depended on the cargo, equipment, and route, but according to records from Bridges I, it took around two weeks to get there.

"Alright. I gotta take a Q-pid there anyway," Sam agreed.

"Oh good. That's great." Mama's expression suddenly shifted like a shadow had been cast over it. *Is there something about the Q-pid repair that she isn't telling me? Maybe she's worried that something that worked perfectly on paper won't function as she intended in practice? Am I really supposed to continue my journey west as if nothing has changed?*

The baby's cries broke the silence. They were exceptionally loud. So loud, in fact, that they made Sam feel worse, too. The lights that had been stable until just a few seconds ago began to flicker on and off. Mama rushed over and stretched out her arms toward the ceiling.

"Here we go again. I don't know what's gotten into her lately," Mama said, waving her arms around. She looked like she was trying to drive something away. All the lights went out and darkness descended on the lab.

"She's so scared. Look at her."

Sam replaced the BB umbilical cord that he had disconnected and was able to make out the baby's vague outline. He couldn't really tell if the baby looked frightened or not, but Sam's BB began to cry too, as if sympathizing with the fear.

That's when Sam saw a long, slender arm stretch into the room from the crack in the ceiling and try to snatch the baby. Mama was trying to bat it away.

"Maybe the other side wants her back." Mama was dragging the baby toward herself on her tiptoes, and held it close to her chest. "Or maybe she wants to go back."

The baby's small hands brushed Mama's cheek. The lights returned and the Odradek piped down. The menacing arm had vanished.

"We can't keep on like this. That much I know." Mama looked up at Sam. Tears were falling down her cheeks. As she stood there, clutching her specter of a child, she looked like the Madonna, the woman who resists the fate of her child to be taken away.

She looked at Sam. It was like she was silently saying, *You know, don't you?*

"She was due... I was in the hospital, waiting for a C-section."

Mama began to explain as she gently rubbed the baby's back.

Everything had been going to plan. The conception went as normal. The baby grew like it was supposed to. Mama had found out that the child was a girl. People began to tell her that she was looking more like a mother. She had been a little embarrassed by all the attention, but she was happy. Someone had started calling her "Mama" and it had stuck. Hardly anyone ever called her by her actual name, Målingen. It was unusual for a child to be conceived in that colony, so everyone was delighted.

She had decided to use a colony facility rather than one at a knot city because she believed that her experience could provide useful data.

There she was, on the operating table. She was given general anesthesia and fell asleep.

When she woke up, she would be able to meet the baby.

But all that awaited her when she awoke was an unbearable pain that felt like her limbs were being torn off. She couldn't move at all.

Even when she opened her eyes, it was still too dark to see anything. She couldn't remember where she was. Something was pressing down on her chest and every breath left her lungs burning.

She was lying upon the crushed operating table, pinned down by the fallen roof. What about the baby?

All she could feel was a dull pain like rocks in her belly. She could hear the sounds of explosions in the distance and felt the tremors shake the building.

She didn't even have the strength to ask who could have done such a thing. All she could do was weep. The tears that ran down her cheeks and into her mouth tasted salty. Even at a time like this, she could still taste. She was still alive.

Mama once again tried to cry for help, but it was no use. She was struggling to even breathe. Her breath hung pale in the air. The sunlight that had shone down on her had disappeared. It was already nighttime. The chill that had crept upon her stole her body heat. She coughed violently, and tasted rusted iron throughout her mouth. She couldn't breathe. Blood was filling her lungs and her world was going dark. It didn't matter if her eyes were open or closed. All she knew was that she couldn't let herself die there.

Mama felt something fall on her cheek, and opened her eyes to find droplets of rain trickling down irregularly.

Then she heard a baby cry.

"Where are you?!" Her voice was so loud that she surprised even herself. *Where's my baby?*

She could hear its voice, but she couldn't see it. Crushed by the rubble, she couldn't even turn her head. All she knew was that the baby—her daughter—was crying out for her mother.

"I'm over here!" she managed to shout out from the pit of her stomach. I'm over here. Right here. But her daughter was nowhere to be found.

Tired from screaming, Mama feel asleep. Then she opened her eyes and started all over again. She called out to the baby, she tried to comfort the baby, sometimes she even sang to her. Each time, she heard her baby cry back. Each cry told her that the baby was okay, and each cry also told her that she was still here, too.

It barely even registered when the rescue team arrived outside the building. Mama could barely feel anything anymore. It was like she had gotten used to the cold and the pain. The only sense that was still sharp was her hearing, so she could listen out for the cries of her baby. It sounded like it had begun to rain outside. It was the timefall. It had never fallen here before.

Mama could hear shouts in the distance, beyond the darkness. As she moved her head faintly, a light entered her vision.

"Hello? Is anyone there?!"

Mama's voice was too weak to reach the rescuers, but her baby was crying so hard it sounded like it was screaming. *You're screaming for help for me too, aren't you? Even though you've only just been born. Even though I haven't done anything for you yet.*

"I'm over here! Over here! Please, save me!"

The rubble was carefully removed from on top of Mama and her body was dragged out. The first thing she did with her bloodstained hands was reach for her belly. The blood mainly spread out from her abdomen. It was already black and dried. There was no pain in the now flat area. The baby cried.

"Thank you."

The hands of the woman who was trying to fix an oxygen mask to her face stopped. She was wearing the red uniform of the Bridges medical team. "Don't worry, don't talk. You've been saved."

"Thank you."

But Mama wasn't saying thank you to the woman on the medical team. She was looking up toward the ceiling.

"Thank you for saving Mama."

As a staff member equipped with a BB came over, their Odradek kicked into life and pointed upwards.

"That's my girl."

That was how the BT baby in Mama's arms had come into this world. Or maybe she had never properly come into this world at all. An umbilical cord extended from Mama's belly.

"And we've been together ever since. But she's a BT. The ties that bind her to this place bind me, too. You could say I've never really been discharged."

This building had once been the hospital, but had now been repurposed into a lab inhabited solely by the mother and her dead daughter.

"And you're okay with that?" Sam asked impulsively, but he soon regretted it. He didn't have the right to ask such a thing. But Mama just turned the question back on him.

"C'mon, you of all people?" Mama was looking at Sam's BB. "Looks like it's sleeping."

The BB's eyes were closed and it was floating inside the pod. Mama rubbed cheeks with her daughter and opened her arms wide.

The BT baby floated slowly upwards. Mama's umbilical cord followed, stretching along with it. It almost felt like both mother and daughter were ascending to heaven. *So, you aren't the Virgin Mary trying to protect her infant from its fate? I see, you're—*

"I just remembered. Deadman told me repatriates have special blood. Mind if I take a sample?" Mama interrupted Sam's thinking with a deadly serious look. "Your blood sends BTs back to the world of the dead."

It was Mama who had created the weapons that had proved it. Those weapons were the reason why Sam's blood was always taken whenever he rested in the porter's private room. So it could be processed and turned into tools to protect him. Sam wondered what else she could possibly want to use it for. Mama ignored Sam's sigh and grabbed his arm. He tried reflexively to pull away, but it wasn't because of his aphenphosmphobia. It was because Mama's hand was so surprisingly cold.

"Stay still." She restrained Sam's left wrist with one of her own cuff links and pricked a vein with an ultra-fine needle.

"I want to run a test. It could result in a weapon for you."

"Mama, are you—"

"There. All done." Mama nodded. Sam had realized that while his breath frosted in the cold air, Mama's did not.

"I'm sorry, Sam. Um, would you mind leaving us alone for a while? You can rest here until the tests are done. You can contact headquarters or work on your equipment, if you want."

An area had been made up into a small private room. The bed that seemed to have been freshly printed from the chiral printer looked brand new. It also looked like some parts of the communications equipment had been upgraded to be compatible with the Chiral Network. But there wasn't a shower booth or an incubator booth for the BB to speak of. Mama didn't need either, so it couldn't be helped. When Sam thought about the distance between here and Mountain Knot City, and the time it would take to get there, he worried about the condition of the BB.

He wouldn't be able to connect the BB to its stillmother and let it rest.

I wonder what kind of bond the mother and this kid share?

Sam had no memories of his birth mother. Neither Bridget nor Amelie had ever told him anything about her. But despite that, the existence of a mother lingered somewhere in his consciousness.

He wondered if a fetus was part of the mother, or whether it became a separate person the moment that it began to grow inside her womb. Whatever the case, a mother was intertwined with her child. Once a child was born, the existence of a mother was essential to it.

Mama grimaced because of the pain in her breasts. Did the programming of a mother kick in whether the mother was alive or dead? Even if she was brain dead and they had no physical contact, the BB's mother still provided an environment for her child. What divides a mother and her child? For Sam, who had never met his mother, that was a knot he would never be able to unravel.

"—so I can't leave."

When Sam looked up, Amelie was standing there. Obviously, she was just a hologram, but her voice and movements didn't quite match. Edge Knot City was still impossibly far away, but even so, the time-lag shouldn't have been this significant.

"Amelie."

Amelie didn't respond to Sam's voice.

"Higgs and the others have finally arrived."

Her arms were moving up and down awkwardly, like a badly operated marionette. She probably couldn't hear Sam's voice. It seemed like it was a one-way transmission.

"They reached all the way to Edge Knot City. I can't do anything. They've destroyed the city and killed everyone here. It didn't matter if they were with Bridges or not."

Sam wondered if the separatists from before, who had taken her hostage in all but name, had been purged too. It looked like there would no longer be any room for negotiation once Sam reached his final destination. He would no longer be able to avoid a confrontation with Higgs.

"We're surrounded by BTs, but somehow I was still able to connect to you."

Amelie's hologram vanished as if it were sand blowing

away, and didn't come back. All that was left was her voice.

"This might be the end. Everything had been going okay so far, but now I don't know what is going to happen. If you can connect us all up to here, Sam, then I can be free. I can go back east with you." A deafening noise filled the room then suddenly vanished. The communications equipment had died. It was no longer emitting any sound at all.

"Amelie!" He knew it was pointless, but Sam screamed into nothingness. Amelie didn't respond, and Sam grew anxious.

—*Sam, I'm waiting for you. I'll be waiting for you on the Beach.*

The voice hadn't been transmitted, but had reached Sam directly. Or maybe he was just hearing things. It seemed like everyone was trapped in one way or another—Sam, Mama, and now Amelie, too.

The monitor blacked out. The electricity to the lab had gone without warning and the backup generator hadn't kicked in. Just before it had happened, Mama had heard the sound of harsh static coming from the direction of the room Sam was staying in.

The lab was plunged into darkness.

Mama had just been telling Sam all about the spikes in chiral density, but they were just a result of this phenomenon, not a cause. That much was clear. Sam must have realized that by now, too.

Mama had no idea why the supercell had occurred, or why Sam experienced what he did (*Liar, you know something*), but she did know one thing. She understood that the source of the weird phenomenon at the lab was herself.

Mama had first seen the signs after Sam had crossed Ground Zero and had begun connecting sites west of Lake Knot City. The area covered by the Chiral Network spread out in twelve directions from each waystation. The intensity varied, but it basically expanded concentrically. Even if Sam wasn't in the area, his influence was gradually getting stronger and stronger.

The farther west Sam traveled, the more he expanded the coverage of the network, and the closer he got, the worse her daughter's condition had become.

It was a fact that the Chiral Network increased chiral density, and that increase closed the distance between their world and the world of the dead. They had been inching closer to the world where her daughter was meant to be.

If she turned a blind eye to all of this, it would result in something that couldn't be undone. The first person who Mama contacted wasn't headquarters, but Lockne, an engineer in Mountain Knot City.

There's a flaw in the Q-pid, just like we feared.

But just as she expected, no response to that text message had come.

We have to fix the Q-pid. I need you.

Once again, there was no reply. It was the same outcome no matter how many times she sent a message. All her voice messages and hologram transmissions had been refused from the beginning. Even headquarters seemed to have trouble making contact.

Time was passing and she still couldn't connect with Lockne. (*You know it'll never happen now, don't you?*) As Sam had steadily made his way over here, the Chiral Network had also come online. Mama's daughter started to cry more often.

In front of Mama there were two unfinished items.

One was the new Q-pid, and the other was a new cuff link. Neither item would have been possible if Sam had never reached the lab. That had been Mama's excuse for putting off her decision.

But Sam had eventually arrived, and thanks to his blood, Mama had managed to complete (*Why did you have to finish it?*) the new cuff link almost immediately.

She had to choose. (*Even though you've already decided.*)

Mama took the cuff link in her hand. Her daughter was asleep, so now was her chance. She would use the cuff link to send her daughter back. If she wasn't separated from her, then she wouldn't be able to repair the Q-pid. She placed one hand on her belly and closed her eyes. Then she activated the cuff link and severed the link with her daughter.

Nothing happened. *Why not? Was there a mistake in my theory? Was I just unable to do it?*

Mama looked closely at the umbilical cord connecting her to her daughter once again. She placed the cuff link on it and slowly began to cut. There was no physical pain, but she still felt like she was being stabbed in the heart. Again, nothing happened.

It looked like her daughter had woken up. Light returned to the darkened lab.

The fact that the communications equipment and all of the devices around the lab rebooted meant that the power had most likely been restored, and the text that Mama had been reading before the blackout was once again displayed on the monitor.

<Give me my daughter back.>

It was the last message sent to her by Lockne.

When she heard the sound of a door sliding behind her, she quickly switched off the monitor. Sam entered the room.

"Did you get any rest?" Mama asked.

Sam just shook his head vaguely. Yes and no. He had equipped the pod to his chest and put his backpack on. He was ready to leave.

"Before you go, I have something I need to ask of you." Trying with all her might to suppress the tremble in her voice, Mama presented Sam with the brand-new cuff link.

"They still work as a communications terminal, but I've added a weapon function. It uses your blood."

The ring opened up to expose a built-in dark gray cutter.

"The outer layer has been coated with metal fibers. These metal fibers are soaked in your blood," she explained.

Sam took half a step back. He furrowed his brow as if he was looking at something that was too bright, and bit his lip. He gripped both straps of his backpack.

"BTs are connected to the other side via umbilical cords, right? When those cords bring the matter of our world into contact with the antimatter of theirs... Boom. Voidout. But your blood has unique properties. It pushes back against the antimatter that makes up the BTs without causing a voidout, so it can be used to cut a BT's cord."

Mama didn't really need to reiterate anything to Sam. It was mostly for her benefit. For her to talk herself into what she was about to do. Mama sidled up to Sam as he turned away from the cuff links.

"Cut the cord of the BT, and it returns to the world of the dead. No BT, no voidout. Win-win."

Right? Mama offered her breast to her unsettled daughter.

"Let's try them out. Cut the cord connecting us."

"Can't you do that yourself?" A vein appeared on Sam's temple. Mama couldn't tell whether he was angry with her or if he had sympathy for her. All she could see was that Sam was trying to suppress whatever reaction he was experiencing. He knew about the relationship between her and her daughter.

Mama tightened her arms as if trying to protect the baby

that slept with its head buried against her chest. It made her hunch over. She must have looked so small right now.

"I'm sorry. She gets scared easily. I know that I'm being unfair. I've tried, you know? But I couldn't do it. It's like I don't have the right to kill this little girl a second time. I tried cutting the umbilical cord by myself, but nothing happened." Mama's shoulders trembled as she continued to hold the baby.

"I can't leave this child's side, but I have to go to Mountain Knot City. Even if you go to Mountain Knot City alone, they'll never accept you. They refuse Bridges. They refuse to join the UCA."

"But isn't that where this Lockne, who's going to fix the Q-pid, lives?" Sam asked.

"Lockne is my twin sister. But she'll never forgive Bridges. That's why I have to see her. And that's why I have to be separated from my daughter. You're the only one who can help me, Sam. Just listen, I'll explain about Lockne and I."

"Before we were even born we were the same person in two bodies.

"In ancient times, two meteorites had struck the earth simultaneously. The two craters were named Målingen and Lockne.

"Before we even came into this world, we talked to one

another. Our counselor diagnosed it as a false memory that we had retroactively constructed, but to us it was real.

"It didn't matter how much we tried to explain it, they didn't understand us. (*Yes, but neither of us even had the words to describe it properly at the time either.*) We had memories from before we entered this world and left our own crater. In other words, we have memories from the time we were inside our mother's womb. We were physically connected to each other inside of her: conjoined twins. When we were born, we immediately underwent surgery to separate us, but we could still hear each other's thoughts and feelings. We had a telepathic twin connection.

"That sense of ours helped us to understand the concept of the Chiral Network. We exist before we are sent out into this world. That is the past that the Chiral Network connects to. Being able to intuitively understand that, Lockne and I developed the Q-pid.

"Then we went west with Bridges I, and that's when tragedy struck.

"Lockne's lover died. It was after we crossed Ground Zero and reached Lake Knot City. We had just completed the South Knot City communications system via Middle Knot City. It wasn't anybody's fault. It wasn't an act of terror or anything. He was in an accident. There were mountains of cargo containers and one day they just fell. Lockne's lover got crushed underneath and died. It probably would have been better if it had been terrorism. At least with terrorists, you have someone to blame. We could have coped by hating the terrorists who were trying to get in the way of rebuilding America, and pushed on forward.

"But we just couldn't stomach how he had died in such a senseless accident.

"We could have asked why for the rest of our lives, but we would never have gotten an answer. It just happened. Just like the rocks scattered across the wilderness—no rhyme or reason. We were told that we were in Bridges and casualities were inevitable. We were reminded that we were tasked with the difficult job of rebuilding America, and that we had to push forward and bear it.

"Lockne couldn't accept it and started to act funny. Why her? Why did she have to put up with just because she was a member of Bridges? Why were they even rebuilding America in the first place? She became trapped in a cage of unanswerable questions and decided to hang herself. I knew what she was planning to do. We were linked, so I was able to stop it. But I couldn't fill in the holes for her. I wasn't Lockne. Even if I could synchronize with her sadness, I couldn't carry her pain for her.

"That's why I proposed something to her." Somewhere in the depths of Mama's consciousness, she wondered if she was being completely honest. *Was that the reason?* "I asked her if she would like to have a baby.

"It might have been a side-effect of the surgery to separate us, but neither one of us was capable of conceiving children. Lockne had an issue with her womb and my ovaries couldn't produce eggs. I had accepted it. I didn't particularly want children anyway. But the same couldn't be said for Lockne. She had fallen in love and wanted the man's child.

"That's why I suggested such a plan.

"I said we should have a baby so that her lover could still remain in this world. Every member of Bridges I was already obligated to donate eggs and sperm to secure genetic diversity for each Knot City, so all I needed was her agreement. I decided to offer my womb as a surrogate for Lockne and became pregnant with her child. The artificial insemination went well, but everything after that…

"Everything fell apart once the hospital I had been admitted to for the birth was destroyed in a terrorist attack. The connection between myself and Lockne was severed.

"For some reason we could no longer communicate as we had. But still, once I had been saved, I tried to contact her. I told her that I was okay, but—I couldn't bring myself to tell her about the baby. I didn't even fully understand it myself. Is she alive? Is she dead?

"I needed time to get my head around it. In time, we grew farther and farther apart, and then eventually our relationship became irreparable.

`<Give me back my daughter.>`

"Lockne demanded I give her back so many times. But I couldn't do anything. So, I set a deadline for the day you reached here.

"Lockne withdrew from Bridges of her own accord and became involved in the decision-making for Mountain Knot City. She was instrumental to the development of the Chiral Network and the Q-pid and, as its engineer, was well aware of the danger they posed, so she was welcomed by the people there. But really it was all because two twins had grown apart and no longer understood each other.

"It's stupid, isn't it?" *Yes, it was.* Mama didn't need Sam's affirmation, she knew what a fool she had been.

"It could have been different if I had just told her the truth. We could have restored the link between us and understood one another.

"But I couldn't. I had fallen in love with this child. I had formed a loving bond with this child that had been inside my belly and wanted to keep her all to myself.

"I need to sever the love and the selfish attachment I feel to undo the knot.

"I need to return this little one back to the other side, see Lockne, and tell her everything. Then we can repair the Q-pid together and reconnect the world.

"I was the one who brought the world to a standstill, I need to put this right. Everything was because of me.

"So please, Sam… do it!" Mama begged as she spread

her arms and released her daughter. She floated gently upwards as she dozed.

Mama gripped the umbilical cord and showed it to Sam. She didn't know how much time had passed. She couldn't hear a single sound. All she could do was stare at Sam's pale breath.

Sam connected the cord of the BB pod to his uniform, and all Mama could do was pray that he would take the cuff link.

"You aren't killing anyone. You're just setting this little one and I free, sending us on to the beyond. I tried to cut the cord myself, but I couldn't because I'm dead. That's my theory. The dead can't send the dead to the other side. No matter how much I try to convince myself, I just can't erase my attachment to this world. If I could have, a BT wouldn't have been born. So please, Sam, I need a member of the living to cut the cord and undo this knot."

Sam's BB became unsettled. It was like it had reacted to Mama's words about undoing the knot. It needn't have worried, she didn't mean that she was going to sever the connection between Sam and the BB.

The cutter that protruded from the cuff link glinted dully. Sam was getting closer. The umbilical cord that was formed of countless writhing particles swayed up to the ceiling.

Mama closed her eyes and a tear ran down her cheek.

She couldn't help, but tightly clench her back teeth. She

held her breath. Sam brought the cuff link down.

The particles that had made up the umbilical cord broke free and began to disperse.

There was a cry from the ceiling. The baby was no longer floating there. Now it was an adult BT with a swollen belly. It was Mama's true self. As the umbilical cord collapsed into nothing, the BT's form and outline began to fade and diffuse, and its cries could no longer be heard.

"Goodbye."

She had finally said it. Mama's body collapsed like a marionette whose strings had been cut. She could no longer support herself. Lying in Sam's arms, her body didn't trigger any of the usual symptoms of Sam's aphenphosmphobia. She didn't give off the warmth of a living person.

"Alright, Sam. Take me home. To Lockne."

MOUNTAIN KNOT CITY

It was ever so sudden. Lockne felt something strange on her left cheek. Like a lukewarm tear. She smelled something off. It was the reaction she had whenever the Beach was near. It had been a while since the last time she had it.

There had been no remarkable changes in the chiral density levels displayed by the monitor. Lockne had been monitoring the changes in density constantly, ever since she'd heard that Bridges II had been dispatched from Capital Knot City and that the Chiral Network was finally being brought online. But she had observed significant changes in the eastern regions. It was just as she had feared.

There were fundamental flaws with the Chiral Network and the Q-pid. It had always been clear that use of the Beach as a communications route would allow its influence to grow stronger. The changes weren't something she had stumbled across after combing finely through masses of data, they were so obvious that they were receiving reports from locals and readings from instruments that had been installed within nearby BT-occupied territories.

Together with her elder twin sister, Målingen, Lockne had appealed for repairs to be made to the Q-pid and for a reduction in the network's scope, but it had all fallen on deaf ears. Die-Hardman acted as the spokesperson for the will of the president and he would not permit any changes to the plan. She had been half-forced to head out with Amelie on Bridges I, establishing infrastructure and organization throughout the scattered communities that lay across this land. Lockne and the others in the backup team had been tasked with completing and maintaining this infrastructure, ongoing research, and development, and investigating the true nature of the Death Stranding.

Along with the progress already made by Bridges I, the increased militancy of the separatists and isolationists had only strengthened Bridges' resolve to rebuild America.

Linking people together with the Chiral Network would help form an impenetrable fortress against threats. Together with the sharing of technology and information, the potential to manufacture any kind of equipment thanks to the activation of chiral printers, and, most of all, their shared goal of rebuilding America, they would be able to stand up to anything, whether it was bands of terrorists or the Death Stranding itself.

But all those claims by Bridges were nothing more than propaganda.

All to bring the people together as one in opposition to a common enemy.

It was stupid. Lockne couldn't help but blurt it out one day. Was it really necessary to go that far just to activate the Chiral Network?

Målingen had once complained about the same thing.

What changed in her? When had they started to call her Mama?

The Beach is linked to individuals. It's why all of our lives are so different, and why we all die alone when the time comes. However, although each Beach is unique to the individual, they are all connected. This was what Målingen and Lockne wanted the Chiral Network to achieve for everyone else. Instead, it was being used as a tool to further the idea of rebuilding the UCA.

This invention wasn't a toy. If Bridges absolutely had to use it, they could use it with restrictions.

Once they had crossed Ground Zero and took over in the central regions of the land, the twins had once again urged their superiors to downgrade the Q-pid and Chiral Network. But both headquarters and Amelie from the advance team dismissed them. The infrastructure they had built was designed to work with the protocols that had been developed previously. They didn't even know whether the Chiral Network would activate properly in those conditions. That's why Bridges said they had to implement it with maximum functionality. Besides, they had already prepared a failsafe other than suppression by the Q-pid. Even if the worst-case scenario did happen, they could still ensure the security of the Knot Cities.

There were a limited number of people who understood the entirety of the system, both because of its vastness and for security reasons. For all their talk about the importance of connections, Bridges seemed to keep a lot of secrets.

Despite this, Lockne and Målingen attempted to enact their own plan to repair the network and Q-pid. Once they reached South Knot City, Lockne and Målingen requested to be stationed at an adjacent colony. It was home to a collider that America had once developed. It wasn't working anymore, of course, but the enormous amounts of materials left behind there were irreplaceable.

They could be used in the redevelopment of the Q-pid.

And, perhaps more than anything, because the sisters—*No, the three of us, including him*—planned to have a child there via artificial insemination.

But the two of them were not allowed to stay together. There were too few people as it was, and changes to the distribution of personnel were not permitted. Lockne was ordered to go to Mountain Knot City.

It didn't matter, though. The two of them had a connection, so they knew they would get through it. They could communicate between themselves using the Beach of theirs that they had both connected to while they were in their mother's womb—*An overlap of our two separate Beaches*—like a miniature Chiral Network.

Thanks to Målingen's devotion, Lockne's wounds began to heal. She made a baby toy that looked like a large old-fashioned thread spool and had it sent to Målingen.

As the baby grew in Målingen's belly, Lockne felt as if it was growing in her own.

She felt it kick. The two of them laughed and shared each other's happiness.

Then tragedy struck. Although it hadn't struck completely out of thin air. At least, not for Lockne. As the birth of her daughter had neared, the bond between the baby and Målingen had grown increasingly stronger.

Even if Målingen had just lent her womb, even if she still

called it "their baby," the only ones connected by the umbilical cord were Målingen and their unborn child. Lockne knew that she was jealous, she knew that it was an ugly feeling, but she couldn't help it.

She hated the fact that people now called her sister "Mama" and, even worse, that Målingen liked it.

When Lockne found out that Målingen—*Not Mama!*— had fallen victim to the terrorist attack in the colony, the first person she worried about was her daughter.

Is she okay?

Lockne sent the thought to Målingen. There was no reply.

Målingen's Beach was closed off. There had been word that mother and child had been saved, but nothing from Målingen herself.

Since she couldn't access their telepathic link, she tried more conventional methods of communication. Holograms, voice messages, text messages...

`<Give me my daughter back.>`

Nothing. At first, she only felt despair, but eventually, the level of hatred she had developed for her sister had grown to match it. As she was kept from the truth, it grew and grew.

Her hatred for Bridges, who also hid information from her, grew too.

That was the reason she first made contact with the group that self-governed Mountain Knot City. Bridges I had urged them to join the UCA, but in the end they were granted a grace period until Bridges II arrived with the Q-pid to decide on whether they would join the Chiral Network and the UCA.

Until then, people from Bridges were to be stationed at the distribution center that had been set up outside of town. But they were not to enter the town unless there were extraordinary circumstances. They were not to interfere internally. Those were the rules.

Lockne left Bridges. It was never recognized officially, but she utilized her skills as a mechanic to remove her cuff links herself.

Then she made sure to tell the people of Mountain Knot City all about the dangers of the Chiral Network, and eventually became involved in its decision making.

That's what her defection was about on the surface, but underneath, she wanted revenge on Målingen and Bridges. If they were going to sever all contact, then she would too.

It was some time after that when Bridges dispatched the second expedition. It was made up of a single man: Sam Bridges.

Tears continued to fall from her left eye. She knew it wasn't because she was sad. She felt a twinge in her abdomen that she hadn't felt in a long time.

<Are you close, Målingen?>

It all came flowing back. The stagnated time that had been dammed up had been released and was now engulfing her.

After that, her tears didn't stop.

✝

As Sam carried Mama there was a change in her spirit.

"Are you alright?" Sam asked, unable to look behind him. The softly falling snow had suddenly turned into a blizzard. The wind was blowing sideways and spraying them with powder. With every step Sam took forward, he would find his leg buried knee-deep in snow.

After leaving Mama's lab, it didn't take too long for the scenery to completely change. The ground was no longer flat, but packed with steep slopes and mountains. Once they went a little farther, all the ground was covered in snow.

The temperature had also dropped dramatically, and the snow combined with the rockiness of the area made for terrible footing. Sam kept walking, but it was as if he was making no headway at all. His suit was made with heat-insulating material and his boots had been treated to be resistant to the cold, but the relentless weather still froze him to the core. He had already lost the feeling in his toes with their missing nails. If he kept this up, he would be risking frostbite.

But his biggest concern was Mama.

When they had first departed, she wouldn't stop talking about Lockne and her daughter, but she had grown steadily more silent.

Maybe the cold was making her sleepy, or she was getting weaker, or maybe what Sam had a bad feeling was going to happen now that she was separated from her daughter was indeed about to happen. It was all just speculation, but Sam suspected that even in this cold and snow, her breath would not hang in the air like his. He only wished he could turn his head to check.

He felt like Mama's body had suddenly become lighter.

"I'm fine, Sam." Her voice was small, but it didn't seem like she was in any pain. "I just thought I heard Lockne's voice."

Mountain Knot City was just over the summit of this mountain.

"Hey, Sam. Lockne has gotten closer. All thanks to you."

The blizzard became even stronger, and Sam could barely make out what Mama was saying.

"I'm sorry. I'm so sorry, Lockne."

MOUNTAIN KNOT CITY

Målingen was almost here. The sister Lockne so despised, yet yearned for.

All of a sudden, their Beaches resonated and their link was brought back to life.

Several scenes unfolded at once like a panorama.

The hospital roof collapsed and Målingen was pinned underneath. Her belly was being crushed and the baby died before it was even born. My baby—our baby. She was rescued, but she couldn't leave the hospital. Lockne watched as Målingen tried every means possible to contact her. (*The same thing happened to me, Målingen. I wanted to talk to you, but I couldn't connect.*)

<Give me back my daughter.>

That was the only message that had reached Målingen. The only message that had reached her twin sister was one of her most hate-filled. Even though Mama had been unable to leave the building, she had still attempted to repair the Q-pid. She had thought of a way to leave her daughter behind and acted upon it just to see Lockne again. She had used Sam's blood to cut their umbilical cord herself, failing again and again. Then she had Sam sever it for her, and bring her here.

So, it was like that. (*Yes, like that.*) We hadn't been broken apart. We were still connected by the same Beach, we had just gotten lost and missed each other.

Lockne ran. She ran out of her room, ran down the basement hallway and aimed straight for the Bridges distribution center. Waiting for the elevator to reach the upper levels frustrated her immensely, and she immediately tumbled out of the doors as soon as they opened.

A porter was stood next to the activated delivery terminal. The snow that covered his head and shoulders was melting and dripping to the ground.

Sam Porter Bridges had carried her sister, Målingen, Mama, all the way here.

"Målingen!" (*I'm finally here, Lockne.*)

Sam laid Målingen down on the stretcher that the staff had run out with.

Bundled up inside the delivery bag with her eyes closed, Målingen looked like some kind of chrysalis. She was smiling faintly.

"I'm sorry, Målingen." Lockne put her head to Målingen's. A black tear fell from Målingen's left eye as another black tear fell from Lockne's right.

"Forgive me, Målingen." (*I'm sorry that I never had the guts to tell you, Lockne.*)

Lockne threw her arms around Målingen.

Målingen presented something to Lockne, gripping it tightly in her trembling hands. It was the toy Lockne had sent her while their link was still open, all that time ago.

"I'm sorry that I couldn't protect your child." (*It's okay, Målingen, you don't need to apologize anymore.*)

Lockne wiped her cheeks, which were now mottled with black tears, and took Målingen's hand into hers. Looking content, Målingen switched her gaze to Sam. Sam offered the one other piece of cargo he had brought along to Lockne.

"Please fix the Q-pid." Målingen's breathing was shallow. *Please don't talk anymore.*

"Lockne, you need to fix his Q-pid. I couldn't save our child, but you can save our world. Only you. I love you, you hear me?" Målingen pleaded.

I love you, too.

Målingen mustered all her strength to take her final breath before her eyelids began to slowly close.

The toy fell out of her hand and onto the floor, where it clattered all the way to Lockne's feet. She felt like she could hear their daughter laughing as it rolled across the floor.

Målingen had finally been set free from this world.

Lockne made contact with Sam in his private room. She had already finished fixing the Q-pid. She had worked pretty fast. It was still only a few hours since Sam had first arrived.

Sam entered the room she had instructed him to come to, which also doubled as Lockne's lab and private quarters. In contrast to Mama's preferred look of a white tank top and work pants, Lockne wore a blue-black cape with a hood that wrapped all the way around her. Mama's body was lying on a simple bed up against the wall. She had a peaceful expression on her face and looked like she would wake up at any second.

Lockne took the Q-pid in her hand and raised it up in Mama's direction like an offering.

"I fixed it, just like you asked me to." Her tone indicated that she wasn't speaking to Sam, but to Mama.

"It's okay now. This should help us to suppress the chiral density."

Sam looked up.

"Surprised that I fixed it so quickly? The hardware had already been repaired to the specification that Målingen and I were looking at before, so all that was left to do was check the code and assemble it."

Sam took the new Q-pid and hung it around his neck. These twins may have disagreed, but they were looking in the same direction, headed for the same destination.

"She died beneath the rubble with our child still inside her. Her *ka* passed over to the other side, but her *ha* remained, bound to our dead daughter." Lockne was leaning over Mama, softly caressing her cheek. "She knew all this, of course."

Lockne looked over at Sam to see if he knew what she was talking about.

"That's why she kept one cuff loose. Didn't want anyone seeing her vitals. Shame she couldn't use her favorite invention." Lockne released the single connected cuff link from Mama's right hand.

"She did all that to keep me and our daughter safe. Even if it was all quite clumsily orchestrated."

A tear fell from Lockne's left eye and dripped down onto Mama's right cheek. It made Mama look like she was crying too.

"Right, let's go. I've spoken to the Mountain Knot City Executive Committee. We will join the UCA. Now you go and use that Q-pid to bring us online." Lockne left the room and they headed to the upper floor.

Stood in front of the activation terminal, Sam showed Lockne the Q-pid in his hand. This was a new knot, created by the twins.

He held the metal shards up to the receiver. Lockne held her breath and looked at him.

The scent of the Beach permeated his nose, together with the usual feeling of floating that Sam experienced, and tears began to fall from his eyes. But it was different to his usual reaction. He was also crying because of the overlying warmth of Mama and Lockne.

"We're whole again. We're one," Lockne murmured almost in song. She crossed her arms, before cupping her left cheek with her right hand and her right cheek with her left hand. Her eyes were now two different colors, one blue and one green.

"Like before. In the womb."

"Yes, I remember."

Lockne and Målingen spoke alternately. All Sam could do was watch. He knew that he would never forget this moment.

He wondered how many times he would think back to it, back to the moment when Målingen's *ka* returned to Lockne's *ha*.

"Thank you, Sam. We're whole again."

He would never forget such a beautiful union.

Lockne and Målingen may have lost their daughter, but they were free from their knot.

And now they had made a brand new one.

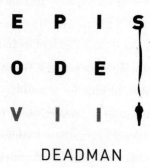

EPISODE VIII

DEADMAN

Sam looked at the BB pod connected to the incubator. He was finally able to let the BB recover in his private room, now that he had brought Mountain Knot City online.

—*She died beneath the rubble with our child still inside her. Her* ka *passed over to the other side, but her* ha *remained, bound to our dead daughter.*

Sam remembered what Lockne had said.

Her daughter was a child who died without getting the chance to live. It was the same as his BB. Killed in her mother's womb, Lockne and Målingen's baby had been stuck between life and death. Just like this BB that they used to sense the other side. They were keeping this one alive. Its ability was why Deadman had entrusted it to Sam. To keep him safe, as Deadman clung to the vague hope that Sam might discover some kind of breakthrough during his journey across the continent. But was this child alive in the first place?

The BB let out a little cry. Both of its hands were pressed against the window of the pod like it wanted something.

The BB's hands began to crumble. The BB's arms disintegrated into particles next, followed by its chest and then its legs. Just like Mama's baby had done.

As soon as Sam made a grab for the pod, its glass window shattered. Both the pod and the BB had vanished. Sam screamed and tried to get up.

He was breathing so hard that his shoulders were heaving. He was still sat on the bed. It looked like he'd fallen asleep.

Realizing that it had all been a dream, Sam looked over at the pod in the incubator. But the entire pod was gone.

"Lou!" Sam shouted, getting up for real this time.

"Looking for this?" a man's voice inquired behind him. A barrel of a man wearing a red leather jacket entered Sam's vision. It was Deadman. He was holding the pod in one of his arms. Sam had wanted to keep Lou's name to himself, but it was too late now. Unable to find the words to gloss the situation over, Sam simply glared at Deadman.

"Surprise! Fragile warped me here. I finally got to visit the Beach. Well, 'her' Beach."

Deadman sat down on the bed. It looked like Bridges were ignoring the concept of privacy once again. Sam's right-hand cuff link suddenly felt very heavy around his wrist. Someone had mistaken the concept of "connection" for "stalking."

"Your beloved BB has a serious issue." Deadman sighed wearily. He was probably worn out from the jump he had just made across the Beach.

"Bridge Babies are quite literally bridges between this world and the other side. Their place is not here with us, nor with the BTs over there. They belong precisely in between, with no greater affinity for one world or the other. But BB-28 here has been 'leaning' farther and farther toward the world of the living. Toward you, Sam."

"That's 'cause we're partners," Sam interjected quickly, but he wavered. The dream of his BB turning to dust crossed his mind again.

"Partners? Sam, a BB is a tool, not a human being. Bridge? Yes. Baby? No." The sweat on Deadman's brow accentuated the long scar that ran across it. This man was anxious. Sam couldn't tell what had prompted the man to come here, but it seemed urgent.

"So tell me what the problem is."

"This tool—this weapon—is transforming into a living being." Deadman wiped away the sweat on his forehead and looked into the pod. "It's gaining weight. Its brain activity is increasing, it's accumulating memories... BB-28 is becoming self-aware—becoming an actual child."

"Doesn't sound like a problem to me," Sam commented.

"It's hardware, Sam. Manufactured for a purpose. A purpose it cannot fulfil outside the pod. The pod is made to feel like the womb of the BB's stillmother, they come as a package. There is a seventy percent risk of catastrophic failure simply in removing it. Which hardly matters, because at this point, it'll cease functioning within a couple of days."

Deadman gently returned the pod to the incubator. The private room they were in was located in Mountain Knot City, which had just been brought onto the Chiral Network. If that was the case, then shouldn't the BB have been able to relieve some stress by reconnecting with its stillmother back east in Capital Knot City?

"I know what you're thinking, Sam, but I told you, the BB is growing. At this rate it's going to outgrow the pod. So, we have to reset it."

Deadman wiped away at the sweat on his forehead with the back of his hand again.

"You'll have to leave it with me, of course. Otherwise the kid's done for."

Deadman had referred to the BB as "the kid." That's right. Deadman also wanted to keep BB alive. Maybe it only seemed like Deadman didn't care. Deadman paced slowly along the walls.

He was looking around the room with interest.

"I'll cut the cord that links the two of you, and then perform an operation that reconnects it to the other side. Think of it as a little tug to correct its alignment—to put it back where it belongs, right between the world of the living and the dead. It'll be reborn as a new piece of equipment. Restored. But like I said, you'll have to be without it for a while."

"You're sure this will work?" Sam asked.

"Of course. One catch, though: the surgery may erase its memories." Deadman's gaze left Sam and wandered toward the ceiling.

"Erase? Lou'll forget me?" Sam cried in disbelief.

"Relax. The BB will still function as intended. In fact, we'll be able to optimize the BB's resources."

Sam had no words. Deadman also shut his mouth and the room fell silent.

Deadman had stopped in front of the shower booth. All of a sudden, he began to remove his jacket and undo the bursting buttons on his shirt.

"Can I borrow this? I'm covered in sweat and chiralium from my trip across the Beach."

Deadman winked as he asked.

What the hell was he talking about? I thought he'd be glad of the chance to hang out with the dead? Sam shook his head, not revealing his confusion.

"Hey, come on. I know that you're worried about the BB, but what about me? Or are you worried about Amelie?" Deadman's eyes weren't smiling. He was being serious. His gaze flitted between the ceiling, the walls, the equipment shelf, the incubator, the terminal, and all the small items dotted around the room before, finally, it returned to Sam.

Sam sighed. Fine. He got up and headed to the shower booth.

Deadman fiddled with his cuff links and released Sam's.

The warm water made a loud noise as it gushed out and cleansed the men's bodies.

Sam's underwear clung to him. As did Deadman's shirt. Deadman pushed his sodden hair out of his face and turned to Sam.

"No one can spy on us in here. It's just you and me. No audio records of what we say... No video for lip-reading analysis. Get closer."

Sam understood, but he couldn't stop the reaction from his aphenphosmphobia.

"Die-Hardman cannot know of this. Understood? There's more you should know. It's about the original Bridge Baby experiments."

Was this what Deadman had jumped all the way to tell Sam?

Did that mean that everything about Lou's condition was just a cover story to pull the wool over the director's eyes? A faint glimmer of hope sparked in Sam's chest.

"Piecing together what little I could find, it looks like they were conducted on the island of Manhattan off the east coast... which was completely and utterly obliterated by what was almost certainly a voidout. I should also mention that the president himself was killed in the blast. It was after his death—when he was succeeded by then Vice President Strand—that the experiments were suspended by executive decree. Documents were shredded, facilities were decommissioned, and every effort was made to pretend that the BBs had never even existed." Deadman inched even closer. He leaned right into Sam's ear so that his lips couldn't be read and dropped his voice. "But the experiments continued in secret."

His words were drowned out by the sound of the water. He was doing everything in his power to avoid any interference from headquarters, or rather, the director.

"On the direct orders of President Strand."

"Bridget?!" Sam gasped loudly.

Deadman clapped a meaty hand to his face.

"They weren't designed just to be BT detectors. The BBs are essential to solving the mystery of the Death Stranding. Bridge Babies are the only bridges that we have to keep us alive from one day to the next. She wanted to incorporate them into the Chiral Network, to facilitate travel to the Beach… But none of her plans ever came to fruition. In the end it was only ever people like you and Fragile, who were afflicted with DOOMS, who could sense BTs and use the Beach. That's why Bridges were so enthusiastic about having people like you in their ranks. It took a while, but in the end they managed to organize an expedition to reconnect America and a team to head west. Meanwhile, BB tech fell into terrorist hands."

"What's Die-Hardman's part in this?" Sam asked.

"I'm afraid to find out. I don't know how long he was working for Strand. I don't even know his real name or his face. I thought you might, since you two go farther back."

"He was already wearing the mask when I met him. Something about burning his face." Sam shook his head to indicate that he didn't know any more than that. Was Bridges different from how it was ten years ago? Or had Sam just been naive about the organization's dark sides and contradictions back then?

"Right. Sorry. Any data we have from back then is classified at the highest level. As far as I know, the director is the only one with clearance. But the Chiral Network presents a new opportunity. By compiling fragmented data in the public domain from all across the country... I might be able to piece together a little more of the puzzle," Deadman posed.

Maybe he would end piecing together something even darker than the origins of the BBs. The thought chilled Sam to the bone and made the steamy waters of the shower feel even more blistering.

"Be careful, Sam. They're watching." Deadman stopped the shower and exited the booth. Sam followed. By the time he got out, Deadman already had the pod in his arms.

"Look after Lou for me." Sam bowed his dripping-wet head a little. Deadman gave him a thumbs up to show that he understood. It looked like all the stuff about the BB had been true. It hadn't just been a cover story like Sam hoped. The BB was going to be reset, and its memories erased. The BB would probably forget him.

But when he thought about the kid, it was probably for the best. He couldn't just monopolize the kid's life because of sentiment or his ego. That's what he told himself.

"Sam, I'll have him back to you before you know it. You get on with connecting up the Chiral Network like you have been doing in the meantime. There's no time to rest for porters like you." Deadman winked and began to head upstairs. Sam was worried about Amelie. Deadman was right. He didn't have time to rest.

"Heartman's lab is up ahead. A number of scientific staff from Bridges, like evolutionary biologists, paleontologists, and geologists, are working on an excavation in the shelters around it."

"Excavation? What kind of excavation?" Sam asked.

"Isn't it obvious? They're searching for clues to help unravel the mystery of the Death Stranding. We need you to deliver some cargo to them and get them up on the Chiral Network. That should help us get a good look at the events of the past, and we'll be able to dig up any buried research results. Die-Hardman wants you on that, too. Got it?" Deadman waved himself out with one hand and held the pod in the other. It seemed like he wanted Sam to act as if the doubts that he now had about the director, Bridges, and even Bridget, didn't even exist. Sam could see it as Deadman walked away.

Alone once again in his private room, Sam looked at the empty space where the pod had once been connected to the incubator. He felt like the emptiness was swallowing him up. It wasn't simply a matter of Lou being gone—Sam felt like all the darkness that Bridges was hiding was completely overwhelming him.

(To be continued)

For more fantastic fiction, author events,
exclusive excerpts, competitions, limited editions and more

VISIT OUR WEBSITE
titanbooks.com

LIKE US ON FACEBOOK
facebook.com/titanbooks

FOLLOW US ON TWITTER AND INSTAGRAM
@TitanBooks

EMAIL US
readerfeedback@titanemail.com